Other books by Randy Thornhorn:

THE KESTREL WATERS
A Tale Of Love And Devil
(sequel to *Wicked Temper*)

HOWLS OF A HELLHOUND ELECTRIC
Riddle Top Magpies & Bobnot Boogies

THE AXMAN'S SHIFT
A Love Story

Visit Randy Thornhorn online at

www.thornhorn.com

Rosasharn Press
244 Fifth Avenue
Suite C-118
New York, N.Y. 10001
www.rosasharnpress.com

ISBN 978-0-9916496-3-1

Printed in the United States of America.

First Edition

for Barbara

WICKED TEMPER

by

Randy Thornhorn

Table of Contents

I wus starin' an' wonderin',
w'en a voice whispered low in me ear:
'Ther Valley o' ther Shadder o' Death,'
'n I knew 's I'd come ter ther valley
o' ther lost childer
--which wer' named ther Valley o' Light.
Fer ther Valley o' ther Shadder,
'n ther Valley o' ther Lost Childer
come end to end.

William Hope Hodgson

Little girl, rise and be healed...

J. L. Swaggart

STEP 1

This hand? This be my hand. This be all the roadmap what matters. Here. Take this hand. Come with me. You thirsty? We'll tend to your thirsty in due time.

You know how that Tizzy Polk went, don't you? I know you do. I can tell. Don't worry it. I ain't one to ask how you come to know things. Maybe you just better than most. That's a possible. That's always a possible.

I'm liking your hands. Turn them hands over. See? Everything you be—it be carved in them hands. You know that? Yes. I reckon you do know. If you look careful and close, that hand there tells everthing worth telling about where your road begin and how. When I look in your hand I see your road. Right there, carved in the flesh, bone, and gristle. Even if your road ain't on no map to speak of. Hands are like that.

That's why it ain't no secret. Not to me. I know how Tizzy Polk's road went.

What say? You trying to tell me something? What's got your tongue? You know how she went, but not how she come to be? I thought you were better than that. It ain't no secret. Just drop your finger on the map. Wherever it be, you won't be far off.

I believe I'll drop my finger on that Skawmarry Holler Road. It's as good a spot as any. I'm tapping my finger on that night when them two birds got kilt. That night her Preacher-Daddy got kiltered. It weren't nothing new for the Preacher. For them two birds, it was a different story. Here is how it went.

Two dominica chickens got run low by a '49 Studebaker pickup, shortly after the amen. Them chickens got mowed down loud by that truck. Bloody feathers flew. At the dimming of day, it was. Hosannahs were happening when it happened. Then the church singers sat. The Preacher, he rose up. Them bloody feathers rose up too. Every soul winner and the Rebel Yell's pickup truck was rolling in the glory.

Tizzy Polk sat down, front pew center. This was her place, she knew it true. Young Tizzy, she might have heard the howling of his horn. But she would never be the one to tell it. She was not that kind of girl. You know the kind.

Hell, spake her Preacher-Daddy, his hands upon his pulpit.

"Beasts of Sodom, *I say*. Brother. Sister. My rapacious chilren," he boomed, his eyebrows tangling as the pickup truck trumpeted out there. Hell yes, it trumpeted then sped away. "I am naming my text this evening. The Book of Malachi and the Book of Revelation. Chapters four and twenty-two, respective. Fer *behold*, the day cometh, that shall burn as a oven, and all the proud, yea, and all that do wickedly shall be stubble: and the day that cometh shall burn em up, saith the Lord of hosts, that it shall leave em neither root nor branch." The Preacher found another leaf, removed the ribbon. "Blessed are they that do my commandments, fer they git rights to the tree of life, and may enter through the *gates of the city*. Fer *without* are dogs, and sorcerers, and awhoremongers, and murdrers, and idolaters, and whosoever loveth and maketh *a lie*." The Preacher's goatee lifted. Dour he was, locked in eternal scorn. "As ye know, we lost another child last night. Mister and Mizz Blue, they little boy Murphy Bob is gone missing. Murphy Bob. Poor, poor Murphy *Bob*. That's the irony ain't it? Bob unto Bob. How many Murphy Bobs gone missing now? My heart be heavy. Yes, my heart be heavy. Well, let me show ye something you ain't never seen before."

Suddenly Preacher Polk's nails clawed a handful of pages from the Bible. Ripping tissue, he flung the pages away.

"That could not possibly make any difference to most of *you*. Most of you cain't read. I don't know whose fault that is. It's not mine. But do you *hear* the *word*? I don't think so. No. I do not think so. *Outside* is where your stench must remain. Outside with the blackest heart that walks this earth. These hills. Cayuga Ridge." A cruel chuckle, he wiped spittle from his lips. "Shit, man, don't flirt with the sluts of perdition. You must *eat* your own venality. You must *drink* the blood of God's own son—the *New* Testicled Son of the Great God Jehover. That's the *true* Jehover. Not none of these horned gods hereabouts, who steals our Murphy Bobs. Let me tell you the true story of Aaron and Zedikiah—" He faltered. He eyed his flock warily. "No. No, I don't think I will tell that story on this day. Never sleep with a monkrat in your bed on the *half* moon. You'll catch the narcolepsy. Fer there's no place you can *hide* when *God* is out to git ye. He's aknowing it all. He's aseeing it all. He's atelling it all. To me, brother. He tells me so many things. Teensy-tiny things. And I am his Revolting Angel. See? And I have come to offer you—an Alky Seltzer. Fer ye own stupidity. And ye bellyaching. I'm sick and tired of it. I'm tired of waiting. He's tired of waiting." The Preacher's brow sagged in defeat. "Why not let tonight be the night?"

Something awful crowed out in the churchyard.

Preacher Polk shot an eye down at the front pew, at thirteen-year-old Tizzy. His eye hit her and Tizzy hung her head. She disappeared into her will o' the wisp smile, as always.

Now, don't worry it, that voice in her head said. Don't you worry it.

STEP 2

I been seeing it done for years.

And Tizzy? Tizzy Polk knew how it went. She knew her place. She stood and sang *I Shall Not Be Moved,* like all the other childer of Cayuga Ridge, big and small.

> *Just like a tree standing by the water*
> *I shall not be moved...*

After vespers, that Tizzy girl stood in her buckletop shoes beside the pilot coat and round hat of the Preacher Polk. She swatted chiggers from her legs as the old clergyman shook each Magee's hand, each Lufkin and each Witherbaugh. He greeted every fat brother of that ponytailed hag, Shonda Jo Biggs, and—while he was at it—even Shonda's fat Methodist Aunt Prin from Ewe Springs. Tizzy knew most of them were scared to death of the Preacher Polk. So they came and sat their pews, took what he dealt them, then took off running when he bade them go.

Tonight, Preacher and daughter stood in a pool of grassy lamplight. Kids in good hand-me-downs played hop frog in the dark. Church singers made for their pick-ups and buggies. From these carriages ladies fetched jugs of cider, molasses cookies, and pie baskets, filling their husbands' arms. Cayuga Ridgefolk twittered in the pines. Deacon Willy Jay lit a big fire over on the school-yard. The Preacher Polk reached out to shake Lemuel Baywright's knotty hand.

"Ask Winterhaust blessings fer us this evening, Lem. Over at the potluck."

"Willingly, Preacher, willingly. Say, I wanna bring my boy Elmer Lee over to your place and let ye talk at him. He ain't worked a day in over a year, maybe two. Something chawed off the tip of his nose. Coon or monkrat maybe. He drinks, ye know. His mama says he'll come around, but I don't believe he will."

"Anytime, Brother Lem."

"I don't believe he will. Them young'uns of his ain't got no shoe leather. Another barefoot winter, them babes will be bad sick with the ague."

"Hurts me to the quick, Brother. I'll come take a word with the lad."

Polk moved him along. Old Lemuel paused over Tizzy, peering down at her.

"I said my piece," Lem told Tizzy. "I'm his daddy an I don't believe he'll ever go back to work. He used to be a star ball jumper, back in the day."

Tizzy drew a blank, staring up at the elder fellow. In all

her thirteen years Tizzy might have spoken three words to the man. Her fourth was not forthcoming. Sister Lucille Weeks was now begging Preacher Polk for a prayer and bed call on her mama, who was lingering in the last lap of consumption. Sister and Preacher confided in soft tones. Tizzy was watching Old Lemuel shuffle off—when a growling echo caught her ear. Her head turned. Her gaze drifted out through the oyster dusk, her eyes falling on the Skawmarry Holler Road—the road rounding the Livery.

Light struck Tizzy. Headlamps lit her face. A revving motor mill filled the churchyard.

A slate-grey Studebaker pickup was coming fast down the road. It slowed. Church folk watched as the truck rumbled by, making a big show of it. Out of the truck's window hung the lanky likes of Matthew Birdnell. Pure-dee defiled trash, he was. He was nineteen or near enough. Wagging his tongue, the bespectacled Birdnell leered back at Tizzy. Then that Birdnell did a peculiar and amazing thing. He opened the truck door. He stepped *out* of the rolling rattletrap. The truck kept going as Matthew Birdnell danced. He danced a fast buck-and-wing jig in the road—in his white-top spectator shoes— and he never lost his crazy grin at Tizzy. Then he quit and raced after the pickup. He barely caught up in time to leap back into the cab. The truck door slammed shut. The truck sped away.

Tizzy gasped. So did the other kids.

Their folks were less impressed.

"Fool kid."

"Birdnell boy. All them Birdnells come dumb like that."

"I be after some of them shoes."

Tizzy had to admit—they were flashy shoes. Scuffed black leather but white on top. Tizzy looked up. Her Preacher-Daddy was deaf to the blare of muffler pipes, blind to hot shoes. Sister Weeks murmured at him, tugging the preacher's coat sleeve. The Preacher kept nodding back.

Sneaking a second glance, Tizzy spied the Birdnell truck as it wheeled fast through the Mercantile—around the gas pumps—then here that truck came again. Revving back toward The First Reconstructed Church of Cayuga Ridge, the truck suddenly swung to the roadside.

Just shy of the churchyard, Matthew Birdnell hopped out. He whipped off his dirty undershirt then flopped his leg over the fender. The moon caught the dangle of his white-top shoe. His ribs stuck out, sickly pale. His horn-rim spectacles were bent, held together by electrical tape. A match flared. He lit a ready-roll. Every move was wiry and sudden, like fire ants filled his britches. Matthew took a deep drag, still grinning at Tizzy from afar. Smoke leaked out of his teeth.

Tizzy saw all this and—after a tick or two—she grinned back at him, in spite of herself.

She knew she was not pretty. Sometimes she felt like a boy. When Tizzy Polk looked in the mirror she saw a dough-glob with Shanghai chinaman eyes and black hair that always looked cut to fit a mush bowl because it was. But right now, Matthew Birdnell was smiling at her.

Lord knows why Tizzy would smile back at trash such as he. She must have been bedeviled. And she was still smiling when she looked up and locked her brakes. The Preacher Polk was staring down at her, glaring down at her, a nail-driver in a black hat.

Tizzy's face fell. Her head dropped. She tried to disappear.

But she could still feel him. She could still feel her Preacher-Daddy up there, nailing her down.

Tizzy knew she was the devil's toy. How could she forget? Her place was here by her Preacher-Daddy. How could she still slip and backslide and fall like this? Just look at her now. No, her head was full of holes. How could she forget she was but a wee whore unfit for any man? Tonight, beside the Skawmarry Holler Road, Tizzy closed her chinaman eyes and tried to ignore the loud but fading trumpet. Her ears denied the roar of tailpipes in retreat.

This was no baby game. This was her road, lest she forget. The road she was born on and born to. This was the way of all flesh.

The third-grade classroom was brightly lit and festooned with chains of colored paper and crayon drawings of stout turkeys and pilgrims with hatchets. *Farmer in the Dell* tinkled from a wind-up Victrola. Grandaddy Griz

Turlington overflowed his bib denims on a tiny chair at a tiny table in the corner. He shuffled the dominoes and kept yarning bull with the other big men at the table.

"Don't like no radio," he said. "Never did, never wanted to. Cain't pull no signal under Ole Riddle Top no how. And fer my money is jist as well. Keeps them radio waves from acutting through ye all the time."

T. Wayne Law was on a wavelength of his own:

"I heared that Vinson girl crawled outa bed one night last week," T. Wayne was saying. "Jist up and gone. Nobody got a bead on her neither."

"*Hell*," Mr. Soaks muttered, scratched, then played a deuce. "How many zat this year?"

Tizzy hugged close to the woodstove, catching the heat and eavesdropping on the men's language. Tizzy noticed a Nestle chocolate bar peeking from the side pocket of Mr. Soak's coat. The blue wool coat hung on the back of his chair as Mr. Soaks leaned forward, counting spots in the domino boneyard. The room was stomping with baby kids. They fooled around doing dumb baby dances for Mrs. Tesher, the third-grade room-mother. Mrs. Bowdrenaire and Miss Crowell had a table of older babies busy carving pumpkins. Little Rafer Don Pitt kept climbing up and down the teacher's chair, sticking his jelly-stained fingers into Granny Raminy's German chocolate cake. The teacher's desk was somewhere under all those sweetcakes and berry pies.

Behind Tizzy Polk the coal warmed her hands and bottom. It had a thick oily smell Tizzy did not care for. She preferred hickory. She preferred the company of nobody compared to that of children. Murphy Bob was likely absent from class tonight because he felt the same way.

Just then—*"Beasts of Sodom, I say"*—she heard her father's damning brogue. The Preacher Polk was thundering up the backdoor step of the classroom with some deacons in tow. He was a lightning rod on legs. This meant her daddy had forked his fill of deer sausage and cushaw squash and now came come courting a berry pie. It was time to praise the pie but blame these lazy young folk for this year's pumpkin crop. It was a tired old refrain, and Tizzy knew it too well.

The children began to sing.

> *O watch your step, step, step,*
> *Watch where you wander little lamb...*

Tizzy took off. She slipped swiftly through the babies and domino shufflers. As she passed Mr. Soak's blue coat, she quickly relocated the Nestle bar from his pocket into hers, hiding it deep within her dress with the napkin. Her eyes swept the room to be sure nobody saw her take it. Tizzy ducked out into hallway.

It was dark here too.

Her steps made a hollow sound. The rest of the feast and fire were all outside. It was chilly with autumn cold. Both doors were open at the hall's far end, down by Teacher Sue's first grade. Tizzy lingered outside the principal's office. She peered into the glass trophy case at ballplayer pennants and greenish brass cups from years gone by, all won by the Cayuga Ridge Bearcats. Each plaque, each flag, featured the school mascot inside a rusty orange circle. The official bearcat was almost cross-eyed, his lower jaw jutted forward with both lower fangs rising over his upper lip like a werewolf. Tizzy stood and imitated him with her own lower fangs, her gaze glittering over the dark trophies.

"—*an ungrateful, rapacious child.*"

Her Preacher-Daddy's damnations rose again, back in the classroom.

Tizzy came out the front door of the school and hit the bottom step with Shonda Jo Biggs descending upon her.

"Where ye been hiding your hide, Tizzy Polk?" Shonda asked in a voice so loud Tizzy wished her dead.

Thankfully, nobody took notice. Most of the Winterhaust revelers were hymning and hawing around the bonfire betwixt the school and church. Tizzy was headed for her own dark corner of the playground, where the pilgrim oak grew. She was going there to be alone, and not with the likes of Shonda Jo.

"Shush, you gristlebone. You know my daddy," Tizzy said, eyes straight ahead. "He allows I should stay close."

They were the same age, but Shonda Jo had big bosoms for thirteen—bosoms she already used for barter with boys of all ages. Shonda's mama even let her come to class during Indian Summer wearing her brother's overalls and nothing underneath but her monthly sickness. Tizzy's desk sat next to Shonda's and Tizzy would never have believed Shonda could get riper than she already was. Tizzy planned to forgo such foolishness. Especially after Shonda's brother said Tizzy's face looked like a mashed apple.

"Ain't it jist awful about Murphy Bob Blue?" Shonda Jo squawked.

"Yeah, I reckon."

Up ahead, the gnarled pilgrim oak spread limbs in the dark over three teeter-totters.

"Hey, Tiz, you missed all them boys—"

"What boys?"

"Horny boys. They come over an asked did we wanna sniff some Energine cleaner. They had rags of it."

"That's the most dundered thing I ever heard. Don't tell me you fell fer em, fat calf."

"Well—"

"Shonda Jo, you need another bath. You're ripe again."

"Really? You think so?"

"You always letting them holler boys mess with you. Energine and rags. I swear."

"Matthew Birdnell has five dollars," Shonda said with glee. "He was one of them boys. I saw him sniffing them rags."

"Where?" Tizzy asked before she could catch herself. At least they were outside earshot of the school now.

"Behind the lunchroom."

"Birdnell? Did you *see* the five dollars?"

Shonda cackled.

"Clary was *right*. You do have a fancy fer that dippy

Matthew Birddog!"

Tizzy wheeled, locking on those rusty red eyes two inches above her.

"I most certainly ain't got no fancies fer that trash. And you best not be atelling nobody differnt. I was surprised he had the dumb gumption to show hisself after what he done at vespers this evening. That's all. Matthew Birdnell better walk soft or my Preacher-Daddy's gonna break them long legs of his and use em to beat some Jesus into him."

Shonda Jo was a mouth breather. Her brain was dulled by the Energine and the visions Tizzy had just blown into it. Shonda repositioned her bosoms with her upper arms.

"I think you would be correct in that assumption," Shonda said. "Tizzy, I'm gonna git me a butterscotch pudding."

Shonda Jo lost interest and lumbered away, nettle scratches all over her plump thighs. Tizzy watched her go. Some folks were too dim for disgrace. Shonda Jo would never learn. Not with a noggin-load of cleaning fluid. There would be no place in heaven for girls who backslid all day in the nettles.

Tizzy would have none of that. She had her own beezwax to tend. She crept over to the oak with her napkin full of pumpkin seeds.

There was a mama coon who lived in this tree. The mama foraged the woods along this dark corner of the playground. Only a low stone wall separated the yard from sugar-pitch pine. Hunters never put their dogs to scent till they were up the draw from Cayuga Ridge, so a coon was fairly safe here. Tizzy had come to know this coon well. She first heard the trill of little coonlets last Friday during recess. But Tizzy still had not seen them. Their mama only came down at sunset. Preacher would not allow Tizzy a pup and he poisoned all cats that came around by tossing out fish heads laced with lye. He said cats were shifty and would betray a trust.

These coonlets would have to stay a secret.

Tizzy squinted up into the high branches as she approached. She was careful not to bump the teeter-totter that lay against the roots. Tapping her ballooned cheek, she made a chitting noise to call out the mama coon.

Then she heard something. She stopped tapping her cheek.

It was running water.

Tizzy heard the splatter of running water, splattering on the backside of the pilgrim oak. She heard shuffling feet and a wheezy snicker at some private joke.

"Who's there?" Tizzy whispered.

Edging around the tree, Tizzy saw the hunched shadow shaking his privates at the root and bark. He was peeing on his white-top shoes. His pee flow stopped and Matthew Birdnell turned to face her.

"Hey there, sugar lips, I been alooking fer you," he said, buttoning his flap.

Then Matthew hooked his arm on a low limb and swung around the tree trunk like an ape. Tizzy fell back against the oak.

"Ain't you even gonna wash your hands?" she sputtered up at him.

"What fer? I'll jist dirty em again." His eyeglasses were crooked over his lopsided smile.

"What's that smell coming out of you?"

"Why, I believe that's words of fond affection you'd be smelling."

"Smells like kerosene to me. Or cleaning fluid. Leave me alone," she warned him. "I'll holler."

"Aw, I cain't let you do that."

Tizzy's fingertips gripped the bark behind her.

"Why not?"

"Because I done got the drop on ye. This is a stick up."

"A stick up?"

"Yeah, I thought I might steal a little sugar lip from you." His head hung over her, his eyes bleary behind the hornrim County spectacles. "Ever give up any sugar lip before, little gal? Naw. I reckon you ain't."

"Listen, you dang dumb gristlebone," she said, gathering her wits. "You better start walking soft or my—"

Matthew swooped in and kissed her.

Tizzy froze like she had salt on her tail feathers. Why wasn't she shoving him away? That's what Tizzy wanted to know.

He finally let her lips go.

"Oh me," she said, still frozen. "I seen a dollar bill once but never a five..."

Matthew gave a snort, a half-smirk, like he was a little ashamed but not much. Tizzy watched his head loll back. Was his neck broke? How did his eyeglass lens get chipped like that?

"One dollar, two dollar, three dollar, five," he said. "It's all dirty money."

Another little snort, then he came back for more, kissing her again.

This time Tizzy's lips began to work with him. She could not help herself. She felt his bitter tongue force itself betwixt her teeth. After he had tasted plenty, Matthew's head lolled back again. Tizzy tried to look up into his eyes to see how he felt. She could see his eyes trying to get a fix on her.

Yes, Tizzy thought, he's broken, he's bleeding. A red drip of blood began rolling down out of Matthew's left nostril. Tizzy knew she must warn him. She must warn him before he got that blood on his white-top shoes. But he was already coming back for a third helping of sugar lip. She must warn him.

Before she could tell Matthew a bloody thing, a hand grabbed the scruff of his scrawny neck. The hand ripped Matthew away.

"*Laggard punk—*" Preacher Polk snarled.

The Preacher flung Matthew sidelong across the teeter-totter. Tizzy heard the sickening snap of Matthew's spine, then the echo. Then the teeter-totter tottered up and down. The bonfire burned. The schoolhouse was singing, laughing, clomping.

Under the great pilgrim oak, the Preacher's wild eye nailed Tizzy hard. So did the back of his hand.

STEP 3

The night got a lot longer. Back at home, Tizzy got a good stropping for her wanton transgressions. Preacher-Daddy used his studded gunbelt, as usual. He nailed Tizzy inside the tiny kitchen coal box, then slapped his padlock on the box's hasp and locked it. This fulfilled his need, for now, and their ritual was complete. Sometime in the wee hours Tizzy got hungry and ate the Nestle bar she had hidden in her dress pocket. Not long after that, Tizzy soiled herself, as she so often did. This meant, come morning, Preacher clawed out the nails then stropped her again before he sent her off to school in the foul dress. Tizzy always tried to wash away her stain in the creek on the way to school. She knew the kids could still see it. None of them made fun of her, though. Most took no notice. They were used to seeing Tizzy Polk arrive on the playground with her lunch bucket and badge of shame.

But this was not just any morning after the coal box. This morning Tizzy arrived to find a damp coonlet dead under the pilgrim oak. The coonlet had died nursing the tip of its tiny ringed tail. Had the wee thing fallen from the tree, perhaps during last night's scuffle? Tizzy scooped out a place alongside the nearby rock wall and buried the fallen babe. Tizzy heard the other coonlets chittering up there in the limbs and wondered if the mama coon was watching or suffering over any of this. It was sad to see newborn life cut short and consumed so soon by cold earth and white wigglers. Tizzy drew a cross in the ground, across the top of the little grave. She murmured prayers over it.

But her prayers were cut short too—by a red-faced Matthew Birdnell. Last night, Matthew hightailed over this school fence and lit for the piney deep. This morning the schoolyard laughed as Matthew and his little half-breed Pappy passed by, down Skawmarry Holler Road. They were chasing their fleet of hogs on foot. The Birdnell hogs must have overrun their pen again. That, or somebody had not latched the hog gate properly while sneaking through the Birdnell's back fence long after dark, after the other Birdnells were all asleep.

This was none of Tizzy Polk's beezwax. She would sail her ship alone. It was all that grunting and squealing that made her peek from behind the pilgrim oak. Nothing more.

Matthew kept his head down, his eyes on the pork trotters. He popped their little hog butts with his birch rod and pretended he did not care about all those eyes watching him.

"That's humiliating, ain't it?" Tobe McCoy said quietly,

sitting on the teeter-totter. He said it to nobody in par-
ticular, but Tizzy thought it came from inside her head.

Tizzy got up from her tiny funeral. As he hustled by,
Matthew glanced over at her. He could not help himself.
Tizzy dropped her eyes, as if she did not see, as if she
might spare him. Matthew and his Pap turned the hogs
up the holler toward home and the bell rang.

Later that afternoon, in Miss Cockelbay's class, Tizzy
sat at her desk daydreaming about the fate of the other coonlets when—out the window—she saw the Birdnell pickup rattle past the school again. Miss Cockelbay
thumped her on the head. There were new sums on the
blackboard and that's where Tizzy's mind should be. Tizzy might have spied Matthew Birdnell coming and going
another time or two in the days to come, she was not
sure. Matthew Birdnell was not her concern. Tizzy might
have learned that Matthew was a junior gravedigger when
he was not herding hogs. But you heard lots of things in
a lunchroom full of jabbering kids. Tizzy could not care
less. That was his dirty beezwax, not hers.

Only Matthew Birdnell could know how many holes he
dug or hogs he slopped. Only he could know how much
hate he sweated and heaved while cursing sweet Jesus in
heaven.

A week and a half went by. It was late Wednesday
when Tizzy came home to an empty house for a change.
She left her books and lunch bucket, then went walking
barefoot along Pearlwick Road. Tizzy seldom escaped the
eye of the Preacher-Daddy anymore. Her only escapes

were on afternoons like this, when he was off visiting the sick, the near dead, and the stranded elders.

It was warm on Pearlwick Road, for an autumn eve, and a cur dog kept his distance behind Tizzy. The scalawag was black, mostly, with tan paws and tail. Every so often Tizzy would pick up a pebble and toss it at him, but not too hard. She kept telling him to go home. She wanted to love on that cur dog like she wanted to love those coonlets up the tree. But it did no good to attach herself to cur dogs or anything else she could not keep or care for. Tizzy needed an angel to save her. And angels didn't come with tan paws or tan tails or long floppity ears. Angels came with white feathery wings. Kind of like chickens.

A dusty lance of sunlight lay golden betwixt the peaks, cutting across Tizzy's path. Up ahead, the grade of the pike rose around the Jenks's leaning barn, climbing toward Coffin Holler and Tutweiller's Snoot. Tizzy glanced back at the dog. The dog cowered and slunk back, sensing Tizzy's dilemma.

Tizzy took a few more short steps. She stopped. Her eyes slit. What to do? She took quick stock of the mutt behind, the road ahead. Then, like a shot, Tizzy broke from Pearlwick Road, running off through the thicket to the left. Befuddled, the dog did not follow. The brush thinned as Tizzy flung through tall darkening timber, snapping pine boughs, then rose-briar. Finally, her bare feet came flying into a family cemetery—a hidden garden of rest—filled with crumbly gravestones. She stopped fast and spraddle-legged.

The sun was seldom seen in here. Tizzy felt the lurking chill. She should have worn her shoes. Blue fleece would soon fill the air, settling in the hollows. This garden of graves would grow colder still. Tizzy knew she must return home, but this was not the homecoming she had in mind.

Her left hand touched a low statue. She looked down when she felt it. It was a cherub angel in Plaster of Paris, dotted with dark, fuzzy cutworms. The unmoving worms clung to the moldering cherub face and wings. Tizzy had wished for an angel, but this angel she let go. She stepped slowly into the graveyard, each dusky grave and stone creeping toward her. Sharp birds spake from the shadows.

Tizzy caught her toe on a digger's spade. She flinched, spooked, and called out:

"*Who's there?*"

Ahead in the dead grass, Tizzy saw white-top shoes. Imagine that.

Matthew Birdnell was lying here on a grave, his head resting against the carved stone. His horn-rimmed eyes were closed, his arms were crossed. He lay very still and very quiet, with a serene smile.

Tizzy was not pleased.

She was winding up—about to speak her mind—but Matthew swung out and nabbed her ankle.

"*Grrrrrr,*" he grrrd.

Tizzy fought hard. She began a barefoot siege on his

face and sickly ribs, kicking with her free foot, attacking this Birdnell fool with all her might.

"*Cutterout, cutterout,*" Matthew laughed. "Stop your stomping."

"You retarded thang. *Think you're hot?* What if you was flopped there on your grandma or grandpa? It ain't no funny, it's jist *papist pagan.*"

Matthew snagged her kicking foot with his other hand, lifting it until she was struggling for balance.

"Hold on ladybug. We gitting *nasty* now. We gittin' fast and nasty now."

"Let me *go,*" she cried, hopping on one leg.

"Do your jig fer me now. I never knowed you could jig so good—"

"Let me go, you burr-headed *hogboy.*"

Matthew lost his loutish grin. He yanked Tizzy's leg up hard. She landed flat on her back with a thud. Matthew leapt to his feet, dismissing her with a wave.

"You're a stupid little chirp," he snarled, pacing away. "You don't know nothing worth nothing. I'm about through with you."

Tizzy was choking.

"Uh—uh," she gulped for air. Where was her voice?

Hitching his pants, Matthew's white-top shoes began to strut back and forth across several Vertlyk family graves.

"Right now you're on the brink of history. And you're too punk to know it."

"Help—" she wheezed.

Matthew spat and kicked a gravestone. "Yeah, about had it with you and all this cockydoodlydoo." A new thought struck him. His head wobbled, pondering his destiny. "*Hey. Tizzy.* I got something you ought to see."

He wheeled in a long stride toward the plaster cherub angel, jumping over Tizzy as he went. Matthew flicked a cutworm off the statue. Alongside it, a child's grave with a small stone were overgrown with weeds and saw-grass. Matthew knelt, brushing clean the inscription on the stone. The light was failing.

BABY O'KONNOR
BORN AND DIED   MARCH 25, 1898
"An Angel Passing Through"

Tizzy rolled onto her side, then up onto an elbow. She felt her chest.

"My heart's afumbling," she told herself.

Matthew riffled through the weeds. He found an old pistol hidden there. Shaking it off, Matthew eyed Tizzy. Tizzy watched as Matthew dropped her another loose grin, then spun the pistol's cylinder.

"Whatcha think? Huh?"

He spun the cylinder again. Tizzy could tell he liked the spinning, clicking threat of it.

"What are you doing with that?" she asked. She liked that clicking a little too. She forgot about her fumbling heart.

"Honey, when this boy starts hitting them banks for all

that big money, they'll think Dixie done riz again. They'll be calling him Rebel Yell Birdnell."

Standing, Matthew shoved the gun into the front of his belt. He struck a wild pose, one hand shifting his cods. Suddenly, he jerked out the pistol and fell to the ground, rolling until he stopped on his belly. When he stopped he had Tizzy in his gunsight. Rebel Yell leered down his barrel at her.

"Where'd you git that?" she asked again, with a slow smile. "I swear..."

Matthew found his elbows and knees, crawling excitedly toward Tizzy's grave.

"I busted in the schoolhouse last night. I took her right out of Mr. Wainwright's desk." He arched a lewd eyebrow. "Took me a stack of wicked magazines too."

"What kind of wicked magazines?"

"Ole boy and a ole gal going at it. Two ole gals going at it, too."

Tizzy was wide-eyed. "Two *ladies*?"

"Well, they might of been ladies. Maybe. Once," he grinned, enjoying himself. "Looked more like two ole gals aslurping on each other to me."

His hornrims were up in Tizzy's face now.

"Matthew could you git me some cigarettes?"

"Anybody been slurping on you lately, baby?"

Tizzy did not like this bead of thought.

"I ain't your baby and I ain't got *ears* fer your filth."

Matthew went bug-loony.

"I hope you live forever," he said in a hush. "Forever

and ever. And I hope you live hainted by the things you done said to me."

He sprang and paced angry some more, spewing venom under his breath.

Tizzy winced and sat up, brushing off her dress and hair. Nothing more could be gained by this conversation. Matthew was too far gone. He was too mad to get her cigarettes now, like a mad cur dog in silly shoes. She expected him to start slobbering suds any minute now. Tizzy crossed her legs, dropped her hands into her lap. She sighed. She was bored.

"I was thinking about taking you with me," Matthew began to blather. "But now you can jist turn tail and scratch it as fer as I'm concerned. They's gals more perty and gals more frisky on down the line. Gals with *great big titties.*" A fever took him. "I been to the county seat. And I been to Bowling Green, Kentucky. You didn't know that, did ye Miss Sweet Patootie. I took the Trailways down to Bowling Green when my sister died—me and Mama. And one or two gals did occur while I was there."

Tizzy gave her verdict: "You're crazy Matthew. Crazy as a sprayed roach."

"What's the difference? What's the difference if'n I am?"

"You are utterly depraved."

"Maybe. You prob'ly right. But they's a few things I ain't. I ain't fat. I ain't happy. I ain't nigger stupid or nigger rich. And I sure ain't no fucking *pig farmer.*" He spat again, this time in her direction. "Ye got that?"

27

She got it. She had no choice. They both sulled up. *Kuhcaaaw.* An inky blur swooped out of the pine then up across the new risen moon. It would be dark soon. Soon, by suppertime, Preacher Polk would return from making his calls on the ailing and elderly. He would expect to find Tizzy at home.

Tizzy tested the back of her sore head with her fingers. She had her regrets. "I didn't mean to hurt your feelings you know."

But he was not listening. Rebel Yell Birdnell was gone, adrift in his rebel mind. This would not last long. Nothing ever did with Matthew. Tizzy knew that much about him by now.

Suddenly, to hammer home the point, Matthew twitched. An odd tilt took his head. He took new interest in some movement in the surrounding wood. He cocked his body, sniffing at the wind. Matthew ducked low and stealthy, cat-walking to the brink of the narrow trail which led to Pott Ridge Cemetery. He detected little—nothing really—his superior radar scoping down the deep ruts which bent from view. His back straightened. He held the pointed revolver closer to his side. Matthew shielded himself behind the thick trunk of a yellow locust tree. His big-eyed spectacles strained to see something, anything, out there in the pitch of thick undergrowth. He sensed unspeakable secrets and heard nightly chitters quickening out there. These woods ran north, beyond Choat's Peak, climbing up the deadly ravines of Old Riddle Top. These woods knotted and spread and ran higher toward that godawful summit until you could not run anymore. Matthew Birdnell knew these woods. He had the blood of the Osage buck in his veins.

Matthew's mouth sagged open. He uncocked his body and his gun, pulling his eyes from the forest. He looked back at Tizzy who was way past curious now. She was on her knees, ready to jump and run at any moment. He had put on quite a show.

Matthew relaxed, returning with his sheepish grin.

"Awww, yeah," he admitted. "You jist fail to grip the magnitude. That's to be expected I reckon."

Tizzy knelt at his feet, her eyes glistening. She was kind of cute in that cornflower dress. Slowly, Matthew held forth the pistol.

Tizzy reached out and took the barrel in both hands. Matthew let the weapon go. Tizzy's eyes left him to look at the gun. The gun felt cold and stolen. But a part of her wanted it.

Matthew dug a news clipping from his shirt pocket, thrust it at her.

"Know who that is right there?"

Tizzy studied the frail photo then shook her head.

"No. I don't reckon I do," she said.

That lit something new in Matthew. Something soft and scary danced across his horizon as Matthew squatted down. A dirty fingernail stroked Tizzy's cheek.

"Well, mama—" he spake. His eyes searched among the dead, then looked back at Tizzy. "It ain't no secret. That's Mr. Johnny Dillinger."

She brightened a stitch. "I've heard of *him*—"

Matthew was nodding.

"Ye heard of Alvin Karpas? Clyde Barrow? How about Big Chester Wilkes? Heard of him?"

"They's bad men ain't they? Gangsters?"

Matthew's voice got heavy, just like her Preacher-Daddy.

"Chester Wilkes stuck up a bank in Elk City, Oklahoma. Three years ago. He took her five minutes afore quitting time. That day was his last day on this earth. His last day as fer as J. Edgar Hoover knows, that is. Because ain't nobody seen Chester Wilkes *since*." Twelve thousand frogskins, jist like *that*. To spend on anything he wants." A nervous tic began nagging Matthew's left cheek. "Well, he accidental shot that shoeshine boy in the back of the neck and it's a crying shame. Yes, it is. But Long John Dillinger had to shoot one or two G-Men who got lost along the way."

"Was that shoeshine boy a G-Man?"

Matthew snatched the clipping from her. It went back in his pocket.

"That ain't the point. Now is it? Wanna know something else, mama?"

"What?"

"Give me six months—remember I said this—six months, and Matthew Birdnell's shooting to the top of the F.B.I.'s Ten Most Wanted. I can assure ye."

"Goodness..."

Matthew boggled his head, eyes to the sky. Yes, he

was sure of his magnitude, sure of his fate and his glory. He was sure as any righteous rebel must be sure.

"That's the way it be and will be. Most of these folks here, in or out of this dirt, they don't figure much. They won't be missed. Well, I don't aim to miss.

The wind moaned in with another screeching, flapping thing in it. An old smell swelled up inside Matthew. The evening star glinted in his eyeglasses as he looked across the pearly tips of timber. There was nothing out there but one mean ridge after another.

"Doll-baby," he said, "that devil done *shat* on these mountains."

Tizzy had never felt such awe and inspiration. She was not sure what she saw in this boy. But it was new and it was shiny. She took his unclean hand from her cheek, laid the pistol in it.

"Don't talk ugly, Matthew," she whispered.

Matthew studied her.

"Your daddy's crazier than I am."

"I know it."

"Tizzy, I'd bulldoze Cayuger Ridge if I could. And burn it."

"I would too."

"Now, I ain't figured how to do that. Not yet. But I gotta do something."

"Matthew, you said, you wanted me going with you?"

"Aw, it crossed my mind the other day."

It crossed his mind. Well, how about that? Tizzy was tickled. She had crossed Matthew Birdnell's mind, but not that Tizzy Polk in little Cayuga Ridge. Matthew had paused in his masterly plans to sketch her in. Tizzy had never met anybody who saw her in faraway places with patent leather shoes. Cayuga Ridge, these dire mountains, they grew distant now.

"My daddy would come undone..."

Matthew tossed off a shrug.

"I don't give two tin shits."

"I think I love you."

He laughed.

"Tizzy, are ye a Christian?"

"Huh?"

"Do you believe in Jesus?"

"Sometimes I do."

"Well, some days I believe I might die from the blue balls. That's what I believe."

"What are blue balls?"

His smile hung looser.

"I think it's a damned blood condition. Don't you?"

Tizzy's eyes drifted up to the moon. There it burned, deep red in the clear patch of night sky above them. How could she forget? It was the first moon of the Winterhaust, the hunter's blood moon. This was the first night when men with guns went hunting these woods for winter game. Children were warned to keep safe inside.

She reminded Matthew of this danger, but he shrugged it off with everything else. He had a hole he wanted to show her, he said. It was a hole he just dug for a crippled man who could not get up from his nap today. They held hands and looked at the hole, but Matthew left it at that, treating her right. He was treating her with true respect now—or so it seemed to Tizzy. Tizzy told him it was as good a hole as any she had ever seen. Matthew mumbled a thank you. He even seemed a bit tender, a bit clumsy, having unreeled so many of his innermost desires and secrets. They hugged, but did not kiss, and Tizzy made it home in time to set the table.

STEP 4

Fortunately, the Preacher Polk was late from sick rounds. He did not climb the step until well after dark. By lantern and moth, they sat in clenched silence, eating turnips and cold soup.

They seldom spake out of turn during meals or at any other time for that matter. Sometimes an entire day with the Preacher-Daddy might contain four or five pointed grunts or half-words in a tongue befitting a varmint or Lych clansman.

The Preacher was long in his pilot coat, like a burnt stringbean, and when he removed the round hat indoors it revealed a white-stubbled dome. The chin bore a jutting tuft of fur like Tizzy had seen in pictures of sea captains in her school primer. Grim and staring at the salt mortar, his leathery mouth worked the hard turnip like a cud. His eyes and long nails were tobacco-yellow. Tizzy doubted there had been many words betwixt the Preacher-Daddy and her mother, a girl only three years older than Tizzy was now. Her name was Latisha, and she had died in childbirth. So said the Preacher-Daddy. Tizzy could never envision how such a thing had come to pass.

"Lord, we've come hungry, hungry for you," the Preacher said through his turnip, without looking at Tizzy.

"Father, meet us in our weakness," Tizzy recited, looking down into her bowl.

"Come my servant, spake the God of Abraham."

"Wounded, scarred, and broken."

"Come into my world, battered and bruised, spake the God of Abraham"

"Wounded, scarred, and broken."

"You cipher your sums today?" he asked, still not looking at her. "You'll need ye sums to tend the church ledger."

"Yessir."

"You keep clear of that boy?"

"Yessir."

"Well. Keep it so. He will steal the pennies off your eyes."

Watching her Preacher-Daddy eat, Tizzy began to feel like her very existence was proof of divine interference. Tizzy herself was the proof writ small. Tizzy did not know exactly how old the Preacher was. But, to her, he seemed like an old taproot who walked upright and rocked the heavens with each thundering prophecy. Most Cayuga Ridge folks seemed to be scary of her Preacher-Daddy but wanted him enough to tolerate him. They wanted his Sunday morning and Sunday night thumpings and his Wednesday night thumpings too. Tizzy sometimes wondered where all that thumping stuff got started.

Tizzy knew she was dirty and born that way. But she did not understand how Cayuga Ridge folks could be all the things her Preacher-Daddy said they were—and still be good folks, fit to be around. If they did not trust his judgment they wouldn't keep coming back for more, would they? And if they were all so scattershot bad because of the bad things he said they were up to, why didn't they stop doing those bad things?

"Salt," he said.

Tizzy slid the salt mortar over. He sprinkled his turnip. He was thinking bad things about the turnip too. She could tell.

Matthew Birdnell might be up to no good in the eyes of some. He was up to no good in Tizzy's eyes, probably. But Tizzy knew why he wanted gone from here. All she had to do was look at all these bad thump-loving folks, folks Tizzy didn't like much either. All she had to do was look at her Preacher-Daddy here, chewing his cud, to understand why Matthew wanted all the things he wanted.

Still, this Birdnell boy was going about it all the wrong way, wanting to point guns at people and rob banks and do wickedness like that. Why, if you were careful about it, a small pilfered thing was enough to lighten your load. A bit of candy could get you through a night in the coal box. The longer Tizzy was away from Matthew Birdnell and his graveyard full of excuses, the more Tizzy came to her senses. She realized that she could not let Rebel Yell Birdnell do crazy crimes against this world or any other. There had to be a better way to go.

"Clean up this mess," the Preacher said, rising from the table. "Git yourself ready fer the bed. Pray right."

Tizzy could hear him in his bedroom dropping his boots on the floor as she cleared the table. As she scrubbed the dishes, Tizzy arrived at a decision. She was a bad girl, but she was not as bad as that Birdnell boy. Tomorrow she would have to tell somebody before Matthew went flying off the handle. She would warn the school principle or Constable Newburn. They would clip young Mr. Birdnell's wings before he could go sticking up banks with his half-cocked pistol. But, still, she would say a prayer for Matthew. He couldn't help himself.

Tizzy blew out the kitchen lamp then headed for her bed. She would try to pray right before she got into it.

Tizzy did not have a room of her own, exactly. She slept in a storage closet, just off the kitchen, behind locked door. The closet was narrow with a high window. It held layers of folding chairs leant against the wall, stacked hymnals in peach crates, along with church decorations and the like. In a spare corner was Tizzy's cot and her clothing crib.

Beside the cot, on her only chair, lay Lou-Lou.

Lou-Lou only had a head—a cracked doll face—but she was enough for Tizzy. The crack split Lou-Lou's plaster forehead, like a thunderbolt betwixt her blue eyes. There was little red left to her lips. A few blond curls were all that survived of her hair. None of this bothered Tizzy. Lou-Lou was the only true friend Tizzy Polk had ever had. And she was Lou-Lou from the moment Tizzy could first form a gurgling word. Lou-Lou's body had been torn asunder long ago.

Tonight, like so many nights before, Tizzy sang herself to sleep by singing a song to Lou-Lou. Hugging her pillow, Tizzy sang, *"there was a little ship and it sailed a honey sweet sea."* Tizzy's voice was almost as flat as her face, but Lou-Lou did not mind. They drifted away together, in a ship and a shaft of moonlight. They both knew the song so well. It helped them ignore any rustlings outside the door.

The hall clock struck ten chimes, then eleven chimes.

In the parlor Preacher Polk sat staring at his front door. The room was dark and he was naked. From his couch, he could hear the crickets screaming through the keyhole. Those crickets were taunting him as he shook and shivered and gulped from his fruit jar. The drink poured down his whiskery chin, glistening on his sunken chest. A few rivulets settled in his privates like cold, burning titillations of Satan. Tonight, like so many nights, he sat here for hours, trying with all will and drunk ordination to smite that chirping chorus of crickets that screamed through that tiny hole in his door. There was no denying them, he knew this. They spake for the horned gods. They came to remind the Preacher-Daddy that they were all around him, everywhere in these hills. The Preacher and his flesh-root scepter and his lone god were no match for them, they screamed, laughing all the while. They gave him no rest. He felt himself slipping, losing the battle, night after night. He took one last burning slurp. Rills of the white whisky slithered the length of him, burning into his groin. He suffered it and liked it. The fire below gave him strength.

"I'll pluck out ye eyes," he slurred. "I'll gouge em out."

With divine method, Preacher-Daddy replaced the lid and screwed the fruit jar tight. Rising from the couch, his bony feet shuffled across the room and into the kitchen. He put his jar back in the floor, under the loose board beneath the stone crock butter churn. He crept back through the house, into the hall. The hour was late. The time for the roll call of Philistia was nigh. The Lord created deadbolts for a reason. There was only room for one Lord in her life. She must be kept safe from all those horned god screamers outside his keyhole.

The hallway boards were rough and creaking. His yellow nails raked along the wall, feeling their way through the dark until the Preacher stood outside Tizzy's door. But her door was not locked as it should be. The iron deadbolt was slid back. This revelation brought a flood of demons rushing up through the Preacher-Daddy, tempting him, seeking to destroy him. He pressed his wet lips against the woodwork, sucking at the gap in the doorframe. A thin line of moon divided his features, his breath came ragged.

Inside, Tizzy drifted off to sleep, eyes heavy as a low moan came through the doorframe.

In the hall, the naked Preacher carefully lowered onto his hands and knees. He must not let those howling horn voices catch him or crucify him or glorify him beyond recognition. He must hide himself until they were washed away by the dawn. In foul desperation, the Preacher-Daddy began to crawl along the floor, muttering, scurrying like a monkrat. If he could only find a keyhole where he could crawl inside and hide.

"*Don't be touching her,*" he hissed.

Suddenly Tizzy was awake, her eyes wide and grey. She heard mutterings, shufflings, the clink-clank of glass.

Outside, the crickets stopped.

Outside, hooves went clopping by, as a hunched man rode his glass-clanking mule past the dark parsonage. A magpie spake down to him from the weathercock.

In time, Tizzy slept again. She dreamt of a mother she had never seen, not even in a photograph. She dreamt of a beautiful mother who looked like Lou-Lou and taught her kindly tunes in a kindly voice whilst sailing south into a warm honey sea. Tonight, like so many nights before, Tizzy heard her mother saying, "*Honeygirl, you are so rare, so fine and refined.*"

Just after midnight, something muffled and strange caused her to stir once more.

A torn whimper came from within the bleak fibers of the house. Tizzy's head felt thick as honeycomb. The heel of her hand rubbed an eye. She threw back the covers. Her bare feet touched bare floor.

Tizzy found herself standing in her father's doorway. She had heard him. Hadn't she? So she came to her father and here he was.

He was still naked, and still wet. He was bathed in sweat, liquor, and tears.

The Preacher-Daddy lay knotted on the bedspread. His eyes were squeezed shut as he sobbed. *Horrible, horrible trees of life*, he cried. *Coming through them keyhole*, he cried. *Don't touch her, don't touch her*, he cried. Curling himself tighter and tighter, his fingers locked together, catching his tears. Strange scripture rasped from his gibbering maw.

He was sleeping. He was praying in his sleep. Tizzy could see that.

Ooooooh, the treee, cried he.

Tizzy stood and looked for as long as she could stand it.

She could see the naked snakes writhing inside him. His serpents hissed, they spake, they wept in words Tizzy did not want to know or understand. She only wanted to flee this house, this place, these people. But Tizzy was afraid to move. *I shall not be moved*, the song sang out, the song they taught her. But Tizzy wanted to move, to be moved. She was not a tree.

"Don't ye touch her—"

Still, she stood there—rooted in his doorway—for as long as she could stand it. She watched as he coiled, his naked snakes wailing louder and louder, until those wails of woe exploded in his bed. The explosion blew the white hairs out of his head. His skin began erupting with white wigglers.

Tizzy fled her Preacher-Daddy's door. She ran for the coal box.

STEP 5

Matthew swung his feet over the edge of the rope bed and sat up. He was about to step out of line. Whoever came next, it would not be Matthew Birdnell. Reaching underneath, he grabbed his white-top shoes. He was careful not to disturb his golem brother, Pug Lyle, who lay alongside the other two Birdnell boys. Pug Lyle was a rank moron.

Matthew checked his shoes for spiders. Fiddleback spiders liked to hide in shoes. Slipping them on his feet, he looked up at the shadowy ceiling—at that fiddleback spider up there. Ever since Uncle Mance's rooster cut loose up the holler, Matthew had been lying here, looking up at that fiddleback. That spider made lazy progress, in no hurry at all. Matthew knew he was looking at a killer. Fiddllebacks were the copperhead snakes of spiders. You did not want one in your shoes or even in the room with you. They were hard to see and waited for you in dark everyday places. As that rooster crowed and the spider crawled, Matthew Birdnell finally heard the morning news.

He was next.

It did not matter if you were first or last in this life if you were next. Being next made nothing else matter. If he kept lying here in this rough bed, not of his own making, next is what the Rebel Yell would be. Next.

"Wave bye-bye, little brother," Weldon told him the night the County nurse took sister Rose away.

"Why?" Matthew asked, playing mumbly peg, his back to the County jeep. "She won't know the difference."

"Well, Rosie is a sweet thing and we ain't never gonna see her again," Weldon said. "They're gonna keep her fer us."

Matthew flicked his knife into the ground, then reached down to get it.

"Sweet? She's deef, she's blind, and she cain't talk. Hell, she weren't never even here," he said, then flicked the knife again.

"That's hard, Matt. Hard. Yeah, what the hell. At least they come got her before some Booger Bob did."

Uncle Mance's rooster kept crowing and Matthew wondered how that cock would like a bite of spider for breakfast. Buttoning his shirt, Matthew checked the ceiling again. Yeah, that spider might be next. But the odds were against it.

A button snagged Matthew's split thumbnail and he almost cussed. That wouldn't do. He didn't want to wake anybody. Matthew studied the damage, sucking at his thumb. It was black with throbbing blood and reminded

Matthew of brother Weldon's big toe. After Tizzy went home last night, Matthew bunged his thumb bad trying to skeedaddle out of that dark graveyard. That spade split his thumb to the bone. It was the last nail in the box. Waxy Jack would have to hire some other Birdnell to work his shovel for six-bits a hole.

There were plenty of them, right here. Four to the bed, Matthew's Mommy and Pap and all these brats kept snoring. Baby Abe was gooing in the bottom drawer of Mommy's chiffonier. The chiffonier was Mommy's dowry and, over the years, eight babes gurgled and snored in that drawer before Abe. Abe was short for Abel, and Baby Abel had the same inbred, lumpish face as most of his clan. More than one snothead in Cayuga Ridge had confused a Birdnell child for a scary Lych child. Matthew had whipped many of them for that mistake. Matthew was lucky. He looked normal. Not too scary at all.

"Them Lychs, they can't help what they are neither," Weldon once said. "Even if they is hiding weird in your woodshed and seldom seen."

Weldon had that kind of, saintly streak in him. And a real practical joker, he was. Weldon was Matthew's older brother. Weldon's eighteenth birthday was two days away. Weldon was all there. He looked normal, just like Matthew. With his jet-black hair and square jawline, Weldon was near to good-looking. Like Matthew, Weldon hewed close to their Osage tribal bloodlines before wormy white men came back in here and spoiled it. Matthew was confused at times on this issue. He liked being white, but he also liked the Osage buck in him. The panther spirit. And Matthew liked being the other Bird-nell with smarts. Him and his big brother Weldon. There were no worms in Weldon's helmet. Back in the summer, working for Pap under the noonday sun, Weldon's funny-bone got the best of him. Hour after hour and day after day, Weldon broke his back behind that old ox, Duggum. Then one hot morning, while the rest of the house was still asleep, big brother's big toe tripped upon a solution to all that backbreak. He played his little joke on Pap—on the whole funny-looking bunch. Weldon went out back of the house and blew his wormless brains into the stock pond with a shotgun. That twelve-gauge blast rippled up Skawmarry Holler for every sleepy ear to hear. Matthew woke up to find a note in the white-tops by his pillow. Weldon had left him his favorite fancy shoes.

It was an unfortunate, predictable, and silly solution for Weldon. One that set Matthew's wormless brain to working on his own plan of escape.

He would start by stealing the truck. He would not steal the ox.

He would steal the truck and hope Pap did not call the law. It was a risk, but Pap always said you had to stick thick with your own kin, else they'd put you in a jacket and take you away. Pap might miss his Studebaker pick-up. But he would be intolerable without his big ox Dug-gum. So Matthew figured Pap was getting the best end of the deal. Matthew thought about taking both—truck and ox—and unloading Duggum somewhere for gas money.

Waxy Jack still owed him five dollars and six bits. But he took pity on the runts. Six little Birdnell bellies gnawing through wintertime was easy for Matthew's brain to ponder. He knew that hunger. These runts would be depending on what Mommy canned and pickled—canned roots, fruits, and vegetables grown in ground plowed by old Duggum. They would thank brother Matt then—the runts.

"You're welcome," he mumbled and stood. Otherwise, he disowned every goddam one of them.

Matthew crept from the room, hitching his britches as that fiddler crept down onto the wall. He went to the privy, cleaning his rear with a page from *The Queen's Saxonican Juris Dictionary*. It was a very big book. One of the kids had swiped it from the heretic Jake Shea's house during a graveside service. Such a heavy read would be good for years, through many trips to the outhouse. Matthew wasn't much of a reader, so he decided to leave the *Queen's Dictionary* for Pap to practice on. He would let Pap read the big book until he read Rebel Yell's name in the newspaper.

Matthew sacked up a chunk of scouse and some pone. He pocketed thirteen cents from the tin behind the clabber urn and, on this morning, he gave the truck a little push. Easing the truck from under the chinquapin tree, he let it roll down the holler a ways. Matthew popped the clutch just past the smokehouse, well out of earshot. The Studebaker belched black and blew out its pipes. The thin tires slid through the shallows then zipped out onto the market road.

Opening up the throttle, Matthew took his first nip. The gun was in his lap. The radio was just static. But he didn't need no radio to hear the news. He was borned bad and borned ready—ready for anything. Ready for what the hell. And, whatever came next, Rebel Yell knew it would be legend.

Tizzy hovered near the pilgrim oak, looking for her mama raccoon. She wished the school bell would ring and restore the order of things. Across the schoolyard Shonda Jo stood gnawing the bone of a raven-haired beauty who just moved here from Ewe Springs. The new girl was Shonda's new girlfriend.

"Her name's Vistalyn Ray," Tobe McCoy told Tizzy when she arrived. He pointed from his seat on the tee-ter-totter. "She and Shonda sure hooked up fast. I kinda fancy her."

Well, of course he fancied her. Just look at her.

Shonda's new girlfriend was too pretty for words, with alabaster skin, cherry lips, long black hair, and Tizzy did not like her one bit. Tizzy had not met this Vistalynn Ray, but did not need to. Shonda Jo might be too dim for disgrace, but she had no beezwax with a new best friend when she had Tizzy Polk. Ignoring Shonda's bosoms whilst reminding her of her backslides was a big part of Tizzy's daily ministry. Every schoolyard had a pecking order. If somebody stepped out of that line or messed up the order, then things did not work right and nobody knew who was next in line. Even Shonda Jo ought to understand that much. Instead, she was over there at this very moment, with that pretty Vistalyn Ray, fawning over that good looker Tom Braxton—when she was not pointing in Tizzy's direction, that is. Tom was a star ball jumper who flashed his teeth a lot and at least had sense enough not to point. And Shonda Jo was even more stupid if she couldn't see that Tom fancied Vistalyn Ray's new round bosoms, not hers.

Tizzy screwed up her face and squinted up through the gnarling oak limbs. No mama coon or trilling coonlets offered comfort. No sounds of life trickled down from the tree. She held her eighth-grade hornbooks tight against her flat chest, trying to squash out all these serpents, pretty white wigglers, and night goblins plaguing her blood.

Her Preacher-Daddy sat down at the table this morning, dressed head-to-toe and looking like he always did. His dome of white hair was all there. What Tizzy could see of his skin had nothing jumping out of it. She didn't know what to think. Was that crybaby preacher she saw last night just a nightmare, a holy vision of things to come, or was Tizzy's head just full of holes? Whatever it was, the Preacher never spake word one in his passing. He ate his bowl, grunted, got up, and walked straight out of the house, headed for The First Reconstructed Church of Cayuga Ridge. Tizzy did not matter. Not at home and not even here on this schoolyard anymore. Tizzy had no notion of anything she expected her Preacher-Daddy to say. In truth, she was glad she did not hear word one from him. But she wanted to hear these missing coonlets this morning, needed to hear them.

Instead, Tizzy heard the Studebaker before she saw it.

His brakes squeaked and there he was. Matthew Birdnell idled in his pickup outside the stone fence

They all saw Tizzy go out the gate and cross the road to his running board.

"Matthew—"

"Lookee here," He hung a folded roadmap out the pickup window. He showed her the pencil circle. "They's a savings and loan. Down in Shepville. Ain't she cute?"

"What are you up to now?"

"Snuff. I'm up to snuff. But first I'm agonna git me some of that money."

"This is your daddy's truck. You cain't jist steal it."

"Well that's what I'm fixing to do."

His motor died. Tizzy tried to take it as a sign.

"Matthew, I saw a sign in the winder at Willy Jay's store. They's needing missionaries to dig irrigation and water wells in Korea—"

"Korea, my white ass."

"You'd be helping out kids, Matthew. Hungry kids."

"Korea *kids*, my white ass."

"You could turn ye life around."

"Or I could jist turn around and rob me this bank. Same turn around. Faster delivery."

"Well, I cain't respect nobody what don't respect his

mama and daddy. This truck don't belong to you."

"That's right. They ain't nothing belongs to me. Not *yet*."

"But, I—" There was no other way to put it. "I thought maybe I did. Ain't we in love?"

He shifted behind the wheel, tossed the map on the dash.

"I reckon you could say that. Sure. Why not? But love don't git the groceries, gal. Besides, I got my horrorscope to think about."

"Your horrorscope?"

"Yeah. When I was down in Bowling Green that time with mama, saw me a gypsy gal. After we got done, she took a look at my hand. She said my horrorscope was one in a million. She said I was headed for fortune's fat pocket."

"Yeah?" Tizzy wasn't buying it. "How much her fortune cost you?"

"Two bucks and a cup of beer."

Tizzy didn't care about any of that really. She couldn't think right now. She wanted to worry about those coonlets, not this. Why was her blood so cloudy?

"I cain't go with you, Matthew. This ain't a good time."

Matthew cranked his motor, revved it loud.

"I ever ask ye to go with me? Huh?"

"No."

He took a flask of liquor from betwixt his cods. Swilling it, he replugged the cork.

"Then don't," he said through a whisky sour face.

"It's just witchery."

"Witchery? I don't git ye."

"Your horrorscopes. It's just witchery."

Matthew arm-wrestled his gearstick.

"Fare ye well, mama. I'll see ye in the funny papers."

Tizzy stood rooted as a tree. Matthew drew a finger-bead on her, making a pistol with his hand. He chuckled, gunned the engine, then popped the clutch.

The pickup shot forward—*baaarooooom*—Matthew raced the truck down the asphalt to the end of the schoolyard. A schoolyard of kids turned and saw blue smoke when he hit the brakes, squealing the truck around. The truck came rolling back towards Tizzy.

As he coasted past Tizzy, Matthew leapt from the cab and ran to her.

He kissed Tizzy hard, forcing his tongue.

He let go.

His feet flew back down the road.

Matthew caught the truck just before it hit Miss Rebekah's mailbox. The tires were weaving wild as he dropped into the driver's seat. Regaining the wheel, he punched the horn then sped away.

Tizzy's head cranked around to see Shonda Jo, pretty Vistalynn, and Tom in stitches over what they had just seen. Tizzy looked back down the road as the rattling Studebaker rolled out of sight.

Bye-bye, my Matthew.

Morning's lessons had begun.

As first recess approached, Tizzy was mooning her way

through Miss Cockelbay's history lesson. Miss Cockelbay was a stout maiden lady who made proper tones Tizzy hardly heard. The teacher was saying something about Yankee lies and Colonel Nash Renfrew. She was unaware of that ring-tail-tooter Ludlow crouched out of her sight in front of her desk. Ludlow kept peeking underneath at Miss Cockelbay's personal beezwax then making bug eyes back at the class. The room was awash with sniggering and snorts. It was a good show. But Tizzy was too busy fretting over Matthew, and herself, and sneaking eyes of wanderlust out the window. Time stood still now. Tizzy's life was wasting. She had not moved. Nobody cared. Brock McCoy sucked a cough drop. Vistalynn Ray sat pruning her widow's peak with tweezers, arching her slender neck at different angles in her compact mirror. The raven-haired Vistalynn Ray had introduced herself during show-and-tell then showed off her grandma's opal ring. It was a good show too.

As Miss Cockelbay broached the question of Negro servitude, Tizzy spied her father. Preacher-Daddy strode down the empty road past the school. His head bent, his long face and legs driven with purpose, the Preacher was headed back to his church. Tizzy knew he and his book must be coming from urgent matters—the last gasp of an elder or some drunk that needed to be terrorized. Her daddy did not fiddle around.

A blast of laughter brought Tizzy back to the here and now. The class was in uproar. Miss Cockelbay had finally snapped to the nasty antics under her drawers and had that carker kid Ludlow in hand.

"*Lud Prather*," she shrieked. "You perverted little *thang*. Git up off of this floor. Up. You're penitentiary-bound, boy. If ole Bob Knott don't git you *first*." She made Lud yelp, shaking him by his red hair. "You git yourself down to Mr. Wainwright's office. You tell him to give you thirty licks—*hard licks*—with his elem cane. You tell him. Or I'll make it forty. *Tizzy Polk*."

Tizzy blinked.

"Tizzy, you go with him. Make sure he gits there." Her handful of Lud's hair shook another yelp out of him. "Hear this, Ludlow T. Prather: I've had my yard of you youngster. You and me gonna dance with the devil. Now git on down there."

Shonda Jo Biggs blew smooches off her palm as Tizzy went past her desk. Vistalynn Ray giggled. They both caught an icy blast from Tizzy Polk's eyes before Tizzy and Ludlow went out the door.

"Y'all *shut up*," Miss Cockelbay hollered.

And they did.

Alone in the hall, Lud was already trying to wipe a booger on Tizzy's dress.

"*Tizzy pokypoke*," he teased, grabbing at her.

She shoved him away.

"Ludlow, *quit it*."

The front school doors were open. Twin bars of soft light streaked down the short corridor. Tizzy and Lud started slowly for the principal's office.

"Them little grunts back in there?" Ludlow jabbered.

"They be better off saying prayers to Lord Tarzan Ape Man. Ever one of them little grunts is got a gret, gret, gret, gret granpappy chimp who come down from the trees. It's in a book. *Ask Charly Derwin.*"

"Shut up, Ludlow. I'm gonna tell my daddy you said that."

"Tarzan now—weren't he the lily-white chimp Jesus? Weren't he though?"

"I'm telling Mr. Wainwright."

"Wainwright? He knows all about The Lord of the Ape. See this green one on my finger, Tizzy pokypoke? That's a juicy. Yessir. The day before Wainwright got borned his baboon pappy went bye-bye. It's in a big book. I'll show it to ye. Jist like I showed ye this juicy."

Here was principal's door. They stopped.

The door had frosty glass with painted letters.

P R I N C I P AL - Q.L.Wainwright, Jr.

Ludlow deflated. Tizzy felt squeamish herself and wondered why. Wasn't there something or someone else she was going to tell the principal about today? Whatever it was—whoever it was—had slipped her mind now. Her head was filled with holes. Tizzy felt cold comfort that she was not the persecuted for a change. Ludlow Prather was. He was hard to pity when he puffed up and poked at Tizzy again. She flinched, whacking him back. Ludlow ate the juicy and turned the knob.

Inside, the room was freezing.

Baldheaded Mr. Wainwright was sweating. He was tugging at his string tie as he looked up, dozens of rubber bands on his forearm sleeve. The other hand dropped some photographs into his lap. The electric fan whirred on his perfect desk.

"You knock on that door before you open it, *buster.*" Wainwright was in a mood. He was always in a mood. The Wainwrights were a stingy clan.

"Mizzz Cockerbay sent me d-down,"

Wainwright considered him for a fatal moment.

"Good. Git back to class Tizzy."

Tizzy smiled back at Mr. Wainwright, wondering if he had missed his wicked magazines yet. She traded dire eyes with Ludlow then left, closing the frosty door behind her.

Outside, she waited and listened. She heard nothing except the murmur of eight classrooms. Tizzy gazed down the dark hallway to the double doors, open at the far end. Two long shafts of light streamed the length of the floor, toward her. Then—in the double doorframe at the end of the hall—Matthew Birdnell's pickup pulled into view. The trucked stopped down there, square in that doorframe.

Whack.

Tizzy cocked her head. Yes, it was Matthew's pickup. Slowly, she began moving down the hall. Behind her, the *whack-whack* of a whipping cane tickled her ears. After the first swats, Ludlow began to repent, loud. But no matter. *Whack.* Tizzy ignored this as she came toward the light. *Whack.* Reaching hallway's end, Tizzy moaned. She found herself on the front steps, staring at Matthew, staring at his pickup. Things dark and wiggly were boiling in her blood. Serpent things. Goblin things. Tinglings. It was clear morning. There sat Matthew, idling, grinning back from the window of his truck. *Whack.* The whipping elem cane was an echo far behind her. Stop. Distant howls of pain. Don't. But the spell was cast.

Tizzy came off the steps and struck a trot across the schoolyard. She rushed up to his pickup. She *punched* Matthew's dangling arm. He winced but took it. The school bell began to ring.

"I hate you. I *hate* you, boy."

Tizzy ran around the truck, yanked the door, dropped into the passenger seat. Matthew set crazy eyes on her. *Brrrriiiing-iiing-iiing.*

"*Git,*" she said.

Matthew was cackling, the pickup was screeching away.

He punched the horn again, a long pealing ruckus as kids poured from the schoolhouse. He left children in his dust. The bell kept ringing. Shonda Jo saw blue fumes from the step while kids squealed past her. Rebel Yell's muffler was cracked, his pipes were loud.

Tizzy twisted to see out the back window. Matthew's truck careened past the white steeple—The First Reconstructed Church of Cayuga Ridge—his horn blaring like an angry angel's trumpet.

In his church sanctum Preacher Polk lifted a bleary eye. His fruit jar quaked, there was an ache in his gourd. Bitter tears stained his rectory desk. He sensed the brash and fleeting trumpet and he knew the serpent's tongue sang from that clarion. This was no drunkard's dream. He knew dogs, idolaters, sorcerers and whoremongers dwelt outside the kingdom of the city, where the murderer and beast of Sodom held sway. The Preacher-Daddy's keyhole had been blown wide open. They had slipped through his fingers. All rapacious children were in the hands of the horned gods now.

STEP 6

They sped the best they could, until the first curve. It was hard to race headlong for long on such a crooked road. The truck wobbled bad. The front wheel alignment was out and the Studebaker's tires were contrary sizes. Still their wheels kept threading unsteady through hills and gaps, two hearts pounding inside the fleeing pickup. And, for a time, this mountain-cloaked passage was all theirs, curve after curve, mile after mile, a lost and winding river of asphalt.

"We gittin' fast and nasty now," Matthew hooted, swilling from his bottle.

One tiny shack gave way to the next, each shack with its small barren field, desolate dead cornrows littered by blackbirds and autumn leaf. Morning's frost was burning off as the shadows grew short. This was nothing new to Tizzy and Matthew. They had lived lives of fleeting light. Each day brought brief respite from these mountain shades when the sun had no more ridges or peaks to climb. But one stubborn hump held the darkness longer than any other. Ahead, on Tizzy's side, it loomed. Riddle Top rose high above them. A great black crag with bristle hairs, it gave up sunlight like a jagged miser then quickly stole it back.

After their first outburst, the two rode silent for a long while. They kept swaying, nervously watching the rearview mirror. The road split and a sign pointed up the right fork in a scrawling hand: **RiDDLe ToP**.

The Studebaker pickup branched left, shunning the right fork and its twisted sign.

Tizzy saw an old fruit stand and tried not to think of how hungry she was getting. She played with the radio dial but got nothing much. Radio was bad up here. Finally, she clicked it off.

"*Hill-a-billy boogie, hill-a-billy boogie—*" Matthew bopped, hoping to fill Tizzy's need. She said nothing, so he quit bopping.

Soon Tizzy began to whistle a flat rendition of *I Shall Not Be Moved*. Five more minutes and Matthew threw his empty whisky flask out the window. When she heard the flask shatter, Tizzy stopped whistling.

"I want some Lucky Strikes when we git to Shepville," she said.

"Ready fer your coffin nails, huh?"

"Shuddup."

"Yeah, I should of dug you a hole while I was at it."

"You're a half-wit." She was fuming, "I want my *own gun* too."

He laughed.

"Bull*sheeit*."

Matthew saw the notched timbers of a covered bridge ahead. He perked up, sped up, and shot through the bridge like a demon.

"Okeedoke. She's right up here."

"What?" Tizzy asked.

"This is the joint."

"Which'n?"

"I figure we got thirty-four mile to go." Matthew pointed at the gas gauge. "Ye see that?"

Tizzy looked. The needle sat near Empty.

"We gotta buy some gas," she said.

Matthew's grin got lopsided and fell into a funny voice: "We gotta git a job first. Stupid."

The gravel lot was empty, like the road. Matthew wheeled in and slid to a rock-slinging halt outside the roadhouse. The joint was low and long, shored with rusty corrugated tin, tarpaper and beer signs. Busted neon over the door called it Bull's Gladiola Lounge. A roly-poly sedan sat off alone by the woodpile.

With his permanent smirk, Matthew leaned across Tizzy and opened the glove box. The pistol was inside. Tizzy could tell he liked the heft of it in his hand. The cylinder was spun and slapped back into place. His eye winked at her through chipped glass.

"Wait—" she said.

"Daddy cain't wait no more."

"We ain't sure—"

"Ain't sure of what?"

"We don't know what we're doing."

"I know what I'm *fixing* to do."

"But—"

"I'm agonna run in here and rob this ole boy. And after that I'm gonna rang up the Louisville Gazette."

They both looked out at the windowless juke joint. Tizzy felt trapped.

"Well I ain't agoing with you."

Matthew kicked open the truck door.

"Ye never was agoing with me, as I recollect. But we-uns is *gone.*"

He fell from the truck, loping over to the roadhouse door. Tizzy panicked, running her eyes up and down the road in case somebody was on to them.

"No, I'm coming—" she said.

Tizzy leapt out to join him. Matthew did not seem surprised. This riled Tizzy even more but Matthew shushed her with a barrel to his lips. A test of the door found it open. He was inside before she could squeak. A moment later Tizzy was behind him in the dark building, looking at the first payphone she had ever seen.

The long bar stood empty. Tizzy made out a boar's head over the whisky bottles. The long dance floor disappeared into blackness. Upended chairs hung on the tables, ammonia and dirty mop water hung in the air. The place felt clammy, like it had never seen a speck of sun. Matthew slid a foot forward, feeling for table legs. Like a mine sweeper, he pressed his luck, waiting for his weak eyes to adjust behind his spectacles. Ahead, behind the bar, the dull outline of a door became visible. The door hung slightly ajar.

"They're closed," Tizzy was saying.

"Shhh. Of course they're closed," he whispered. "Joints like this don't open afore the dinner bell."

They slipped around the barstools. There was a fancy old cash register with its empty drawer sticking out. Matthew gave it short shrift. Tizzy could not understand why her feet felt funny, until she realized she was walking on fresh sawdust. She had never seen a sinner's den like this.

Matthew was getting away from her.

The hinge barely whined as they eased into the back room. The room was cramped. A backward man knelt behind a desk. A mandolin sat in his chair. His khaki-covered rump met them in the amber of the dangling bulb.

"Right *there*," Matthew barked with a sudden twitch of his gun. Tizzy twitched with it.

The man turned his khaki shoulder and looked at them. He was elder enough to be Tizzy's white-haired grandpa. This grandpa had fleshy jowls and somewhat surprised grey eyes set wide over spider-veined cheeks. Tizzy hooked Matthew's belt loop for greater safety.

"Who're you, son?" the man asked, his voice steady— so steady it rattled his intruders. A shock of his white hair hung over bushy eyebrows. He held a small strong-box in his left hand. His other hand lay on the open hatch of a floor safe. The rug was rolled back.

"Let me see them hands, and *shut your yap*. I'd hate to kill ye—" Matthew grinned. "—but I'll kill ye."

"I can see that," the man answered.

Tizzy marveled. Why, Matthew was doing all right for himself. His throat had lost the jitterbug. Tizzy let go of his belt loop.

"Awright, daddy, you *stand up*. And fetch over that moneybox."

"Ain't no money, son."

The big khaki-clad man rose, not trying to hide the arthritis in his knees. He faced them full on and they both saw the star. Matthew's jaw sagged. Tizzy bit her lip. There was a shiny five-pointed badge pinned on his shirt pocket.

"Aw gee, mister..." Tizzy said.

"Who're *you* now?" Matthew demanded. Suddenly his gun thrust straight out from his body, holding that badge at bay. "*Hell—*"

"Sheriff Bull Hannah, from down in Ewe Spring. This is my place. I own it."

"*Own* it?" Matthew yelped.

"Since before you was a seed, boy. Sheriffing don't fill the corncrib."

Matthew's eyes lit up.

"That's what I told *her*." He glanced at Tizzy. "Ain't that what I told ye?"

"You said it don't git the groceries..."

"Same damn thing." Matthew asked the Sheriff, "Ain't that the same damn thing?"

"The money, Matthew..." she whispered.

"Aw, yeah, now *howzabout that money, mister.*"

The Sheriff dropped his strongbox on the desk blotter. The lid lay back, the box empty.

"Like I say, they ain't no money hereabouts."

"*Whyzzat?*" Matthew cocked back the hammer. The Sheriff froze.

"Whoa there, sonny, I got mouths to feed. I just come back from the Farmer's National Bank of Roanoke. I make the deposit twice a week."

"Matthew, maybe..."

"Shuddup, Tiz. Mister, you best not be arazzing me. I got plans fer that *money.*"

"I copy that. We all do young'un. We all got our plans. But how can I oblige?"

To Tizzy he seemed rugged but kind, a kind smile half hidden in his face.

"Silver. Copper. Pocket change—" Matthew mustered, new options dawning, "—you gotta make change fer your people."

"Back at the house. In my wife's purse."

"Christa*mighty,*" Matthew swore, nudging back his specs with a sweaty middle finger, smearing a lens.

Then Tizzy Polk whispered something cute.

"His billfold..."

"Oh, yeah—oh, *yeah.* Howz about that billfold Mister High Sheriff. Just lay her right on down fer the count." Matthew saw the man's hand start to move. "But you *watch* yeself now. Don't go fer no *razor* or nothing."

67

The iron gaze held steady under the bushy white brow. "No. I would not do that."

Sure enough, the Sheriff handed a wallet over to Matthew and Matthew flipped it to Tizzy. It was elk hide and worn to a shine.

"Any cash in there?" Matthew asked.

Tizzy opened the wallet and saw green.

"Yes."

Matthew got happy and wagged a finger at the Sheriff.

"Awww, Mister Sheriff, you figured to make a fool outa me?"

"I would not do that either. I plumb forgot."

"Hell, yeah. I wonder what else you plumb forgot. Howz about ye stepping on out here and we'll take a gander at that fancy till of yourn. Maybe you plumb forgot that double-false bottom full of hunert dollar greenbacks."

"Son, how many you know around here with a hunert dollars to they name?" the Bull asked.

But this meant little to Matthew. He had Tizzy check the empty floor safe for secret buttons and compartments. Then he guided Sheriff Bull out to the long bar and the fancy cash register. It was folly. There were no trick deposits to be found.

"Awright, you stay right here, Mr. Bull," Matthew warned. "And don't be raising no ruckus till we got a good running start. You best give us a hour—*naw*—make that two hours. Or I'll come back here and shoot ye children. Ye hear me?"

"I copy that, son. I hear you." Sheriff's hands were high. "You sure you wanna go through with this? Don't I know you? What, you're maybe seventeen? Eighteen? And you're putting this little girl in a world of danger."

"*Hell's bells.* She likes it thisaway, we be partners."

"Partners?"

"That's right, partners in the crime," Matthew said as he and Tizzy backed toward the door. "Come to think of it—they's a Nash Rambler outside. I'll be wanting them keys."

The Sheriff unclipped the ring from his belt, tossing the keys to Matthew.

"The phone..." Tizzy remembered.

The phone? Matthew caught her drift, whirled, and smashed his gun hand into the wall phone's bells. His pistol went slithering across the dark dance floor.

"Oh, Lord," Tizzy said.

A ridiculous racket ensued as Matthew dashed for the gun.

Tizzy glanced at the Sheriff. There was a window of opportunity, just a moment when the Sheriff could have taken a chance, made his move. But he did not. He held his oats, unflinching. He watched the kid recover the rusty weapon.

In that instant, Tizzy also saw a green bank note deep in the boar's gullet, above the Sheriff's head. She said nothing. She felt sorry for the poor Sheriff, even though he did not need it. The Sheriff's eyes kept track of Matthew's runaway revolver until full recovery was made.

At last Rebel Yell got his gun and rebounded to Tizzy's side.

"Don't you fret about me, kids," the Sheriff said. Y'all jist drive careful."

"*Shuddup*," Matthew snapped. He ripped the phone line from the wall. "Heed my words ole boy—"

Tizzy felt Matthew fall against her. They burst into the sunlight. Outside they ran for the pickup. Matthew flung the Sheriff's keys across the asphalt into an elderberry bramble.

"Cain't ye stay outa the way?" he snarled.

"Cain't you hold onto your own gun?"

"Keep talking, Tizzy. *Keep it up.*"

Bounding into the truck cab, they tore out of the parking lot, out onto the highway. Behind them, Sheriff Bull Hannah squeaked the front door open a few inches. Stern now, the old warrior watched them go.

Roaring hard down the road, Matthew was soon slaphappy. Tizzy kept grinning with glee at the rearview mirror. Nobody appeared in the cracked mirror, so their happiness grew.

"He knew I'd of *kilt him* if I had to," Matthew whooped. "You see his eyes? He knew I was bigger stuff than he could handle. Hell, I got a genius fer this. I *like* it."

"That *was* kind of fun," Tizzy allowed.

"Kind of? It was *bucketloads* of fun. How much did we git?"

A bottomless gorge opened up on one side of the road as a railroad trestle bent to meet them. They heard a high-pitched howl, panicked, then saw the freight train appear. Chugging black smoke, the train cannonballed along, pacing the truck. The train howled again and Matthew howled back. Tizzy counted.

"Fourteen dollars," she said.

"What ye mean?"

"It's fourteen dollars."

Matthew got unhappy again.

"She looked like a lot more'n that."

"*She* did? Well *she* ain't. It's all in one dollar bills."

"*I'll be cockchafered.*"

Tizzy was fed up.

"Well you're jist gonna have to stop and count it the next time, ain't you?"

Matthew punched the windshield. The train chugged off, disappearing into at tunnel. Tizzy let Matthew stew. She made no mention of the greenback she'd spied in the boar's gullet.

"Fourteen jack," Matthew muttered. "I could of counted all day and night and it would still be fourteen. Counting don't change nothing. Stupid you."

"Retard boy."

"Stupid split-tail you."

They drove silent for another half hour of winding road. They met no traffic except for a pair of nosing goats headed for Cayuga Ridge. The goats came, the goats went, then Tizzy pointed up at the cracked reflection. They were being followed.

"Model A..." Matthew said.

A flivver pickup had appeared, put-putting sprightly in the rearview mirror. It had a lot of power for an old flivver. Matthew slowed so he was not speeding. Then he slowed some more. A yawning farmer finally pulled along beside them, waved, then spurted ahead. Two miles later the flivver turned off at a pasture gate. Tizzy sank back in her seat.

Suddenly, Tizzy's window swept past a dark rider: a hunchman, astride a clanking, clopping mule.

She had been so intent on the flivver pickup she had not noticed the rider up ahead—and now behind them. Now there was just an echo, like the clopping and clanking outside her window the night before. Today, in the rearview mirror, Tizzy noticed a stringer of junk bottles across the mule's flank and the shadowed, half-hung face of a Lych under a straw cap.

"Ole Ephran Lych," Matthew said. "Packrat. Scrounges glass scraps, parfume flutes and such, fer small change. Sleeps Sundays."

"Jist Sundays?"

"Well, all day Sunday."

Tizzy looked again. The mirror was empty. The Lych and mule had vanished in a curve of blue mountain haze.

"I want something to eat," she said.

"Yeah, I knew you'd wanna fork three plates a day."

"You're all dumbass, hogboy."

Matthew Birdnell *slammed* his brakes. The wheels

locked. Clutter flew off the dashboard and into their laps. The map blew out of Matthew's window. The truck fishtailed to a stop in the highway. He sat there seething down at Tizzy. She studied the scenery. Matthew made his mad dog moves. He growled—put the gear shift through its pattern—then popped his clutch. The truck lurched forward. They were off and running again. Tizzy scrunched up her nose.

"Matthew, I swear. You are utterly depraved."

They rolled on. Matthew kept sucking his sore thumb. Tizzy laid her head against her door as her spirits began to sink. These were the same hills and hollers, they never seemed to end.

"I wanna go home," she heard herself say.

"Naw, ye don't," he said. "Ye think ye do, but ye don't."

"How far is it to Shepville?"

"Twenty-six mile."

"Maybe we can git on County Relief or something. I could babysit."

"Hey, ladybug—"

"What?" she answered dimly.

"We're fixing to gas up. Ye still hungry?"

"Of course I'm still hungry."

"Well, you're in fortune's fat pocket, doll baby. They's a jelly biscuit and a gas pump up here. But we cain't tarry long."

"Don't call me doll baby."

The Studebaker left the road again at Hayden's Crossroad. The pickup eased past a big parked tractor and stopped at the pumps of Kinebrew's Grocery & Gas as the station's screen door flew open. Out came a clean-cut young fellow in snowy coveralls rolling a dolly-load of empty milk bottles. He was smiling at some private joke, unfazed by the Studebaker's arrival. Tizzy and Matthew watched the fellow jockey his cases of clinking glass over to a white-paneled truck.

GOSPELTIME MILK - "Sweetest O'er The Land"

Tizzy read the side of the milk wagon three times before she noticed the young milkman was beaming back at her now. As soon as she noticed, his smile got bigger. Tizzy hesitated, but did not return the favor for fear that Matthew would flip. Still unfazed, the white smiling fellow started loading his empties into the rear of the Gospeltime Milk truck.

Matthew cut the engine. Tizzy leapt out and walked around, but Matthew was not with her. Tizzy stopped, looked back, and asked through the pickup glass what he was dreaming about. Looking up from his lap, Matthew belched and said, "Sure, why not?"

He got out and joined her.

There were voices within.

"We was at it all day yesterdy and today on the hide," some child-woman was saying inside the store. "I cut my hand open—"

The store was well-lit but dark with the scent of sorghum, damp tobacco, and a million mornings of woodsmoke. Tizzy let the screen creak closed on her heel.

She was in a tight maze of tools, hull-sacks, and canned goods. Matthew was already fingering a harrow blade. Two girls in overalls, both over six feet tall, were leaning like big bookends over an old lady at the cash register. The black-headed sister nodded while the sister with strawberry curls and calamine lotion on her chins held up a bandaged hand.

"Mama double-stitched it with silk thread," the strawberry blond boasted in her man voice. "Silk thread melts the scar."

"Sakes alive," the tired old lady said, shaking her noggin.

Tap. Tap.

What was that? asked Tizzy's ear.

Tap.

Tizzy squinted to see and saw.

A silver thimble on the lady's old finger tapped the register, once, twice, three times more.

Tap, tap, tap.

Tizzy drifted into the racks, hoping to disappear. There were rows of canned cling peaches and sardines and sugar beets. Black Draught. Tube Rose Snuff. A Bubble Up soda pop box and candy rack were braced along the counter. Matthew's arm was already swishing the icy water inside the drink box. He caught Tizzy's eye and smiled. It was no Gospeltime milkman smile.

"—God amighty if he weren't the hairiest shoat I ever had to stick," the big strawberry blond was saying.

"Hairy like a witch baby," the black-headed sister said.

"Mama said she come up on a piggy when she was a little girl, she come up on it an that piggy was reading the back of a old coffee can. Paw-Paw bled that piggy and burnt it. Right off he did it. He give mama the burnt ashes in that can and she throwed em down a dry well."

"You're a liar," the other sister snipped back. "She give them ashes to Aint Willa an Willa made a real strong cough serum. That was that serum what saved Paw-Paw an Uncle Bennie from the yeller jaundice."

"Oh me..." wheezed the old tapping woman.

Tizzy wandered through the grocery shelves, mute, memorizing all three women over the top of the bread. Below the bread were fried pies and packaged pastries.

"Uncle Bennie?" the strawberry blond pondered, hooking both thumbs in her overalls. A confusion of freckles mingled with her bug bites and pink dots of calamine lotion. "Uncle Bennie was down with the *dropsy*, Katy. I'm perty sure."

"You're perty sure of what? You're perty sure of nothing. Paw-Paw an Uncle Bennie both catched that yeller jaundice the week afore Christmas. Let's see. Nineteen-aught-seven or eight it was. Mama writ it down in the book. Nineteen-aught-something. I cain't seem to recall right now."

"I think Uncle Bennie give Paw-Paw the infection, Kate—"

"Shut up Myrna."

"It's simple arithmatics—"

"*Myrna.* Ignorant *ox.* Granpaw would tan you, not

that shoat, if he knew how *pu*rile you was."

"Oh me... my word..." went the old spinster.

The strawberry blond laughed, whacking her sis hard on the arm. "Settle down, big sister. Daddy loves ye and I love ye. You're a keeper. Granpaw loves ye and Miss Doobelle loves ye too. Don't ye, Miss Doobelle?"

"Lord yes, hon," the wrinkled Doobelle exclaimed. Tap. Tap. "You're a prize tomater and we love ye to death."

Matthew snickered at them. Tizzy held a pecan roll. Nervous, she glanced up. Miss Doobelle smiled at Tizzy from behind the counter. It was Tizzy's day for smiles. Tap. Tizzy smiled back.

"That ain't the *point*, Myrna." The jet black hairs stood up. "You're telling tales after school. Tales what ain't fit to tell, you little fool. Change the subject."

"Okeedoke. I'll change the subject. Y'all hear they caught and kilt Big Chester Wilkes down in Joplin on Tuesday? Newspaper say he spent all them bank bucks he stole having his face cut up and sewed back so's he could hide out as somebody else."

"What's your point now, Myrna?"

"The point, Kate honey, is that's why it took so long to catch the fat rascal."

"Hmmph. Still ain't much of a point. Jist a fool tale to tell."

"Haw. Maybe that's how went Murphy Bob Blue," Myrna said playfully.

"And that proves you the biggest fool to tell. Some-times I wish Boogery Bob Knott woulda come got you instead."

Myrna curled her lip at big sis.

"Doobelle, how much are we owing?"

Doobelle came to life. She ran a feeble hand over the goods on her counter.

"Oh me," she warbled. "We've got a two-pound rice, black pepper, and coffee, Wine Of Cardui—"

Tizzy's hand exchanged the pecan roll for a small sweet potato pie in cellophane. Timid, but quick, Tizzy slipped the pie under her dress and into her panties. Matthew sidled up the counter to press flesh with the boxy girls.

"Hell, no need fer Cardui," he cracked like a parrot "Nigger gals chaw that ginger root when they monthly pains come. And they does it fer free."

"They does what fer free?" Myrna asked him.

Mathew winked.

"Well, that all depends. Now don't it?"

Nobody laughed. Black-thatched Kate growled from her belly, still peeved. Old Lady Doobelle was straining for good humor. But Kate looked downright surly. Her eyes bid upon Matthew like she was sizing him for slaughter.

"Ain't from this neck. Are ye?" Kate decreed.

"Aw, sure I am, sis," Matthew said, swilling his unpaid cherry pop. "Jist up the road a piece. Skawmarry Holler. Jist the other side of Cayuger—"

"Well, we don't cotton to that kind of unfit talk around here. Not around ladies, we don't."

"Well, do fergive me, Kate honey," spake Matthew, taking another swill, still grinning.

Nobody but Matthew seemed satisfied by this. So he ceased to exist for the big girls. Snubbing him, they paid their chit and left. As the door jangled shut, Matthew set his half-empty pop bottle beside the register. Doobelle nodded like her head was on a loose spring. Tap. Tap.

"Honeybunch?" Rebel Yell called out to Tizzy. "Ye want that jellyroll?"

"Nope," Tizzy said, approaching the counter. The old lady made precious eyes at her. So did Rebel Yell.

"Ye want some crackers or a sody pop then?"

"Nope." Tizzy had all but disappeared again, into her will o'the wisp smile. Her mind seemed distracted by the hametugs and tack on the wall behind Miss Doobelle.

"Nope?" Matthew mocked. "Hell, I thought you was hankering fer a bite to eat?" Matthew said.

"Well, I'm not."

"Howz about one of them new fleet trailer homes an a three-tube Zenith radio?"

"No."

"*No?*"

"No."

"I swan," Matthew swore to the lady. "Young'uns these days. Well, I'll jist be a minute, gal—" his eyes locked on Tizzy's, "—better wait out in the truck."

"Okay," the Tizzy said, obedient in mixed company. Her hands were clasped primly across the lumpy tummy of her dress. She went. As Tizzy opened the door she saw the big chugging diesel tractor turn the crossroads, headed elsewhere. Kate was driving and Myra sat alongside on the big fender.

With Tizzy out of the store, Matthew lolled his head back around. He hung half-cocked against the register, mooning over Miss Doobelle with strange expectation.

"Anything else?" the old one asked.

"Ah-yuh. I could go fer some of them Camel ready-rolls. Two packs."

"Surely. There ye go. That will be six bits. Plus a nickel for the cold drink."

"Aw—" Matthew snorted. "You're ajaping me."

"Do tell?" the lady said, looking spry and stupid to Matthew, like a hopsack scarecrow. Tap. "Did you fergit somethin'?"

Matthew slid the pistol from his shirt.

Her rheumy eyes got bigger, wiser, less stupid.

"No, sweet mother, I did not fergit nothing. *You* did. You dang near fergot to fork over the take. The booty. Now *open her up.*"

His pistol jerked at the register. Doobelle got the message.

"Oh me..." She fluttered. Tap went the thimble. Her bony digit released the drawer. Jittery hands spread the cash before him.

"*Wait,*" Matthew twanged, his pupils dancing wild inside tortoise shell frames. "Count it. Count dat money."

Fumbling, Doobelle tried to please. "Thirty-nine—forty—forty-one. Forty-one dollars. Do ye want the silver?"

"Let the devil take your silver, ole darlin." Matthew snatched the greenbacks from her. He balled up the cash crudely and shoved in his pocket. Now he was retreating through the hull sacks.

Doobelle's thimble dropped off. It tapped its last and rolled. Her mouth was agape, afraid.

Matthew opened the door.

"Now don't ye holler—"

"Oh me, no, I won't—"

"Ye ain't agonna holler on me?" His tailbone hit the screen.

"I won't holler—"

"Naw, I reckon ye won't."

And his gun exploded. *KA-BANGGG.* His trigger tripped before he knew why for or how. A bloody hole bloomed betwixt Miss Doobelle's eyes. She fell.

Cackling, Matthew flew out the screen door.

Tizzy heard the pistol's report, a clattering screen. She sat in the cab with gooseflesh sweeping her as Matthew landed behind the wheel.

"What'd you *do*?" she bleated.

"*Watch out,*" Matthew said as the engine cranked.

Dumbstruck and dead ahead, the Gospeltime milkman stood in the windshield: his milk wagon and cases of fresh glass bottles blocking their path.

Matthew ground into reverse, backing from the pumps in a streak.

More grinding, and the pickup gunned forward, kicking gravel, fast and hot for the road. But that milkman was in the windshield again!

The milkman had cut in front of them, waving, shouting, shouting something Tizzy couldn't understand like *"stopweseenyou"* before Matthew cussed and dodged him.

The gravel began to skid again when Tizzy saw the mule and man passing on the road. There was Ephran Lych, bent on his mule. They were about to run Ephran down.

Tizzy grabbed the dash, the pickup sailed across blacktop, the brakes locked. Tizzy felt the pickup's rear-end slide around as they careened broadside into the mule and rider.

"Mamaaa—" she squealed.

Her window smashed into the hairy belly and trouser leg. The beast bellowed and squealed with her, glass flew, and Matthew fought the wheel.

BAAA-ROOOOOOM.

Lych and his mule were crumpling like shadow puppets. The truck lit for the crossroads. But a horse-drawn hay wagon was crossing the crossroads. On it, four young farm boys stood paralyzed—staring head on at the barreling truck—staring at Tizzy and Matthew terror-riven in the oncoming windshield.

Matthew locked brakes again. The Studebaker pickup reeled around, full circle, smoking and screeching. He gunned the engine.

And they sped away—speeding back to where they came from—him berserk, her door stoved in, leaving fresh devastation in their wake.

Bloody, she screamed in his ear.

"Gristlebone. We still ain't got no *gas."*

STEP 7

About halfway back to Bull's Gladiola Lounge was the cut off where the dirt road ran up the branch to Ewe Springs. They left the asphalt and ventured in a good hot hurry, raising dust along the draw, past a few fancy gabled houses. Folks lived a little better over in Ewe Springs.

Suddenly Tizzy did not want to go home. She wanted to die. And disappear. Now. Home was impossible. She could never return, for that would be worse than eternal damnation. She thought about the Preacher as she picked glass shards from her scalp. She did not whine and she did not make tears. She had a pretty good idea of what happened back there, inside that store. That old lady was gone. Deader than Dixie. Lych and his mule might even be dead. And Matthew, he looked scared alright, gripping the wheel, tongue working, lips dry with that gun in his lap. Tizzy didn't like the way he kept nudging his eyeglasses back up his nose. It scraped at her nerves. She also didn't like the way Matthew kept breaking into stray chuckles now and again as those eye-glasses bore ahead.

"*Ye gone an done her now,*" he kept muttering, "*yep, ye gone an done her now...*"

That said it all. Matthew was gone when he got up this morning. So was she. And that set her straight. Tizzy Polk never cried over spilt milk. She remembered the coal box and the back of her Preacher-Daddy's icy, hateful hand. Then Tizzy knew. Her milk was spilt for good.

Their hearts raced for several more speeding minutes before they heard the first sputter. Matthew pumped the pedal anyhow as they flew, then coasted, then died on the roadside. Getting out, Matthew pushed the empty truck into a dry, brushy creekbed.

"That tailgate. They can still see it from the road," Tizzy said.

"Ain't nothing to be done about it."

The sun had shifted in the sky, they were moving into afternoon. Matthew mentioned a driveway he'd spotted just before the gas ran out. They trotted back down the road. Matthew made no effort to hide the gun. Tizzy's side ached but she kept up with him. They wasted no time.

A blue Packard convertible sat on the gravel drive with its top down, bright autumn leaves littering the seats. It was a nice, two-story home, not too big really, with an alcove and black shutters. Each shutter had a white star. There was no key in the convertible's ignition, but Matthew heard a splash. He slid over to the birdbath, peeking along the side of the house to the backyard. He glimpsed a toddler in her frilly polka-dot skirt. A woman's echo caught his ear, and giggling children.

Tizzy knit her brow, watching Matthew skip onto the porch. She did not tarry when she saw him sniff sideways through the screen door then slip inside. It was open. And she went in after him.

They moved fast and quiet across the grand hook rug in the parlor, past the phone nook in the hallway, past the open Bible on the kitchen counter. It looked like a nice family lived in this airy place with doilies and crayons and hardwood floors. It was good not to meet them. Over the sink, on a cup hook, Matthew found car keys.

"Yes, princess made magic bubble..."

It was the woman's voice again.

Matthew looked out the sink window and saw the young mother with her three children. The squirtlings were blowing soap bubbles in the backyard. Twin boys and a girl. And one lovely mama in sandals. The mama was young and tanned with tawny tresses. And when she bent to grab at her children's bubbles her ripe bosom floated free inside her husband's plaid flannel shirt. Matthew loitered at the sink, watching those bubbles float. Tizzy did not like how he watched them, with mama and kids so blissful, so unaware of his hungry eyes.

"Come on," Tizzy said quietly, pulling him away.

Matthew's eyes left the window. It was a shame. He might have to swing by for another visit sometime, when he could visit longer.

Together they pushed the Packard backwards down the driveway, rolling it out onto the road. In the dark days that followed, Tizzy often wondered what happened behind them. The pretty young mother must have heard a motor chug to life, not far down the road from her house. She must have looked up from her bubbles for a moment and wondered who that might be, as the autumn sprites sailed away in her Packard.

Lucky for her, her Packard ran beautifully, swiftly. You know the kind. A well-oiled machine. You could call it reckless abandon, or a fierce pledge to pop a bank president, but Matthew was retracing their flight from the store. To Tizzy, Matthew did not seem so broken up about any of this. Not anymore. Even small amounts of money gained—even a newly stolen car—seemed to embolden him. By Tizzy's count, they were forty-nine dollars richer, sixty-three dollars in all. There was no telling what terrible extremes might be achieved should Rebel Yell ever acquire major funding.

"If we can sneak back through the crossroads in this doozy," Matthew figured, "we got a shot at slipping on down to Shepville this evening and catching the train. Git a sleeper car whatsay with clean sheets? One of them red-eye trains to Memphis."

Tizzy did not argue with him. She was too weak and grogged in the warm afternoon sun. The car's upholstery was a soft yellow stitched-leather. It had a shiny radio with ivory buttons and a chrome dial, but this radio did not work either. So Tizzy went back to whistling her flat hymns, cleaning her forehead with spit and a napkin she took from the house. The blood was dry by now. She would recover. Besides, maybe this was a dream, and maybe they could make it all happen. She had never ridden on a train.

A hardtop grey sedan was turning off the Cayuga Road as Matthew turned onto it. The sedan's prissy driver looked cross and distracted beneath his equally grey beard and pinstripe suit. He was paying them no mind. Tizzy entertained notions of ongoing invisibility until they reached the steep knob before Hayden's Crossroad. By then sinister clouds were gusting in through Auld Cloot Gap, the sun blurring into a hazy spot. Matthew braked before the crest of the hill and got out where the Crossroads still could not see them. He skulked low as he hustled to the top of the knob to take a peek. Pretty soon, he motioned for Tizzy to join him.

Tizzy burrowed in beside Matthew on her stomach and her dreams were dashed. Down the grade, flashing in the crossroads, were three patrol cars. It was a black and white roadblock with three bright cherries on top. The Gospeltime Milk wagon was still there. Local folk were milling out in front of the store, talking to several police officers in khaki uniform. One of the men looked a little like Sheriff Bull Hannah to Tizzy, but she could not be sure from this distance.

"Oh my Lord, Matthew, they're alooking fer us."

"No doubt about it," he squinted.

"What are we—?"

"Most likely they got fellers atrooping in and outa Cayuger Ridge by now."

"Then my daddy knows."

"Everbody in your ole sow circle knows by now, mama." Matthew scuffled a few feet back from the crest so he could raise his head. "Listen here, Tizzy. I got me a second cousin, more like a uncle really. Wert Birdnell. He's got a crackling still and a two-room shanty up on Riddle Top."

"Riddle Top?"

She tried not to cringe.

"You bet. An he's hid out pert good up there. It's been a few years, but I believe I recollect the way. I believe he might put us up till this settles down. Hell, perty soon they'll figure we slipped through somehow. They'll find the truck in no time at all, an this car will be reported stole. Folks'll reckon we snookered em and we're long gone from these parts."

"You think so, Matthew? Won't this car look cockeye up there?"

"Aw, we'll hide her out, in some barn or somewheres. We can cover her in pine limb if we have to, till we need the car again. Anybop, them hicks don't git no news bullets up there. You know that."

Tizzy got quiet.

"They say you can always hear something laughing. Up that mountain," she said. "Crying too."

"Hell, them's just tales to scary kids with."

Truthfully, Tizzy did not know very much about Riddle Top. She had heard whispers. Who hadn't heard them? Unpleasant encounters. Odd incidents. Tales of folks disappearing up that dark mountain. But it held little regard in most daily lives of Cayuga Ridge. None they would fess up to. Most of the whispers lacked details. Rumors grew of a secret lake few had ever seen. It was known that most of the Lych clan had trickled down from there. If you stood around long enough, you might hear a rumor or three. But most Cayugans considered themselves too worldly and genteel for idle gossip about such a haintful and unrefined peak.

All Tizzy knew was this: she had seen that great, black Riddle Top looming over her every day of her baby days. And she had never wanted to go there.

No, Tizzy realized, that was not quite right. She knew something else now. She knew that, today, her baby days ended. No more baby days. You could hammer that into a stone tablet and hand it over to Moses. And Tizzy still had no itch to scale Riddle Top.

But today's damage was also done. Matthew was gone. Tizzy's milk was spilt. Within the hour they had returned and were fast approaching the **RiDDLe ToP** turn-off, the rising fork up the mountain. Just before the signpost, Tizzy slapped Matthew's arm.

"I hear a si-reen coming."

The Packard was already leaving the blacktop. Matthew had heard the patrol siren too. He quickly pulled the car behind a boarded fruit stand. A police sedan came from Cayuga Ridge, its siren wailing and cherry-light flashing.

After the police sedan passed, they ventured forth again. They eased back onto the blacktop then turned wide onto the Riddle Top mountain fork. Less than a hundred yards up, the asphalt grew broken, then ended altogether. Now it was just hard clay ruts.

They began to climb.

Minutes later, the Packard sedan began groaning, straining at the incline. They saw no shacks or shanties, no cabins, pens, or fence. The higher they climbed, the darker it got. An early dusk settled in, lingering, roiling as a black storm grew near. Trees began to thrash and rule overhead. Finally, thunderclouds rolled over the peak, meshing with the piney slopes. The air turned electric. Going up and up, winding in and out and around, the road tangled until they got dizzy. Sometimes, remnants of other roads crossed their path, but Matthew did not take the bait. They jounced, they bucked, but they kept to the main drag.

Tizzy had to give Rebel Yell his due. Even with their teeth jarring loose, Birdnell rode on like a champ. Often he had to make several runs at a grade before they could surmount it. Once he had to get out and force branches under a rear tire to escape from a wash-out. Tizzy helped. The Packard was not made for this. In most places the way was so cramped that needles and branchy fingers were scratching the Packard's paint. Riding inside the open roadster, they both got swatted by limbs, but

Tizzy got the worst of it. She could tell this trace was seldom traveled. It was never meant for such a pretty blue car. Or for Tizzy either.

"Dang. My head's bleeding more," she said.

Her napkin was soaked red.

"Let's fix ye up," he said.

"No. Don't stop again."

"C'mon. Let's fix ye up."

Matthew stopped the car, got out again, and found a pine knot on the ground. He heated the pine knot on the motor manifold. Gently, he dripped the pine knot's dripping resin onto Tizzy's cut. It burned a little. They both knew it would. But the bleeding stopped. With Tizzy patched, they moved on.

When Tizzy did finally see the first shack nesting in vine and moss, the novelty of it struck her. How peculiar, she thought. How peculiar that this would be the first homestead since mounting Riddle Top. Usually folks clustered in the lower regions. Soon Tizzy saw another shack, rickety but upright, then another. These three shacks were not empty. Smoke curled from their stovepipes and chimneys. But Tizzy spotted nary a face nor anybody at work or along the roadside. Who knew if human eyes saw them pass? None were stirring. It was all so strange. If there were hidden eyes watching inside those shacks, what they saw must have been equally strange: A squinty, bespectacled boy and a nervous girl. And an urgent blue Packard, climbing this restless slash of road.

They came to a fork where the road split into three. Matthew eased off the gas again and stopped. His shirt flapping, Matthew cleaned his lenses with a ten dollar bill.

He could smell the rain. The clouds hung dark, heavy.

He thought about raising the Packard's ragtop, but didn't know how or how long that might take. Still, he was sick of this grit blowing in his eyes. He put his glasses back on. Tizzy was shivering now. He could see that. They had just skirted alongside a pile of rocks—a cairn of stones that seemed to be some kind of road marker. These two ruts to his far right looked like the spur he was looking for. But hadn't there been an old water tank? He remembered a water tank. Were those wormy cross-ties rotting over there in the laurel all that survived of the tank? Matthew tried to justify the missing water tank and tried to ignore the old rusting tractor chassis at the mouth of the spur. The tractor was sunk to the axles in a mud-baked bar ditch. It reminded Matthew of the fly-blown upper half of a horse carcass he once saw—a horse that got trapped in a peat bog and died there. So Matthew ignored the tractor.

He couldn't explain it, really. It was probably the Osage pathfinder in his bones. But these other two road spurs to the left didn't interest him even a little. They didn't call to him. But this far right spur—it called to him. It was an off-winding spoke of road with a charred dogwood bent over the narrowing spoke. Its ruts rose quickly past the dead tractor, rising into the forest, disappearing.

Yes, that road over there had his name on it.

Matthew Birdnell was six years old when they had toted him up here to see Cousin Wert. His Pap bought some shine and Wert gave Pap a special witching rod for finding water. Matthew did not want Tizzy to know it had been so long. His memory was good. This was where you left the main trail, he was pretty sure. He remembered Pap's truck reaching this turn off sooner. But he was only six years old at the time.

Matthew cranked the wheel, steering the Packard under the charred dogwood tree. Tizzy watched the sunken tractor float by.

"So it's thisaway?" she asked.

He didn't answer.

They hadn't gone far before Rebel Yell had him a few doubts. Maybe this road didn't really have his name on it. Maybe it weren't no road at all. This spur was very poor. In fact, this mess they were twisting and pushing through was more like a gully than a road. The root-tangled walls of it rose and fell and mostly rose. More than once Tizzy had to lift a pine bough by hand, above her head, while they drove under.

"Matthew, you sure he's thisaway?"

Matthew didn't want to admit he was about out of brainstorms and ways to jump. He had exactly one new opinion to offer: Somewhere in this racket of grinding gears, motor, and crashing limbs, he was pretty sure he heard a front wheel bearing going out. Other than that— he was about out of steam. This gully road looked played out and dangerous. They might give up and try to get some help at one of those rathole shacks they passed. But this gully was too tight to turn this blue doozy around. If he had to, Matthew could shift the roadster into reverse and try to hot dog it backwards all the way back down to that three-way. They might even get there before the bottom dropped out of this sky. Or they could pitch camp here and sleep under a hubcap. Either way, when that rain swamped in, this steep gully road would turn into the river of no return. What Matthew really wanted was a reshuffle.

He was about to get one.

Without warning, the car bucked over a steep hump and they were out of the trough. The gully ended. They both breathed easier, but not easy. The ground flattened out, opening into a blustery stand of black gum trees. Only these trees were blacker than most.

"Oh me, Matthew. Them's giants."

They were huge trees, great ghosts of trees. Many were just hollow shells, blackened cinder bark, victims of a wildfire. The road through the black gums was stark, but easier on the shocks and tires. They had not travelled far through this burnt forest before they saw a glint of fire ahead.

The sod-roofed log shanty pressed back against a claybank. Outside in the wind, they could see a kneeling man. He was all legs and arms and seemed to be holding a torch over a stump hole or something in the ground. The man was jabbering down into the hole. When the man heard them coming, his movements got frantic, un-hinged. They saw him spit a few more words into his hole before he quickly raked sod over it and leapt up. He scur-ried inside the log shanty as Matthew and Tizzy arrived. Tizzy was thinking their long blue car must have looked like something from the blue future or Jules Verne to a fellow like this.

Matthew set the brake, then shouted through cupped hands.

"Feller in the house?"

Tizzy's hands were betwixt her knees, trying to stay warm. She forced her teeth to stop chattering as Mat-thew got out of the Packard. She noticed he kept one foot on the running board, like he didn't want to leave home.

"In the house—," Matthew shouted again, *"—didn't aim to scary ye."*

The mossy door cracked open, a sliver of light flick-ered out.

"Hit ain't nunner my done..."

"What?"

"Hit ain't nunner mine, not mine..."

It was just garble, garble coming out of that crack.

"Ask him again, Matthew. Go talk to him."

"Shhhh. I'll handle this, Tiz." Matthew's foot stayed on the running board. He tried again. *"Say there, ole boy?* C'mon on out here and jaw with us. Don't mean no harm. We jist looking fer family."

After a moment, the door creaked and the unhinged man tiptoed out with his pine torch. To his visitors, his windblown tatters were flags of distress. He acted like he was sneaking on somebody. Even the torch seemed odd. It wasn't dark enough to need a torch yet, despite the purly pall in the air.

As the unhinged fellow approached, torchlight flickered across his face—and they saw who he was. He was a Lych.

"Don't," he said.

The rusty eyes were almost webbed shut with what looked to be scar tissue, the abnormous skull misshapen. His left cheek looked melted, charred, as if wax and ash fused too close to flame. Each hand was four fingers and a partial. Watery red eyesacks glinted back at them.

"Don't yer tell, don't yer tell, don't yer tell—" He seldom spake to people. Anyone could tell that. His thick tongue told you that. A kind of smile began to stretch across his face, revealing a pair of brown teeth. "—*peehee*."

It was almost a laugh.

"Matthew, let's go."

Tizzy reached across for Matthew's sleeve.

"We—uh—we's looking fer Wert Birdnell's place. I'm kin. Matthew. His cousin Wilbur's boy. Ain't—ain't sure if this here is the way."

The Lych went rigid. A thousand volt jolt shot through him and his arm flew out. His triple-jointed finger pointed up ahead, up the road, stiff as a stick it pointed.

"Up the—uh—" Matthew stammered, climbing back in the car. "Up ahead, ye say?"

The Lych dropped his pointing finger. The torch

sagged. Something was vexing him again. His head fell and began to drool. He settled onto a tree stump.

"Nunner...nunner mine..."

Were those real tears puddling on those ravaged Lych cheekbones? There would be no lingering to find out.

Matthew released the brake. The blue car hustled off into the wind. Tizzy took a last gander back at the troubled and troubling creature.

As the blue car disappeared into the trees, the Lych looked down at his covered hole. He flipped away the sod, a mad tongue forking his lip.

"Hit ain't nunner my done, dog dang—" he spake to the hole. "I don't knowing how went no tizzzzypoke."

Up the road, Tizzy was riddling with doubts.

"You think he's right," she asked, "yer uncle's on up here?"

"I hope so," Matthew said, steering the Packard out over a cavernous ravine. The ledge was tight. Matthew had begun to leave doubts in the dust and let panic take over. He panicked even worse as the trail cut back into the mountain, leading them inward, twisting deeper into wild forest. They might have ten minutes of any light left at all. Maybe a little more. Twenty at most. This mountain was no place to be after that. Matthew had heard those whispers too. His baby days stank from those whispers.

"Matthew?"

"*Shuddup*," Matthew snapped.

What if Tizzy made tears now? Yes, Tizzy was fixing to fry his nuts in hot tears. He just knew it. She would ask questions he couldn't answer. She would ask things about spidery Lychs while a line of fiddlebacks tapdanced down Matthew's spine. It was hard enough getting this buggy over this hard rock road without a Tizzy in his ear.

Matthew nudged his glasses.

"I *know* he's close. Cain't ye feel it? I can feel it."

Matthew lit the headlamps.

The headlamps lit up a beast, a *wolf* or *panther* or— *what the hell is that thing?* Two feral eyes flashed back.

—Matthew cranked the wheel to miss it.

A big hairy blur bolted off into the woods—

—Matthew's foot stomped the brakes. The Packard slid backward.

Tizzy *squealed*, her rear fender bulldozing into a side ditch.

The car stopped.

They sat at a peculiar angle, motor racing, lights shooting up into the towering pine above them. Things got desperate. Matthew spun the tires, goosing the pedal, but the Packard would not move. After he burned enough rubber into the ditch to convince himself, Matthew quit.

His temper took over. He hopped out, slamming the door.

"What kind of bitch beast of Sodom was *that*?"

Tizzy wished he had not said that. He kept kicking the

fender as she climbed out of the car.

"Matthew, I'm scary," she said. She found him in the near dark and slipped her hand in his belt.

"Now don't fret or start praying to yazoo on me. Didn't you see that curlycue of smoke jist afore that thing jumped us? It was right up this woody slope. Not too fer a piece."

Tizzy shook her head. She was not sure of Matthew. Was he lying to ease her troubled mind? Did it matter if he was? They were spilt milk.

"You sure, boy?"

Matthew knew she doubted his powers. He also knew he was not lying. His specs had glimpsed a tease of smoke, just over the treetops, just before he yanked the headlamp plunger.

"No doubt about her. You can smell it, cain't ye? Hick'ry."

Suddenly, Tizzy realized she could. She could smell it. A faint undershade of hickory on the wind.

Tizzy almost wanted to stop him. She dreaded it, but Matthew killed the lights and kept the keys. He took her hand from his belt and held it tight. There was not much time.

Skrrreeeeekacheeee. Overhead a lost bird thing was flapping, screeching at them.

Matthew left the road's furrow, pulling her up through piney wood. It was ingrown and dank here. The musk of fetid earth, clotted vegetation, and death on the vine overtook them. They climbed a steady slope. Matthew pushed aside limbs with his pistol, clearing a rent through the nettles as they searched the bristling, fading sheen. Both were soon winded, breathless amidst swirls of leaf. Tizzy raced to keep up. And, before she knew it, she saw this Birdnell boy was right about one thing.

There was a shack alright.

STEP 8

"Is this *his* place?"

"Naw, I don't think so. Naw, it ain't."

She tried to slow him but Matthew was already approaching the porch. Hickory smoke spun from a rock chimney, teasing into the breeze. A grasshopper weathervane pointed the way.

The house was sizable, for mountain folk. Well-settled brick pilings supported the tarpaper roof. The wood was grayish, storm-worn. There were four rooms at least and a wraparound porch with cane fishing poles leant along one porch side. The chicken coop was perched just downslope from the cane poles. Under a thrashing hawthorn tree, Tizzy climbed past the upended wheels of a buckboard wagon. Then she began to hang back. She felt queer about the place. Higher up lay bones of a busted gristmill, its mule-harness singletree in splinters. Above that stood a lonesome smokehouse. An inhuman slumber clung to all of it. And, strangely, Tizzy felt like she almost knew this house, this place—like she knew it enough to know something was missing. Something was not right.

But the right or wrong of things did not disturb the Birdnell brain.

Matthew swaggered right up onto the porch. He held tight for a moment, then poked his pistol into his back pocket. Tizzy shivered. Matthew rapped upon the door.

Off in the trees, some meat-eater commenced howling. The meat-eater howled and the wind howled with it. The house slept through the howling and did not hear. The house was asleep. Tizzy felt it.

Matthew rapped again.

Directly, a loud thud met Matthew's ears, a thud from behind the door. This gave way to heavy shuffling, with much creaking inside. Tizzy could hear this quake from way out in the yard. Louder it came, door-muffled clumps, deep from the house's belly. Matthew withdrew by inches. The doorknob rattled.

The quake stopped, suddenly. Seconds passed, a half minute or more, before Matthew heard a voice within.

"Help me," it said.

Matthew did not move. A man. It sounded like a man. Or a bull down a well.

"What?" asked Matthew, throwing white eyes at Tizzy.

"Ain't you gonna help me?" asked the dull burr behind the wood.

Rebel Yell was jumpy. Tizzy could tell. So was she. She felt the woods watching.

"What...what's wrong?" Matthew asked back.

"Push on the door," spake the door. "It's swole up."

The doorknob rattled again from within. The inner command was clear. Matthew could not doubt it. He most certainly heard the words.

"Oh, okeedoke ... sure," he allowed.

"Push it."

Matthew rolled his gaze out to Tizzy. Tizzy took another step back. Then Matthew's specs fixed on the doorknob. Reaching out, he gripped the tarnished knob, and he heaved. Hard.

Matthew braced everything he had against the door. He pushed and struggled. Yes, he tried. Finally, Matthew's breath burst. So he struck a new position. Then he threw his shoulder into the door again, groaning, straining. He winced and Tizzy winced with him. But nothing gave.

Matthew's breath burst out again. Releasing the knob, he fell away, shaking out his hand.

Once more, the voice spake within.

"Git over there—"

"Over where?" Matthew asked.

Unseen things thudded behind the door some more.

"I ain't talking to you," it said.

The heavy door trembled, trembling until at last it cracked open. Bellyaching hinges whined as the door began to swing open wide. Something seized in Tizzy's womb. She swapped troubled eyes with Matthew as he retreated to the top step.

"Baby—" was off Tizzy's lips before she could stop it.

She saw the shape of a man.

A hulking man with lantern jaw now filled the door-way. He wore loose factory fatigues, rolled at the bicep, like a city worker. Tattoos ran up both massive forearms. His face showed fleshy decay, eyes deep and brutish. He brooded over young Matthew and Tizzy for a moment as the wind crashed in around him.

Tizzy knew in a flicker what the man's face looked like. He looked like a stag. A wicked stag with a bad temper.

At the man's flank, a tiny girl appeared. Barefoot and filthy in her ragged dress, she looked about six years old.

The man looked down at his dirty blond child.

"I said git over there," he rumbled. Without affect, the girl-tot turned and trod back inside.

Tizzy heard the porch cringe as that stagman stepped out. He examined Matthew more closely.

"Where's your ride?" the man growled low.

"Do what?" Matthew wasn't sure of the gravity.

"*Matthew—*" Tizzy said in a small voice from the yard. Matthew wasn't listening.

"Well?" the man pressed.

A flush of leaves scoured the porch. Matthew grinned stupid, loosening up.

"Hey, yeah boy. How you doing, buckaroo? We sorry to bother ye. We cain't find Lewt Birdnell's place, ye see? Maybe you could set us straight."

The man's hands hung like hammers. His deep eyes vetted over Matthew for much too long.

"Son, you best tell me now. How y'all get up here?"

"Right. *Right*. Well, this'll stun ye, I know. But me and Tizzy here, we was—uh—my cousin Lewt, he's my pap's cousin? He still lives on up here. Somewheres up-long Holy Creek. Sure. It's all coming back at me now. You prob'ly know the place. They's a red cistern house jist off his back porch. An a bunch of hoodoo gypsies put the abracadabra on him then used his new wife back during that cold spell in—"

Tizzy saw those stag eyes slit.

"We drove up in our car," she blurted.

"—We drove up in our car," Matthew jumped in.

The man came forward, pulling the door closed behind him. He loomed over Matthew, digesting all this. Tizzy could see Matthew's pistol butt in the dusky light and hoped she was the only one that saw it.

"So where's your ride?" the man repeated with less give. Much less give.

Matthew kept weighing his options.

"Tell him Matthew," Tizzy said.

"Aw," Matthew surrendered. "We parked her under a persimmon tree. About three wishes down thataway."

He gestured wild, down toward the road.

"Where's Mister Birdnell's house, mister?" Tizzy asked. She was cold and tired of these mountain gales.

The man's gravity shifted. It shifted down to Tizzy.

"I don't know."

That was all she needed to hear.

"Well, we're sure sorry we bothered you," Tizzy said.

She began to stumble away from the house. First she

stumbled backward, then she turned to go. She prayed Matthew would follow. But where? A frigid night listening to her limbs and thoughts rattle, down in that car, in these woods, was more than Tizzy could fathom.

"Hey, Tizzy?" Matthew called out.

"Matthew, let's go before we git wet."

"*Doodlysquat*," Rebel Yell yelled. "*Tizzy*. I'm atalking to this man. Go or stay. I don't give two tin shits. But I ain't gonna be ready until I'm through talking to this man." Matthew swung himself back around and leered straight up into the man's deep and unforgiving gaze. That gaze made Matthew falter again, for a heartbeat. But he recovered. "I don't think it's any of your goddam business how we got here," he sniped. "All I require of you is some goddam answers, big boyfriend. *Right?*"

For a moment, the whole wide world hung heavy. The man's jaw went crawling, tick by tick.

"What's your name, anyhow?" Matthew persisted, "I wanna know who *you* is—"

Tizzy hated what she saw next.

Standing there in the brewing storm, in the face of Matthew's depravity, the stag-faced man did a terrible thing. He smiled. Slowly, grimly, terribly, he smiled.

"Bob. The name be Bob," he said. Something chuckled inside the drum of his chest. "And I don't know your people. Seriously I do not."

Matthew shook his head in disbelief.

"So you be Bob?"

The man did not answer that. He did not need to.

Matthew just kept shaking his noggin, acting the fool. Tizzy just kept away. Finally, the man who called himself Bob called out to her:

"Who are you, daughter?"

"Tizzy June Polk, sir," her teeth chattered. Oh Lord, there went her school name. "I mean, I mean, we best be agoing."

Then Bob surprised them both.

"That's too bad," he said.

Matthew shifted his hip on the top step, the heel of his hand parked on the pistol in his back pocket. He made no effort to hide it.

"Well I'm atelling ye, Bob. You need to spit shine ye sorry disposition. Am I right? Huh, now?" He moved into the man's shade, rising eye-to-eye with Bob, nose-to-nose. "A feller like you—you best know who you're afucking with. Don't ye think?" Matthew made a wiseass click with one side of his teeth. "So, yessir. We'll be moving on. I've about had my fill of ye."

"Matthew, I'm *cold*."

But Matthew kept poking.

"Jist so happens, Bob, I'm awanted by the law—"

"Yeah?"

"Yeah. You damn right I am. Now I want you to keep that under your cap, *Bob*." Matthew's voice dropped, "That's jist betwixt you and me."

The man stood there and watched Matthew check his cods. Then the man watched Matthew turn and stride right off the porch, his foot missing the step by inches.

Matthew fell hard and face down in the dirt. Tizzy felt the thud and caught her breath.

From the half-shadows, Bob moved to the porch's edge.

Tizzy took a few baby steps. Matthew tried to lift his head, whimpered, then he was out cold in a bed of hen scratches. Tizzy's baby steps stopped.

"Tizzy June—"

She lifted her face, to Bob. His tattoo-riddled arms dangled above her.

"How old you be?"

"Th-thirteen."

"How long you been kiltered with this four-eyed blatteroon?"

Tizzy searched for a good answer. She could not find one. So she picked up the County spectacles instead.

Bob hove Matthew's carcass through the door of the house and dumped him like a slab of butchered pork. Wind gusted in, filling the threshold. Tizzy edged in behind Bob. She saw Matthew on the splint rug, the air thick with wild bits of chaff and twig. Coughing, Tizzy adjusted to a dim flickering room—and the biggest hound she had ever seen.

Before the stone fireplace stood a dark giant dog. Jowly, mottled, with great clumps for feet: this boss dog was a spindling creature almost as tall as Tizzy. The hound stood alert and agitated before a hot fire. Behind the dog, on the hearth, the little ragdoll girl sat cross-legged. She let the big beast growl. Tizzy froze, pale of heart. She was held fast by those black dog eyes. Bob went back to the door. He shut out the weather then snapped his fingers at the hound.

"Uh-uh. *No.*" he said, gutter-deep. His chin jerked a warning.

The dog settled clumsy onto the hearth, keeping a fix on Tizzy. Bob almost grinned again.

"Uh-*uhhh,*" Bob stressed, teasing the dog.

Bob came around Tizzy. He lumbered across the room, avoiding everybody. Tizzy began to fret legions in his wake.

"We're sure hating to *bother* you. We cain't stay on though, not really. It's agonna *rain.* It's gitting *dark.*"

Bob stopped. He looked back at Tizzy. He was mulling something over, resetting his tack. Then an inner demon bit him and he took off again, down a pitch black hallway.

"Dawg damnation," he swore from out of sight.

With Bob gone, Tizzy studied the room. The place was ample but sparsely done, hewn of rugged timber. There was a heavy rocker with a tiny pedestal table and one ladderback chair. But there was not an extra stick of anything. Tizzy wondered if all the rooms were so naked. There would be a kitchen. They must take meals on a kitchen table. Tizzy did not want to see the kitchen, no, thank you. But she did finally spot a standing Victrola phonograph over in the corner of this front room. On the wall above the Victrola, shimmering back at Tizzy, were a couple of stony ancestors: An unsmiling old sir and old missus in an oval photograph. Their faces were hard, and harder to sort out in the dull flicker. But these ancestors seemed to belong here in a way little else did. They were small comfort. They made Tizzy feel accepted in a much different light than the dull lights staring back from the eyes of this girl and this hound. Tizzy did not like being stared at. She was no two-headed calf.

"Mmmmm..."

Suddenly, Matthew's body began to stir on the rug. The butt of his pistol was still sticking out of his rump pocket. Tizzy bent down, pinching a bony Birdnell arm.

"Oh Lord, Matthew—git *up*," she hissed in a whisper.

Matthew sneezed, then slumped back into the wood-planked land of lost boys. The little girl slid him a glance. The child was also in a lost land of her own, unaware of the thump-thump-thump that began overhead. Like heavy fingertips drumming above, rain was hitting the tarpaper roof. And Tizzy realized it was too late now. The rain was here and so was she.

Suddenly Bob was back. He returned from the hall dragging an oily, blunted old broom. His thick-soled boots stopped at the rug. Matthew's snoring body provoked him.

"You think I want you under my roof? I don't want you under my roof."

He looked at nobody when he said it. He told it to mid-air.

"And we sure thank you," Tizzy stammered. "God, I'm sorry, mister. He's afixing to wake up. Ain't he?"

Bob reached down and plucked the pistol from Matthew's pocket. He laid the gun on the Victrola then booted Matthew's tailbone. "Git up, boy."

Matthew flinched. He began moving again. His split thumbnail fondled the raw knot rising over his eyebrow.

"My melon. Busted my melon..." Matthew mumbled, rolling over on his back.

"Eats," Bob said. Bob was still talking to himself. He was ripping the oily broom-straw apart. "Goddam, they'll be wanting eats." Then he looked at his visitors: "Y'all want grub?"

Tizzy began to nod. She had to admit, her stomach had been cranky for hours.

"Hell, yes," Matthew slurred, eyes closed. "I'm powerful hongry."

Bob knee-snapped the broomstick before it hit the fire. He lumbered back down the dark hall. Minutes later he returned with two bowls of lukewarm grits and a hard biscuit each. Matthew was sitting up in no time, sopping his bowl, cheeks stuffed with feed. The dog looked hungry but was not eating. The little girl just looked.

Tizzy nibbled politely, her knees together in the rocking chair. She had accepted the granny rocker though it was not offered. She ate and tried to ignore those watching her do it. Two dark bedrooms opened off this front parlor. Lightning flashed within those other rooms, from hidden windows. The hominy aroma Tizzy smelled and tasted on her spoon mingled with the bitter-pecan scent of these walls. It felt like generations had grown cadaverous in here, grown toothless and mum and died in here.

A blue-white flare lit the front parlor, followed fast by a bullwhip crack of thunder. Tizzy saw the portrait on the wall clearly for a moment. The elder couple in that tinted photograph bore no resemblance to this Bob, or this little girl either. It was a troubling riddle. But not nearly as troubling as the biscuit Tizzy had to soak in her grits to chew. It was rock hard and Bob had used too much baking soda. The little girl kept watching Tizzy dab her biscuit. Tizzy tried to smile back.

"Who are you, hon?" Tizzy asked.

The ragdoll child stood up and left the room without a ripple.

All the while, Bob spake nothing. Their host sat sullen, straddling the other chair, his gloomy meditation shifting constantly from hand to hand, from Tizzy to Matthew. The heavily-sketched forearms flexed, each hand gripping the ladderback chair handles like prison bars. After a while Bob took out a buck knife and began shaving a callous from the left hand's heel.

Matthew sat across the room with his spine against the Victrola. He sopped his bowl and watched Bob groom himself.

"Say, what about you, Bob?" Matthew asked finally, smacking his lips. "What's your *other* name be? Maybe I heard of your clan."

"Lloyd," Bob said as his skin shavings filtered to the

floor.

"Never heard of no Lloyd breed. How about you, doll baby?"

"Nope." Tizzy tried to act like she liked her troubling biscuit and tasteless grits. She tried to look friendly to Bob, now that the little girl was gone.

Bob was having none of it. Those sleepy eyelids avoided her. His beezwax was the buck knife and the job at hand. His eyes retreated in the firelight, disappearing into dark caverns beneath a broad-raftered, bushy brow. His breath came dry and regular as thunderclaps landed on top of each other. Sometimes the stormy grumblings sounded like they came from deep inside this Bob's gullet. The seams of his lantern jaw and cliffhanger cheekbones masked any outward emotion. Yet his mouth had an insolent, almost girlish shape. Tizzy watched Bob pucker and blow a dry skin scale off his blade.

The way he straddled that chair, Tizzy thought Bob looked trapped in a bad harness. His black hair was greasy, long, and swept back. He looked unnatural for such a natural man. In fact, Tizzy began to see that even his tattoos were unnatural tattoos. As her eyes warmed to the light, she began to see how his tattoos were butchered. They were more like tattoo scraps. The leftover illustrations danced in the light: bleached, wrinkly red and blue-green. His skin etchings that had been *almost* removed. They had been altered until they were a twisting, scarred mess of old cuts and hairy remnants of color. Yes, those tattoos had died torturous deaths. Tizzy chewed, trying not to stare. Bob did not seem to care. But she tried not stare. She was pretty sure there was a snip of dragon's tail she could still see, blue and curling up from scar tissue below his left elbow.

"Sure appreciate the supper, sir," she peeped at last. "Is that your little girl? Sure is a cutie pie."

Bob gave a grunt. Matthew tried not to laugh, stuffing it down with biscuit. Tizzy scowled at him. So did the dog.

Bob spake.

"Got a wife. She be her daughter. This'n is just waiting fer her mama to come home."

"Tonight?" asked Tizzy.

"Not too likely. Soon though. We all waiting fer mama to come home." This amused him. So he smiled, like a reptile.

"I'd sure be proud to meet her. Maybe we'll git a chance before—"

"Hell's bells," Bob was booming. "Reckon you two jackanapes can bed down till daylight. I'll study on where that other Birdnell of yourn lives."

The floor timbers groaned as Bob unstraddled and left them. Matthew slid close to the rocker, running his busted thumb up Tizzy's leg. Tizzy swatted Matthew's hand. The dog's head came up. Tizzy stopped rocking. She sat very still until the dog's head went back down. Out in the black unseen regions of the house, doors were opened then shut, a little too loudly. Meanwhile, even that little old ladykiller—the Rebel Yell Birdnell—kept his County specs trained on that hound. That hound did not like him. He did not like the hound. Matthew hoped he did not have to plug this big egg-sucking bastard before all was said and done. There, there, Matthew thought. Nice pupper, Matthew thought. If this dog could read his mind—and the damn dog acted like he could—Matthew wanted only happy thoughts on this dog's radar until the moment the bullet entered the brain.

Tizzy Polk was also trying to have happy thoughts. She knew this dog did not like her either. Tizzy was even glad to see Bob return.

Bob gave a raft of blankets to Matthew, telling him to make his pallet on the side porch swing. This front room was no kind of bedroom, Bob said. Centipedes crept from the wood cradle and the hard stone hearth made for poor sleeping. Especially after the fire died, he said. Especially with this big damn dog here, he did not say.

The little girl had returned by then, carrying a broken Dr. Pilcher's medicine bottle. Bob seemed to think nothing of this as the tot held the jagged-edged bottle by its neck, like a baby rattle. Bob told her to make ready for bed. Then Bob opened the front door and sent his dog outside. This did not please Matthew.

Bob put Tizzy in a side bedroom, just off the parlor. The room had a lumpy bed with nice chenille coverlets. There was an oak bureau, a standing mirror, and an out-side door onto the side porch. Tizzy was surprised and relieved to have a real room of her own, for the first time ever. She almost felt special. Bob pointed through the window at the outhouse. Then, without another word Bob left them there. He retired to another darkened bedroom off the opposite side of the parlor. His heavy boots could be heard by Tizzy and Matthew, kicking things behind his closed door.

Matthew was dicey about the porch swing now. For all he knew, the hound was out there waiting for him. Screwing up his courage, Matthew kissed Tizzy and watched her wipe it off. He wished her sweet dreams mama before he stepped outside, looking both ways—up and down the porch—as he went.

Alone, finally, Tizzy was afraid to blow out the lamp. Wind kept singing through the cracks. After many silent psalms she removed her buckletop shoes. It took another hour and a few prayers over spilt milk to coax herself out of her dress and climb under the covers. She still would not blow out the lamp. But this long and fateful day had taken its toll. Tizzy did at last lose her tussle with the waking world. Only then did the lamp's flame gutter and fail. Tizzy slept for a while. By midnight the rains let up. Atop the roof, the grasshopper weathervane stood dripping, waiting for the next wind to rise. The wait was never long.

Somewhere in the wee hours, Matthew woke up. Lying there, drifting in the porch swing, the new stillness and night chitters began to get to him. After a while, he threw back his blanket, then slipped around to the side door of Tizzy's room. It was open. Inside he found her sitting up and munching on a snack.

"Sweet-potater, sweet-potater, how's my little sweet potater? " he whispered. "Where'd ye git the pie, mama?"

Matthew tiptoed over and slid onto the quilt beside her.

"I brung it with me," Tizzy whispered back. "And you ain't suppose to be in here."

"Brung it from where?"

He was already nuzzling her ear.

"Brung it to school with me, fer dinnertime," she said, smacking away the last stolen bite.

"Haw. No wonder you wasn't so hongry back at that feed store."

He kissed her on the mouth. She let him, for a little while. Matthew wasn't so bad when he tasted like sweet potato. Finally, Tizzy came up for air, catching her breath.

"Gee."

"But you said you *was*, doll baby. Why'd you say you was hongry back there on the road?"

Tizzy had no good answer, so she wiped her mouth with the top of her sock. Before she knew it, Matthew's lips were gobbling hers again. Matthew began snickering while they kissed and so did Tizzy. When it was not a bestial abomination, kissing could be pretty funny, Tizzy felt. Why, sometimes it was okay. Nice as a midnight snack. Until he got fast and nasty, that is, until his hands started scurrying under the sheets. Until his split thumb started fumbling for her nipple.

"Matthew, quit it," she whispered, shoving him off.

"Behave or I'll holler."

"Tizzy hon," he said, his breath hot. "I got me a bad rash, a pod rash. Help me doctor it. I'm going down slow, so help me.

"Hush, you are utterly—"

"Let's play married folks. You can be my *wife*. Fer a little while. I want me some of that punkin pie."

"Matthew, stop your grabbing. I ain't old enough to be no wife."

"Sure ye be. Merf Tuckabee's girl, Ruth? She married that pot drummer last harvest moon. And she was only twelve."

"She *had* to, you ignorant boy."

"Yeah? How's this ignorant feel?" He kissed her again, and his tongue began exploring. After a moment, Tizzy's tongue began to explore back. But she never stopped worrying it. She fretted over every wet inch of his tongue and hers. Maybe the bedsprings were too noisy. And what if their whispers were heard, or worse?

"You *could* be my wife, "he was moaning now. "It's possible. I ain't told nobody up here ye *ain't* my wife. I think I love ye, Tizzy."

They went back at it, swapping tongues and breath. He stopped to nibble and it shot tremors through her.

"I ain't ready. You need a gold rang, and a preacherman," she protested, eyes closed, struggling to keep the blanket.

"Don't need no preacherman, doll baby. This is jist pretend," he said. Then he touched her where she had scarcely been touched. Tizzy gasped.

"*Buuutton?*"

They froze.

"*Button—*"

The bull was out of the well.

"*Buuuuuut-ton?*"

It was him. Bob's voice echoed, deep and mournful.

"*Where is he?*" Tizzy gasped, her arms still hugging Matthew.

"I don't know," Matthew said, breaking free, sliding off the bed.

He dropped down, squatting under the window beside the bed. They heard Bob call Button's name again. Tizzy joined Matthew as he eased the window open a few inches. Their faces pressed against the open screen.

Outside, the night sky was clearing. A shiv of moon pierced the timbers. The air smelled damp and earthy through the window screen. Across the yard, near the trees, they saw dim movement.

"*Buuutton?*"

Suddenly they both saw Bob. And when they did, Tizzy almost yipped.

"*Shhhh.*" Matthew jabbed her but she never felt it.

Out back, beyond the privy and clothesline, Bob was calling to the woods. He stood there near naked except for scanty white shorts cupping his crotch. His body was beefy, almost as pale as the moon.

"Buuutton, goddam." Bob's bare feet trod slowly, back and forth, restless. Then he stopped again and called through cupped hands. "Button, come *on* girl. Come on back in this house now—"

The tangle of pines did not answer him. Not at first. Then a lone hootowl began to hoot back at Bob.

"Button?"

He called a few more times. Tizzy and Matthew whispered, straining to see and hear. Then, after a spell, Bob gave up and strode back inside, slamming the kitchen screen door as he came. Tizzy bolted back into bed, Matthew slipped out to the swing. No other body spake for the rest of the night. Each was left alone, on their own again, on Riddle Top. It was a very long time until morning.

STEP 9

When Tizzy awoke she saw Button. And Button was not lost. The itsy-bitsy girl was outside, hooked in the porch window, watching Tizzy sleep. Through sleep-crusted eyelashes Tizzy detected her. Tizzy sat up fast and the child ran away, chased by a Tizzy Polk yawn.

Lying back, Tizzy rubbed her eyes, cleared her head, and pondered the long night's doings. Yesterday and last night were the makings of a weird whirligig dream best forgotten. If only she could wipe them away like sleep from her eyes. If only she was not lying here in this strange bed in this odd house on this crisp morning with real baby girls in her window. Thank heavens they would leave today. Tizzy wanted away from here, anyplace away. But then, who knew what Mr. Wert Birdnell's hospitality had to offer? He would be, after all, an upcountry Birdnell. And they were not the purest lot. Matthew, for instance. Matthew was from that lot. Wasn't Matthew Birdnell the reason Tizzy lay lost in this bed while little Button was not really lost at all?

Tizzy lay awake in bed a long time, waiting. She was hoping Matthew would come to rescue her, so they could slip away without seeing that near naked Bob again. But Matthew did not come. Finally, Tizzy got up and dressed. She tried to leave through the side door to the porch. But it was locked—locked from the outside. Tizzy jiggled the knob. It held fast. Had Matthew Birdnell been ornery enough to do such a thing? Warily, Tizzy went out into the house. The house was empty. She searched down the hall. Bob was nowhere to be found, not in his bedroom or the other smaller room beside his. Nor was he farther along in the worn linoleum kitchen. The kitchen screen door was propped open with a rock, the pump dripped over the sink. But she did not hear the man's heavy footfalls or any other echoes of life. Tizzy wondered where that little girl Button hid.

There were chickens outside. Lots of chickens. Tizzy found Matthew on the side-porch swing, snoring so loud she was sure he had blown a gasket. Leave it to inbred Matthew Birdnell to greet the day with loud cracked mufflers, a new knot on his head, and clogged up ears. In this ruckus, only a long-legged Mole Boy, born blind and stone deaf, could fail to be roused. A sparrow and several rowdy goldfinches sprang after scattered grain in the yard. They had to be quick and lucky. Otherwise they were beat out by the clucking crowd of white brooder hens which roamed freely. The hens spilled up onto the porch and out into the trees. A soot-black java rooster kept crowing. The rooster sounded ragged, like he had the croup in his chest from a night of rain. Tizzy walked right up to Matthew. She did not try to be quiet about it. Even so, and even with this crowing, Matthew kept sleeping.

Tizzy was peeved that he could sleep through such rooster racket. They should have been gone at dawn. Thankfully, he slept in his dungaree pants instead of near naked in his underdrawers, like Bob. Matthew told her last night that only big city cats wore "jock shorts" like Bob's. That's what Matthew called them. Jock shorts. As long as she lived, Tizzy knew she would never forget near naked Bob, pacing in the pines. The sight of that man, like that, was upsetting to say the least. And once Bob came back in the house, the upset was complete. Lust left Tizzy's bedroom, flying out the door faster than Matthew could flee to the porch. Yet Matthew Birdnell was still mean and salty enough to lock her door, trapping Tizzy inside so she could not escape after him. What if Bob's jock shorts had come visiting her, with no way to escape them?

Tizzy trudged on past Matthew still snoring away the morning in his swing. She had to see how he locked her inside. Farther along, she found the porch door to her bedroom. But, looking at it from out here, Tizzy saw no latch of any kind. She tried the knob and the door opened. It swung inward with little effort. She pulled the door closed again. How perplexing. How rare. Matthew Birdnell was actually innocent of this little crime. Or so it seemed. Could Tizzy's door have been so swollen from rain that it first would not open but now would open easy? Or was that Button girl outside and playing tricks on Tizzy? Somehow Button did not seem like a trickster kind of kid.

Returning to the porch swing, Tizzy poked Matthew in the ribs. He began to stretch. Wings flapping, a white hen landed at Tizzy's feet and Matthew startled, his eyes popped open.

"Whuuutha-hell?" he croaked as Tizzy shooed the bird away.

"Shhh. She's just an ole hen," Tizzy said, sitting on the edge of the swing. Matthew's waist was still rolled in a wad of patchwork quilt. He raised up onto his elbow, squinting around the place at a clouding morning sky.

Tizzy and Matthew did not know it, but the tiny girl—Button—was beneath their feet. Button had crept from the crawlspace, out under the wide cracks of the porch, listening.

"He's gone," Tizzy was saying.

"Who'd that be?" Matthew asked, still groggy.

"Who else?" Tizzy insisted. "That feller, that Mr. Bob Lloyd."

"Oh. Bob. Well, where's he at?"

Tizzy wanted to smack him awake. Matthew did not seem too concerned about getting off the man's place. This did not gladden Tizzy's heart. She wanted to find Matthew's uncle or, better yet, give serious thought to turning themselves over to the authorities. Tizzy had begun to think they might convict her of littler crimes than

Matthew, then send her down to some children's home. Or a reform school someplace in the city. That would be alright, maybe. She could live with either of those. That way, just maybe, Tizzy would never be released back to her Preacher-Daddy. In a few years, perhaps even before she was an old lady, they would have to let her out and she could get a laundry job or do missionary work. She was pretty good at cleaning things. She would probably never have babies or a nice house—no man would want a dried up maiden thing—but Tizzy's heart would not be so full of stain. Her conscience would be clean, washed in Jehovah's blood. The true Jehovah. Tizzy wondered if Matthew would go for any of that.

"Danged if I know where that barebottom Bob is, you gristleknob. Let's just git our shoes and go. That little ratgirl, Button? She dang near scaryed the hoo outa me when I waked up. She was staring in the winder. She's tucked around here somewhere—"

"Well, I figured to git some guidance from barebottom Bob," yawned Matthew. "That storm kinda *bewildered* me."

"You was borned with hookworm and bewilderment, Matthew. I swear—"

"Ain't so sure I'm knowing whichaway to go. Ain't so sure I'm finding Uncle Lewt without some guidance from Bob. Besides, who says I can throw that car back on the road by my lonesome?"

"I'll help."

"Sure thang, mama. A little river bag runt like you.

Naw, I believe we oughta lay back until Bob shows and ask a few dumb questions."

"That should be easy shakes fer you. You're good at dumb questions."

"Lookee here. We probably notorious by now. I reckon our names would strike fear in the loin of Old Colonel Renfrew. And his loins been dead fer fifty year. I oughta know. I took siesta on his grave."

"About like a dunder hogboy. Disrespecting the dead—"

Angered, Matthew started to untangle his covers.

"Jist watch and wise up, doll baby. I'm takin care of business. See? Besides, I ain't so sure he is a Bob, or a Lloyd neither."

"What do we care? Come on, Matthew—let's git *gone*. After some breakfast of course."

Tizzy was hungry again.

"Know where he hid my gun?" Matthew asked, sitting up shirtless and barefoot.

Tizzy did not feel easy sitting flush with a boy's bare white ribcage. Matthew looked kind of rickety and undernourished to her. Teeny red pustules spotted his back.

"I don't know where he put the gun. Somewhere in his room, I reckon. You saw him go in just like I did. His room was too dark to see."

"Yeah," Matthew pondered, putting on his glasses. "What say we jist steal that popgun right back—*shoot— whatzat?*"

Betwixt his dirty toes, Matthew saw a sliver of Button's eye. Then the eye was gone.

"Where?" Tizzy startled.

"It's *her*—" Matthew knelt quickly, scanning from crack to crack. They heard shuffling beneath them—then Button shot out from under the porch.

"Hey, you *nubbin. Git on back here*," he hollered.

But the Button skittered off, leaving chickens in an uproar.

"She was under there snooping on us, Matthew."

Tizzy whistled sharp as she saw Button leap into the chicken pen and squat there. Tizzy and Matthew stood on the porch for a while, studying her. The ragamuffin hunkered amongst the silly birds, eating her goobers one by one, staring back at the two on the porch. Her wee mouth was dirty. It looked to Tizzy like the girl ate more dirt than she did goobers. And even from far off you could tell Button was teetering, about to fall asleep. Matthew called out to her a few more times. But Button did not respond.

Matthew decided they should search the house for his pistol and maybe snitch a bite or two for the road. This was an instant hit with Tizzy. Tizzy had begun to advance the theory that anything that distracted Matthew Birdnell's mind with a chore was of benefit to all concerned. So Tizzy was happy to help steer Matthew into the mundane, beginning with the getting of breakfast. Tizzy wanted her breakfast. At the very least, there were eggs aplenty to be rustled and fried. That way they would be tanked up and road ready as soon as Bob showed his face again.

In the kitchen, they found a pantry and substantial stores. There were canned goods, flour sacks, rice, saw-blades, hurricane lamps, and rat traps like neither of them had ever seen outside a country market. A king's ransom in the house of poor folks. They also found a couple of military canteens, some 20-gauge shotgun shells (but no sign of a shotgun), and a sheathless trench knife with a German iron cross on the handle. Matthew took a shine to the German knife but Tizzy warned him to leave it be, lest Mr. Bob Lloyd notice it missing. It was the kind of thing he would notice, she told him.

Outside the pantry, on the kitchen counter, was an apothecary chest—the tiny drawers stuffed with molded herbs, roots, and tea leaf. Quart jars of dry grain and corn lined the counter left and right of the sink. The jars ended at a drinking water tub and ladle alongside the kitchen back door. Matthew stepped out back as Tizzy filched a tin of sardines and matchbox. Under a tarp on the back porch, Matthew found several crates of bonded bourbon. Tax-stamped whisky was a rare thing in these hills. This much of it was not even rare, it was unheard of. Who had that kind of money? Matthew heard an acorn snap and dropped the tarp. Bob was approaching from the yard.

Matthew did a sidestep, away from the covered whis-key. Tizzy quickly sat on a kitchen chair inside. They waited as Bob scuffed up the back steps. He had a dead snake in his hand.

"Ho there, Bob," Matthew drawled, trailing the man into his kitchen. "That girl of yourn—"

"—Button," said Tizzy.

"Yeah, that Button is out there ahunkered in that pen. She don't come when ye shout."

"Yep. She'll do that," Bob said. He tossed the snake in the sink. "Reckon y'all gotta eat. Eat afore you go."

Bob went back outside and said something at the Button in the chicken pen. Whatever it was, she must have been moved by it. Shortly after, Button appeared in the kitchen carrying a hatful of brown eggs. It was an old blue-straw sunhat, almost falling to pieces. Her tiny bare feet shuffled over to the stove—careful not to drop her blue hat basket. Bob was already frying sowbelly in a huge skillet. Button had chosen wisely. Outside a light drizzle began to set in, turning the mountain place colder and misty.

Tizzy wanted to scoot closer to the stove. But she did not care to hang that close to the man or the strange girl either. At one point, Bob paused, reached in his baggy pants and hauled out the pistol. Slapping it down on the rough table, he returned to the stove.

"There's your piece. Don't lose it."

Sheepish, Matthew returned the gun to his hip pocket. Tizzy was busy dwelling on the little girl crouched betwixt woodbox and stove. Guns no longer interested Tizzy. There was no hickory warmth in them.

"Where'd you get your snake, sir?" she asked.

"Horn snake. Rolled up and took a stab at me."

129

"Hell, Bob. Hope ye stabbed him back," chortled Matthew from the doorway. He was leant there, rooting in his nose.

"Naw, I kilt him with a rock."

"Will you skin him out?" Tizzy asked. "Will you cook him or what?"

"Never eat a snake in my life," Bob muttered, breaking eggs into the grease. "I'll be acutting off his tail stinger. They's uses fer them."

Tizzy did not ask. Button had left the kitchen and soon they heard thin, zither music trickling from the parlor. It was the record-playing Victrola, cranked by her wee hand no doubt. Breakfast got fried and Bob sat down. Matthew and Tizzy elbowed up to the table and ate like wolves in winter. It was good to have meat and eggs.

Bob ate slow, gazing out into the drizzle. To Tizzy, Bob looked like he could see a thousand miles in front of him. She found herself stealing a gander at his lantern-jawed face and the way he tore sowbelly with his bottom bearcat teeth. It was hard to square this man with the naked craw she saw last night, hairy-legged in his underpants. He looked different in his work clothes. Not much friendlier, but different.

The fourth plate sat untouched at the fourth chair. Tizzy asked about Button's breakfast.

"She ain't used to feeding at no table," Bob said.

Every few minutes the record would start over, the tinny music wafting down the hall. It was sad music and felt like a memory. Tizzy wished it would stop.

"Say, where's your birddog, sir?"

"Don't rightly know. He keeps to his own. And he ain't no birddog."

The drizzle had begun to let up. Bob rose, slung his horn snake over his shoulder, and scoured the plates. He pumped water, rinsing the grease off his fingers. Then he took out makings and started rolling a smoke.

"I got business still needs tending," Bob said, his hip against the counter. He struck a match, lit up, and looked at Matthew. "Maybe you could pluck a bird fer my pot, boy. When I git back this afternoon we'll git you outa that ditch. Ain't but one road to your cousin's ridge."

"Sure Bob, I'm able," Matthew popped off, leaning back on his chair legs. A full belly had brought out the lazy in him.

Tizzy wanted no part of it. They were supposed to be gitting gone now. Bob unslung his snake and went out the door. The screen was clapping shut before Tizzy could speak. She jumped up from the table.

"But, Mr. Bob Lloyd—"

She got to the screen door in time to catch a last glimpse as Bob faded into the woodline. He moved mighty fast for a man who moved so slow.

"Keep your woolies dry," Matthew advised, still creaking back lazy in his chair. "We'll gitalong mama. In no time at all. Naturally, I suspect they may be gold hid here somewheres, under a board or something. Could be. What with all these goods and larder."

Bullets were still in the gun. Matthew showed them to

her then they moseyed outside. The ground was wet but hard. Hard mountain earth. Matthew said that was because it was all rock underneath and the hardest graves to dig were in these parts.

"Dirt don't run deep enough. Ain't good for growing nor buryin'" he lectured.

"No matter the spot?" Tizzy asked.

Matthew had to allow that the soil sat deeper in some places. A good digger's feet could tell him. It was the sort of thing you were born with, like nighteyes.

"Ain't no future in dirt-digging skills," she said.

"Maybe not, Tizzy Polk. But cain't everbody de-vine the depths of dirt like I kin."

"Well, I seen a Shetland pony play piano once," harped Tizzy. "But he ain't parked up on a rock farm, running from the law."

"Yeah? I doubt he's got a record label."

"Matthew, I'm bored."

"Me too."

"What we gonna do about it?"

"I dunno."

"Do you wanna kiss?" she asked.

"Naw, not really. How's the best way to choke a chicken?"

Matthew headed down toward the pen, scattering hens as he went. They darted and leapt around him in a flurry of white wings. Tizzy sat hugging her knees on the porch. She watched Matthew rubberneck, choosing his victim. He pointed at a plump hen dithering in circles.

"How's that one look to ye?" he shouted.

"Appears awright to me," she called back.

He leapt for the hen. But the plumper stopped making circles and gained surprising flight before Matthew could reach her. Matthew whirled and locked eyes on another fat mama egg-charmer. She was even strutting toward him, pretty as you please.

"What about *her*?"

"Yeah—" Tizzy yawned. "—she looks perty fair."

Matthew went for her but she was not so agreeable after all. She flew through his hands. He tried another. Then another.

"Aw, she was a loser—how's about that one?"

"Uh-huh, she's perty fair—"

This went on long enough for Tizzy to write her name nineteen times on the roof of her mouth. She could see Button perched on the gristmill watching Matthew scatter chickabiddys. The Victrola notes echoed out the window, twanging, hanging in the trees. Matthew got more red-faced, more gandy dancer, and began to sling sweat. He cornered a young white pullet who clucked up a storm then escaped through Matthew's legs. Tizzy tried not to laugh. Apparently Button saw nothing to laugh about.

But both of them jumped when Matthew unwound and fired his pistol. *KA-BANG.* He missed the pullet but nailed a nearby hen. *KA-BANGBANG.* He popped two more. The yard squabblers took on a new edge as he aimed—*BANG*—and missed one. *KA-BANG.* Another hen flipped in the air and fell dead. He wasted fewer bullets. He shot two more. His sights were getting better. He nudged back his glasses and quickly reloaded. *KA-BANGBANG.* Chickens clashed, white feathers flew. Matthew emptied his second load into the flock, killing four more birds.

Matthew dumped his cartridges again. He was slotting more bullets when Tizzy saw Bob emerge from the woods. Sulphur and smoke swirled around Matthew as Bob approached, smiling.

Tizzy stood up, she did not know what to expect. Close to a dozen chicken corpses littered the yard. Everywhere she looked, Tizzy saw white lumps with bloody-red splotches. They had piled up in a hurry.

Bob came up to Matthew. He stopped and looked around. The thin smile was still there, but fading.

"You like to kill things do you?" he said softly.

Matthew snorted and spun his pistol cylinder.

"Sure do, man. When they rile me." Matthew winked.

"Did they rile you?"

"Damn sure did. But you don't have to thank me, Bob. I figure you got chicken dumplings here for a month of Sundays. Fire up that pot."

"Naw. This is one supper. Maybe two," Bob uttered, thunder rumbling in.

"Huh? How is that?"

"Cain't salt em. Cain't smoke em. Cain't cure em good."

"Ye cain't?"

"Naw. Without no icebox, chickens don't keep. Don't

you know that?"

"I reckon not. Mama cooked. I eat it."

"I reckon the rest these birds will jist go to rot."

Bob was cryptic, his eyes were still lit. But not his face. His face was a mask. Matthew folded.

"I'm, I'm sorry, mister. Reckon I got a mite undone."

"You git undone a lot?"

"Well, I git fast and nasty. Maybe."

"Yeah?"

"Don't mean no harm by it."

"Well. What is it you do mean?"

"I ... I dunno."

Bob looked at Matthew like he was supper.

"Don't worry it none," Bob said, finally.

On the porch, Tizzy felt the first drops. The rain was starting up again. And Bob was coming her way now, headed for the house.

STEP 10

"Set down, Judah," he spake.

Sheet lightning cracked the night. Bob made a crude motion to the dog.

The giant dog came shucking into the firelight, wet and grizzled with mud. He padded to the hearth and settled, with head high. The twin points of his ears were perked, alert to the two strangers still on his ground.

Tizzy had always liked dogs. She admired such dogged behavior. She could even respect the vigilance here in this hound, yet she kept her distance from it. Lolling on her tummy, Tizzy felt reasonably content in the reddish glow of the splint rug. She might as well. They were not going anywhere. Matthew sat sideways on the ladder-back chair, a bare foot across his knee. Behind him, a white-topped shoe was hung on the doorknob to Tizzy's bedroom. Matthew kept squeezing his big toe, trying to locate a thorn he picked up from the porch the night before. Tizzy could have told him not to trot in and out of her bedroom with no shoes. Every so often Matthew would sip from the Old Rip Van Winkle bourbon Bob had poured him. Hogboy swore it was balm for the agonies of thorn hunting. But Tizzy saw he was laughing a little too loud already, enjoying the hunt. Every other sip, Matthew would gouge into the toe with his nickel-handle pocketknife. Over an hour of open-toe surgery and still no thorn. He said he could feel it. Tizzy was not so sure.

Bob sat close by the fire, slumped in the rocker. One hand held Button against his knee. The other hand poured three more golden fingers of bourbon. He took up the glass and warmed to it. Outside was deluge. An earth-shattering show of rain and electric sky was putting the earlier storm to shame.

They all came inside after Matthew's chicken massacre. The rain began to blow, harder than before. Things got threatening. Gullies and streams appeared, cutting through the hillside as black weather pounded roof, windows, and doors. The truth blew in with it and cut right through Tizzy and Matthew. All thoughts of dislodging the car today or driving away from here were dead in the water. Washed away. Bob Nottingham showed no concern in the matter. He hauled in plenty of firewood, side-kicked the hearth to knock mud off his boots, and opened a fresh bottle of bonded whisky. Then he jerked open the front curtain and sat by his fire. He sat and watched the grey out there go away to nothing. The hard spirits in his glass seemed to lull him, just a little. He made comment every so often about the weather and transmission work and the best way to stew a pullet. Tizzy listened. Mostly,

Matthew shot off his mouth and dug his big toe. Lighting flashed, thunder tailed it. The rest of the world was far away and on its own.

"Ain't never seen no hound like this'n here," Matthew was saying. "What's that ye call him?"

"He's a brindled dane. Calls hisself Judah."

Matthew thought that was a hooting treat. Tizzy too was amused. Not many dogs named themselves in her experience. She was not even sure how such a christening would occur, but no matter. At least the beast wasn't growling at her anymore. Earlier, when it first dawned on Tizzy that she was not going anywhere today, she might have growled back. She might have barked and bit. She was that mad about it. But that grew tiresome too. Tizzy had never been one to cultivate anger. The steady rhythms of the rain and this smoky warmth had made her mellow. Bob seemed almost generous and neighborly now. He was not growling anymore either. It was bad news about his dead chickens. But Tizzy could see that Bob Nottingham was not a man to shed a tear over a spilt chicken. And most of his chickens were out there soaked in darkness, blood, and heavy rain. In here, though, Bob's fireside was looking brighter. Wasn't it? His Judah dog was here on duty and licking muck from the talons of a clumpish paw. His girl Button was safe in his hand. Wasn't she?

Sitting on the floor, at Bob's knee, Button did not seem to care much about her own welfare, one way or the other. To Tizzy, behind the dim flicker in Button's eyes,

Button's heart looked flatter than a hoe cake.

"Don't she never talk?" Tizzy asked.

"Not really," Bob said.

"Never at all?"

"Not since her mama run off. She weren't much of a talker before that either."

"Whud happened, Bob? You chase mama bear off widda stick?" Matthew asked, wagging his toe.

Bob seemed to think Matthew was funny, after a fashion. His beetle-brow would crinkle and his mouth would purse when the boy said stupid things.

"Mama lit out on her own. Damaged goods. She been married once already. That's how she got this one here." Bob's fingernails idly raked Button's dirty blond hair. Button took no notice.

"I went to Jackshhhon once," Matthew began slurring. "And my mama's Uncle U.U. had jush found his third wife—April Jan—hiding there after she run out on U.U. with another feller. Perfume dr-dr-drummer from Natchez. U.U. finds em together. Drummer does the talking. U.U. winds up given em both fifty dollars. *Each.* An he buys her a white wedding dress fer their wedding. First one he bought weren't good enough. Shit now. She needed her a *new* one. Soon as the dee-vorce is done, Uncle U.U. starts running with bad company. Colored gals mostly. Takes to dranking hisself to death. They say he'd mostly set with them whoors and cry all night. Making em talk baby talk like *her.* Aunt April Jan's baby goo-goo being forced on them poor gals. Man alive." Matthew shook his head. "Auntie April. What a peach she were. Bitch had a bad conduct discharge from the Salvation Army. If you could of knowed her. It was a twishhhted thang U.U. done to them gals. Goo-goo, ga-ga. Well, friendshhh, some say he finally flushed his love fer April Jan out of his system when he fell in front of that noon-day train on his birtday drunk. Which was perty much like his day-before-his-birtday drunk. Except he hadn't fell in front of that train yit. They say the whistle blew but he didn't hear it, they says. Didn't kill him right off. Nope. Old U.U. is still living in my Grammy Netta's spare room down in Jackshhhontown. But he cain't talk or wash hisself or go to the privy right, so who's to say? Now he don't feel a thang. That's good, ain't it? He's happy enough. Kinda like little ole Button here."

Matthew beamed for a moment, proud of his knack for parallels. Tizzy lay on the floor wishing he would fall in front of something.

"It happens," Bob said

But the boy was not through.

"Then again, whooo really knowzzz?" Matthew meditated further. "Maybe U.U. ain't shed of her at all..."

Tizzy was tired of being trapped indoors with a 90-proof Socrates. But Bob did not seem to be bothered by it.

"Some git they heads kiltered over a woman," Bob said, his eyes off in the ether. "They'll go moon-loony and do vicious crimes. Till somebody else does what they can't do fer themselves."

"End their mizzzery?" Matthew smirked.

"That's about right."

Matthew slurped his glass, pondering love and life, raindrops and vicious crimes.

"Wouldn't that be some fun fer awhile though? Take aholt of this world? Grab her by the tail and holler: lookit me, I'm *hyere* and I'm *gone*. You could hit ever mail train and bank from Jackssshun to Kingdom Come. Run wild like a sprayed roach till ye go out guns ablazing or you fry in the deep fry."

"They don't electercute yu too much fer robbing trains and banks, boy," Bob muttered, his jaw sagging. "You just moulder in the man's jailhouse."

"Shooo, Bob." Matthew slunk forward in the flickering room, his gaze climbing the beefy scar-twisted tattoos on Bob's forearms. "I figure you and me, we seen the monkey show. Bad times, hard-hearted days and a mean p-p-pecker or two."

"Maybe."

"You can bank on dat—"

"Maybe so."

"Come on now, Bob. You're familiar to me. I jist know I knows ye. Who are you really?"

"What do you mean?" Bob's voice was a husk.

"You seen our weapon. We both wise. Me, Tizzy, we gonna git us an alias too."

Boom.

It was thunder.

Boom.

The seams in Bob's face flattened smoother in the

light. He was wearing the mask again.

"Bob be short fer Robert. The name be Robert. Robert. Lloyd. Nottingham." Chain lightning rocked down on the house. "But don't you worry it none," he said.

Matthew sat dumb as a nit. Tizzy was spooked. Something about that name. That name was familiar or near familiar, like something she had once overheard or dreamt of.

"Ye ain't from Ole Riddle Top, are ye Bob?" Matthew prod softly.

"Seems like I've always been here," Bob said, pulling Button's head against his knee.

"But I reckon ye been out and around. Ain't ye? Reckon ye never took no fer no answer."

"That is true, I expect."

Tizzy frowned. She rose onto her elbows, her chin in her hands.

"Was she perty, Mr. Nottinham?"

"Who?"

"Her mama?" Tizzy asked.

"Yep. Yep, she sure was. Pertier than Liz Taylor."

"I'm sorry."

"Aw, she'll be back one of these days. Most likely."

Steel-blue bombs of light rattled the window glass. Bob Nottingham turned his face to the window. A new and pleasant glimmer sat on his lips.

"Come to think of it," he spake, "maybe y'all best stay on a few days and lay low. I ain't so sold on where your cousin's ridge is. I could be wrong. You could rest up

143

here. Do a few chores till the heat blows over. I know what big trouble is like."

"Golly bum," Matthew said, grinning. "We'd hate to shhhtep on your good nature."

"And our car—" Tizzy injected, unhappy with this turn in the topic"—our car is in a bad way."

But Bob did not hear them.

"Besides," he said, purring to the window. "When that sky opens up like this—fer more than a day—why, that ole road just might not be there no more. You don't wanna git caught out on this mountain. Not on this mountain."

Matthew blinked, pie-eyed. "Well if you're of a mind, Bob—"

KER-RRRAAASH.

An *explosion* and the door flew open as a big raven sailed in. Nottingham's hand shot up fast—faster than anything Tizzy had ever seen. He caught the black flapping bird by its throat as he rose from his rocker, snarling. Judah barked. Another *explosion.* A bourbon glass in the flames. Judah barked again. Nottingham stomped out onto the porch. He stood brazen in the crashing storm, a stranglehold on the black-winged, mad-flapping fury in his hand.

"Dawg *damnation,*" Nottingham roared, "I told you to stay *outa my house.*"

Aghast, through the open gusting doorway, Tizzy and Matthew watched the man *hurl* the raven back into the maelstrom. They watched Bob Nottingham come back inside and slam the door, bolting it shut.

A queasy silence fell. His cragged face came around, edging into the light.

"I got another bird to gut," he mumbled.

Nottingham left the room. Soon they heard cupboard doors and cast iron rattling from the kitchen. Tizzy and Matthew were afraid to look at each other. One of them might have to say something.

STEP 11

Morning was hot, crackling hot.

Tizzy lay on her back, both legs propped over her head against a porch post. Where were her hobgoblins, she wondered? As hot as it was this morning, Tizzy's blood was not being stirred in their kettle. At the moment, she felt none of the simmering troubles or hobgoblin doubts about her soul or her savior that plagued her most days. The only fear Tizzy felt at this moment was a fear of falling. She was trying not to let that happen. Because, if she did fall asleep right here, right now, she would be found buried in maple seed whirlygigs. It was a game. When her spirit moved (and this morning it moved slowly), Tizzy would toss a winged maple seed up at her toes then watch it twirl back down. Usually, the warm breeze would carry the whirly off the front porch, into the yard. But not always. A few pods kept landing on her nose or neck or around her bellybutton. She did not brush them off. That would spoil the game. Tizzy wanted to bury herself in whirlys before Matthew returned. It felt good, in a way, to want something for no good reason at all. It was a silly game, for no good reason at all. She had a ways to go and she was trying not to drift off to sleep before her whirlygig desires were met. These desires almost roused her lazy blood troublers. But not quite. It was too datgum hot for that.

Matthew was down checking on the car. Button was around, somewhere. But who knew where that somewhere might be? Maybe the odd little child was crouched beneath Tizzy at this very moment, under the porch, poking her dirty button nose into Tizzy's beezwax. Tizzy did not care. It was much too sultry for such nonsense. Her sleepy head had even stopped seeing bits of last night's half-raw chicken. She could hardly remember the peppercorns in the blood on her supper plate. The kitchen ceiling had leaked and the linoleum had been wet. But right now she did not care about any of that anymore. Not really. Not too much. Tizzy just wished Matthew would hurry on back so she would have someone to talk to, to keep her hobgoblins away. She yawned again. Right now, Lord help her, she was just a sinpot of wanton sloth. What would her Preacher-Daddy say if he could see her now? What would he tell Robert Lloyd Nottingham about such a wanton daughter?

And how could that daughter explain to a Preacher-Daddy that she had slept in complete bliss last night, in this strange stranger's house. She had slept more restfully and peacefully than any night she could remember. Under an eiderdown comforter and blankets Tizzy snoozed and dwelt along a deep honeyed river. In a long and meandering dream, her sweet mother stayed by her side. *"Honeygirl,"* her mama sang, *"You are so rare, so fine and refined."*

Somewhere in the early morning hours Tizzy stirred for a moment. She surfaced enough to hear the backdoor screen creak open and slap shut. Then she sank back into her mother's loving dragon-tattooed arms.

That jug-bitten Matthew Birdnell never heard a thing. He never stopped snoring on the side-porch.

Long after daybreak, a scratchy needle stole into Tizzy Polk's dream and her mother waltzed away. The Victrola was plunking zither chords again. The melancholy waltz kept swelling, fading, swelling. Tizzy finally stretched then slid from her covers. The rain was gone. Sunshine broke through the glass into her room. She had even slept through the doodly-doo of the java rooster.

Taking her time, Tizzy dressed then drifted past Button in the parlor. Button was sitting on the floor, staring into the phonograph's horn, watching the music come out. Tizzy found Matthew in the kitchen eating pone. He had been up since dawn, he said, and had not laid eyes on Bob. Tizzy wondered where Mr. Bob Nottingham went each early morning. She had vague memory of the screen door twang that almost interrupted her mothering dream. What was there to do on Old Riddle Top at such a cold, dark, godforsaken hour?

Matthew had made extra pone, so they managed breakfast for themselves. Afterwards, they went outside and were surprised to see how many chickens had weathered bullets and storm. Everywhere they looked, hens were skipping through puddles, making a gay chicken day of it. Matthew swore there were more of the dumb white clucks now than before he unleashed all that firepower. His pistol had hardly made a dent. From the porch, he and Tizzy could see where Bob Nottingham had tossed the dead hens into a pile beyond the coop. It would not be long in this sun before the pile bloated and stank.

Still, Matthew was never one to rush into the day. He dragged Tizzy over to the porch swing where they flopped and engaged in idle foolishness. They swung with fervor, counting chickens and fussing at each other. They finally tried to make some sense out of Nottingham's stormy explosion the night before. Bob had seemed to enjoy their company. He even extended his hand to them, sort of, offering this place as their robber's roost. Yes, things were looking brighter. So why did that abominable black bird have to come screeching in and break the spell? The way Tizzy saw it, Mr. Nottingham did everything but call that crow by name before he flung it back into the tempest. It was as if crow and stagman were familiars. But there was no telling, Tizzy told Matthew as they swung. There no telling what a man might do when his castle was under siege. At the right place and the right time, any one of us could turn crow-chucker.

Well, do the hillbilly bop, do the hillbilly boogie, was Matthew's answer to that.

Responding in kind, Tizzy began reciting King Solomon's Song of Songs. Let him kiss me with the kisses of his mouth for your love is more delightful than wine, because of the savour of thy good ointments thy name is as ointment poured forth, therefore do the virgins love thee.

Hillbilly boogie, all night long, Matthew responded.

Dark am I, Tizzy informed him, yet lovely, daughters of Jerusalem,

Such morning chitchat made Tizzy feel almost civilized until Matthew kissed her on the mouth with more delight than wine. Quickly, he got too randy trying to see how dark this daughter of Jerusalem was up her leg, under her dress. Queen Tizzy had to banish the boy from the porch swing. The Victrola had fallen silent by then and the Birdnell got fed up with her entirely. He decided this was the right time to check on the Packard.

Matthew had been gone the better part of an hour. Tizzy knew the woody slope was steep down to the road. It was dense thicket at best, and probably slick with mud and matted leaves. But he should have been back by now.

Tizzy tossed up another maple whirligig. It spun and bobbed on air. She hummed softly, singing a little tune in her head.

> *O watch your step, step, step,*
> *Watch where you wander little lamb,*
> *O, to a promise land...where...where...*

To a promise land where *what?* It was an old song, a

baby song, and she ought to know it. To a promise land—
where?—she could not remember the rest. It dangled on
her tongue. This lapse was peculiar, seeing as Tizzy had
heard it sung since the crib. She was getting thirsty. The
water dipper was on the other side of the house, waiting
by the sink in a tub of cool well water.

O watch your step, step, step,

Squabbling chickens took flight—and Tizzy left her
daydream. Behind her, Mr. Nottingham came around the
smokehouse, from the woods upslope.

Tizzy squinted upside down, shading off the glare.
She called out over her eyebrows to him.

"Mornin, Mr. Nottinham—"

"Yuh," Nottingham said. He stomped onto the back
porch holding a coil of wire.

"We already eat some pone." Her feet came off the
post.

"I figureed so."

Tizzy jumped up, shedding maple whirlys as the
screen door twanged shut behind Bob. Tizzy heard limbs
thrashing over her shoulder. She glanced around and
saw Matthew, breathless, slogging up from the car. He
had just cleared the trees in time to see Tizzy shrug at
him from afar. She pointed through the front door, then
went inside.

Halfway down the hall, Tizzy spied Button through a
door crack. The girl was curled asleep inside the hall

closet. She almost looked like a cherub angel, or an un-washed baby bird sleeping in its nest.

By the time Tizzy reached the kitchen, Nottingham was plundering the pantry. He moved an unlit brake-man's lantern from the floor to a hanging meathook, then dragged down a frog gigger from rafters overhead. Tizzy sidled in, trying not to arouse his ire. She sat with her bare toes perched on the rungs of a chair, watching him tug and tug at the gigger. He made soft curses. The gig-ger was tangled. His mind was elsewhere.

"My word, what is it keeps you so busy of a morning, Mr. Nottinham?"

"Nothing much. Tracking fer game. Things of that nature."

"Without no gun?"

"Depends on what you hunt, how you hunt. I deal and trade. Do a goodly bit of trading with hill folk." He stopped, looked Tizzy over for a second, then went back to tugging. "Some folk—if you gonna catch em—you got to catch em early. Afore they gone for the day."

"Are they that far?"

"Yep."

"Well, I'll do ye a favor, Bob," Matthew wise-acred, coming in the backdoor. "Help me encourage that ole se-dan outa that bog down there. We'll wipe off them soggy seat covers, and I'll chauffeur ye right to Cock Robin's doorstep. Folks will stay home just to see you arrive in such *high style.*"

Matthew wiped his face with his shirttail then dropped

onto a chair.

Nottingham lay the frog gigger and wire coil on the table betwixt his two guests.

"Your blue ride needs a road, boy. Where I go, they ain't always no road, see? Besides, you done me enough favors already, thank ye."

This was a curious observation, Tizzy thought. Mr. Nottingham had never seen their car—so how did he know it was a blue car? Had he inspected the Packard in his nightly wanderings? Yes—Tizzy decided—of course he had visited their car. Mr. Nottingham wandered all over. Each time he returned to the house, he emerged from a different pocket of woods. Did he not?

"What ye got in mind fer them, Bob?" Matthew asked, eyeing the coil and gigger.

Nottingham was washing his hands at the sink, pumping and lathering the gritty palms. "Aw, I might make a swap with an ole boy over in Johabeth's Holler. Swap him fer some willer tar and pounded saltpeter. I catch him things he likes."

"Saltpeter? Hell, what ye gone do with that?"

"I don't know."

"You want any breakfast?" Tizzy asked. "I could fry an egg."

"Naw," Bob said. "Ain't hungry just yet. Storm took a flap off'n the roof. I aim to nail it and clear that brush blowed under the porch."

Nottingham drank some coffee then went back outside. His ragged-out black rooster followed after him through the remains of a summer garden. From a small shed on the upslope side of the house, Nottingham took a heavy roll of black roofing paper. He put Matthew to work snagging dead branches and snarled brush from under the house and porch. Then Nottingham got a ladder, climbed it, and hammered on the kitchen eaves. This took most of the morning, with Tizzy passing tools up to Nottingham and Matthew doing a piss-poor job clearing out fire hazards underneath. Toiling in the crawlspace was sweaty, cramped labor and Matthew did not cotton to it. Matthew dragged out his ordeal until Nottingham finally finished the roof then came down to help. By high noon the dirty work was done. The sun and last night's rain were building up a head of steam, so everybody went inside for a cool drink.

Tizzy checked on Button. Button was still curled in the closet, sleeping, like she had been out gallivanting all night. Bob Nottingham opened a can of cold beans and spooned them straight into his mouth.

"I got other business to tend," he told them, leaning on the kitchen counter. "I'll be back directly. They's plenty of the vittle. Bacon up in the smokehouse. You need eats, you git it. The hand be the mother of the deed."

"The hell ye say, Bob," Matthew laughed. "The hand be the mother of the what?"

The mottled hound Judah bounded onto the back porch, big paws clumping like drums. Fresh from the woods, his black eyes gleamed. He drooled sorghumy slobber and barked.

Nottingham set the can in the sink. Snatching his frog gigger and wire, he went out to meet his hound.

"Judah—ho now," he commanded. The dog reeled, peeling off across the yard, back into the trees. Nottingham turned and spake through the screen. "Back by supper. You might tend to them dead biddys."

"Sure thing, Bob. No big deal."

When Bob spake, he meant Matthew and Matthew knew it. Tizzy knew it too. Chickens rotting in the sun had never been far off Tizzy's mind as they had toiled away the morning. Now she could hear the cicadas out there, rising on the heat. She and Matthew stood on the back porch, watching Bob stride slowly past two burnt trash barrels. He moved with sluggish rhythm, as if his muscles ached deep and he had all the time in the world. Tizzy wondered to what purpose those tools in his hard hands were intended. What was that Mr. Nottingham had just said? The hand be the mother of the deed? This was a new bit of scripture. A verse Tizzy had never heard.

"How was the car?" she asked Matthew, after the man had gone.

"Awright. I reckon. The mud was riz up nearly to the fenders. Best git her out soon."

"Matthew?"

"Yeah. mama?"

"I wonder if they're alooking fer us still. Down there. I wonder about my daddy and Shonda Jo and all them."

"To hell with hot chickens," Matthew snarled, scratching furiously. Then he shot the sun a finger-fuck.

"And that sheriff we done robbed. Wonder if his kids got enough to eat. Wonder if he's out ahunting after us too."

"Ain't likely. Besides, ain't nobody gonna look fer us up here. You know your damn daddy ain't coming up here. Preachers like him stay off'n Riddle Top. So they say."

"I suppose they do," Tizzy said, sitting on the stoop, her Preacher-Daddy vivid in her mind. "I'm good riddance anyway. To him, I'm sure."

"And we ain't got to worry by my pap. Pap ain't got much but he's got a opinion. On everthang. And he don't cotton to townfolk or lawmen neither. He'll jist run em off with his 30-30 and some twenty dollar words. Even if he is shy a field hand. What the hell. He got his pickup back by now."

"They prob'ly done forgot about us."

"That's right."

Eventually, Matthew gave up. He could fight it no longer. He found a spade in the shed then headed down to the coop. He would inter those rain-sodden chickens before they burst with maggots in this heat. He would bury them and be done with them.

There was no percentage in watching Rebel Yell say last rights over a chicken grave, so Tizzy went back inside to rummage the drawers. She ate a stringy snap bean while she nosed through the bureau in her room. Her bureau did not disappoint. Each drawer was heavy laden. She found a lavender lace tablecloth and some jewelry boxes, some crumbling postcards from Fern Lamb to Lucan Vitus Merriweather Jr., a pocket compass, and a sewing kit with several embroidery samples tucked inside. In the bottom drawer, Tizzy uncovered a family Bible, with several pressed lilies gone brown betwixt the brittle pages. The pages also held locks of rust-red hair wrapped in tissue paper. Two yellowing photographs were filed in the fourth chapter of Deuteronomy. One picture was of a curly-headed baby with the name—*Lonny 6wks*—inked on the back in a precise hand. The other picture was an anniversary tintype of the same elder couple Tizzy had met before in that parlor portrait. But the elders were surrounded now by sepia kith and kin, including several youngsters with cowlicks. Rusty red cowlicks, Tizzy would imagine. They all scowled at her, washed out and faraway looking.

Nope. Mr. Nottingham did not favor any of them. This gave Tizzy another idea. She got up off the floor.

Bob Nottingham's room was spare, more spare than the parlor. The once-white window curtains looked like they had never been washed, ever. The locked closet door beside his bed might have been cheerful once. Now it was a dull yellow. Yes, this yellow door was locked tight. Bob's iron bed-frame was rusting, with only an oil lamp and soapbox table to keep it company. There was a nubbly olive-drab blanket smoothed and folded beneath his pillow. It was not like Tizzy's nice bedroom at all. There was no table doily or out-of-date bank calendar or dreamy half-robed damsel on a rock at sunset gracing the wall, like in her bedroom. There was no cedar hope chest like she had in her room.

Tizzy turned. She saw an oak chest of drawers.

Without knowing the why for, Tizzy felt a disturbance as she approached the chest of drawers. Yes, she felt deep disturbance, from inside herself. She hesitated before touching the face of the top drawer. With great caution, she slid the top drawer open. It would have been empty—except for that rolling tiger's eye marble. The gold marble rolled and banked off the inner edges of the top drawer.

"Tiiiizzzy—"

Whap. Tizzy jammed the drawer shut and was back out in the hall with hardly a ripple. Dang that dumb hogboy and his hollering. The hall closet was closed shut now. Tizzy turned the knob and took a quick peek. Button was not inside.

"Tiiizzzzy—come quick."

Tizzy hoped Matthew Birdnell did not expect her to come running every time he got a weavel in his ear. Maybe that silly little Button was down by the coop and he was pestering her. Tizzy would have to put a stop to anything like that. After all, they were company in somebody else's house. Hogboy tended to forget things like that.

Tizzy shuffled down to the chicken coop. She felt too warm and faint in this swelter to get in a big hurry. She found Matthew behind the coop in the hot shade. He was standing over a fly-buzzing, feathery lump of chickens beside a moist hole.

"What *took* ye so long?" he demanded.

"I was coming," she whined.

"Take a look at this—"

"What is it?"

Something was wrong. Suddenly, Tizzy saw how shaken he was. Matthew dropped to one knee, raking back his sweaty hair.

"I de-vined it. My digger feet de-vined it. Like I done a hunert times before. My feet says to dig here, right here. So I took to digging. Real soft ground. Ain't even hit rock yet. And I find this here—"

Tizzy bent forward, peering into the hole. She saw something spindly, chalk-white, caked with earth. She looked closer.

It was a hand. A skeleton's hand.

"Oh me," she exclaimed.

"Soon as I spotted it, I dug out around her best I could. They's a lot of roots down there. Anyways, they ain't no more to it. It's jist a hand. Or hand bones, I mean."

"Ain't never seen the like—" peeped Tizzy. She felt her throat tighten. Her toes crept back from the edge of the moist maw, away from the skeleton hand within. The bony claws were bent. They seemed to bite into a deep clay gullet down there, seeking eternal shade, clawing after it.

"Looks to of been dead a good long while," Matthew said. "Ain't no flesh to it."

"Oh me."

"What we gonna tell Bob?"

"Oh, we can't do that." We ain't gonna tell him nothing," she answered, without stopping to worry it.

"And why the hell not?"

"Oh me. We can't do that. Maybe he put it there."

Somebody started laughing. Ragged rooster laughter. *"Haaaaw-dee-haw-haw-haw."*

Who was that laughing? Tizzy and Matthew raised their heads and their eyes together. They knew before they saw.

It was Button. She was laughing. The little girl was perched up on the gristmill, where the rooster crowed himself sick each morning. She even sounded like the rooster. Her face goggled at the sky and she was laughing.

"Haaaw-dee-haw-haw."

"It's not funny," Tizzy trembled to nobody. "Make her stop that."

Matthew, he did nothing. He just watched the ragdoll laugh. .

"She's tetched," he whispered, finally.

Button stopped in mid-cackle. From her perch, she looked down at the two. She was wide-eyed and blinking. Could she have heard them? Then her cupid mouth exploded again. She started up again. She looked up and laughed and laughed, as if she saw a jack-in-the-box in the clouds.

"Haaw-dee-haw—"

The sky and trees above echoed with the sound of zither strings snapping and unstringing. Tizzy and Matthew knelt there, stupefied by this crazy child, not looking in the hole below them.

Neither of them noticed as the skeleton forefinger tapped once, twice, three times.

STEP 12

Nottingham left the great spreading oak. Judah ran ahead. Nottingham had let the dog scout as far as Pucker's Knob before he reined the booger in. They had work to do. Farther down the leeside of the wooded slope, Nottingham stopped and knelt. He sifted the loam, tasted it, and found it to his liking. If he seeded this earth with acorns and bone, when the moon and the signs were ripe, then an oak—or just about anything else for that matter—would grow itself, rooted deep. His progeny would grow until tree and mountain were one, alive and entwined like muscle, rock and root, almost immortal. But you had to be careful, the moon must be ripe, or the thing you grew could sour and turn on you. Some just wilted, shriveled away. Some had to be dealt with and brought low.

From beyond the green-draped chiney briers, Judah's peculiar voice echoed back to Nottingham. Even toads with stones in their heads could not foresee Bob Nottingham's advent upon the slew and the village. He might even steer clear of Johabeth's Holler this eve. Judah had never given a damn about Johabeth, and Nottingham did not tolerate Johab. No, he never cared for Johab at all. Nottingham did not suffer or keep those blatteroons with no sense of humor. He had never met a Lych yet who had one.

He scooped up an angleworm, pinched it in half, then returned both ends to the soil. Now there were two. Rising, Nottingham opened his buck-knife and continued down the slope. The dog must not get too far afield. It was a hot harvest moon, and the soul of man kept calling.

STEP 13

True to his word, Bob returned at sundown in time for supper, without the gigger or wire coil. His hands were empty. He bore no willow tar. He had no saltpeter to speak of, pounded or otherwise. Nobody picked his brain on the subject, nor did Tizzy or Matthew mention their skeletal findings behind the chicken coop. Matthew almost kept the skeleton hand as a keepsake. But after very little persuasion from Tizzy he dumped chickens on top of those boney fingers and buried them all.

The next few days were much the same. Nottingham would slip from the house in the dark, predawn hours, and return later, usually after breakfast. He would busy himself around the place, doing repair work or sharpening tools on his grindstone wheel. Once, Tizzy joined him. She did not know why, since Mr. Nottingham disturbed her in so many ways. Yet she was drawn to him like a moth to a guttering candle. Cross-legged, she watched Mr. Nottingham hone an adze hoe blade on his whirring, spinning wheel. They both looked up when Matthew lost his temper at a stump that tripped him on the way to the privy. A hissyfit ensued, with Rebel Yell kicking and sniping at the wily stump. But the boy did not interest Nottingham for long. He went back to pedaling his grindstone.

Tizzy asked if he often got riled himself. He said he did not. But Tizzy had her doubts. Surely he had his hobgoblins too. Didn't everybody? Surely his wicked goblins could run boiling through his veins, on a bad rainy night, with bird in hand. So Tizzy dared to ask him. Was he sure?"

"Ain't no temper left," he said. "Maybe I burnt it all up."

Tizzy doubted he was doddering or losing his memory. So she changed the subject.

"Mr. Nottinham?"

"Yuh?" he muttered, sparks shooting off his wheel.

"They ain't no road to your door."

"Naw, they ain't. Used to be though."

"Well, whatever went with it?"

"Roads git lost sometimes. They's always another one to be found."

"I only seen one road up Riddle Top. They's more? Down into them gaps—and the valleys?"

"You know it."

"I declare."

"Girl?"

"Yes, Mr. Nottinham?"

"Ain't no *bad* nights to speak of."

He seemed to be telling her something. So, mostly, Tizzy left him alone. He seemed to stew better that way. Occasionally Nottingham would settle on a box on the front porch, brooding in the heat. He would sit there, fixed on Tizzy and Matthew while they fed the flock of biddies or picked at each other like snot noses worrying a scab. Tizzy could always sense him watching. She could still hear him telling Matthew not to worry it. ("Don't worry it none," he said.) When her hobgoblins got busy, when she was not hearing Button's laughter in her head, Tizzy heard those words. Don't worry it none. Mr. Nottingham did not seem to worry it up on that porch. He would just sit and watch them, unmoved, while the Victrola's zither notes and grooves went round and round. Then, sometime in the afternoon, he was bound to leave them alone on the place. "Look out fer that snake," he would often say before departing. But Tizzy never knew what snake he meant and she did not ask. Yes, he had his private little jokes and he was always back by supper.

It was strange, but Tizzy always felt safer then. She did not like it when he left them alone with this house.

More than once, while Mr. Nottingham was gone, Tizzy thought she saw phantoms—or sly country boogers who slipped around like phantoms. They would slip by the house, like passing murmurs, just inside the trees, from tree to tree. She would hail them but nobody showed themselves.

One gloomy afternoon, Matthew was suffering over the sink—and letting Tizzy know it—as she pinched lice from his scalp. His dignity was doing most of the suffering.

"Lice is a Birdnell blood condition," he told her. "I cain't help it."

"I reckon you're right," Tizzy said, poking through his dirty hair. "If going to bed with too many of your kinfolk counts as a blood condition."

"Keep it up, Tiz. I just need me some turpentine."

"Nope. I ain't gonna watch you light up like a candle in the parlor. Vinegar and lye soap is what you need."

A soft knock-knock came down the hall.

"What's that?" Matthew asked, swatting away her hand.

"Somebody's knocking at the dang door."

Tizzy could tell it came from the front door.

Tizzy and Matthew went into the parlor. They were almost to the front door—when another knock came from within her bedroom. This meant the visitor was now outside the porch entrance to Tizzy's room. They changed kilter, both moving cautiously into Tizzy's room. When they opened her bedroom's outside door—there was nobody on the porch. But they were just in time to see a decrepit stranger's backside disappearing into the forest. In a glimpse, they could both see the stranger was bald as a coot and wore a scavenger's patchwork coat. They would both agree on that much, when they retold it later.

As their visitor disappeared, Matthew hollered a hello then ran after him. When Matthew finally returned from the trees—a quarter hour later or more—he swore there was no hairless tramp to be found. There was no one lurking in those woods, not a whisper.

"Oh, fergit it," Tizzy told him. "You jist didn't look hard enough. If you weren't so lazy and you'd found the feller we can be sure of one thing."

"And what might that be?"

"He ain't got no headload of lice.

Matthew did not lock horns with her over it, not much. He wanted to believe she was right. Even though he knew different. He knew how hard he searched through those empty trees.

Mostly, while Nottingham was away, Tizzy and Matthew spent hours in uneasy distractions, forgetting bad jokes or playing hangman and ticky-tac-toe in the dirt. Matthew was not so good at hangman since he did not really know his words or alphabet. He had dropped out after third grade. He always wanted her to play mumble peg with his nickel-handle pocketknife. But Tizzy was not too keen on Matthew Birdnell's knife-throwing skills, even if he was aiming down into the dirt. Besides, it was a boy's game. And, being a boy, Matthew would not stop angling for another game of mumble peg, despite her refusals. Besides, there were other issues. Tizzy was usually barefoot to preserve her buckletop shoes. Whereas Matthew had the leather of his white-top spectators to protect his toes and his legs could stretch farther. More often than not, Matthew would get mad, give up, and go nap on the porch swing, fanning off flies in his sleep. Up here it was unusually warm, like a late echo of summer, an Indian-giver summer, with too many flies for this time of year.

Tizzy tried to nap in spurts, but the heat was too much for a decent snooze. So she would whistle flat hymns and delve into her bureau drawers, fondling the tarnished jewelry and old photos, bewildered by each mystery. She had not returned to Mr. Nottingham's room—not with that slaphappy Button poking her little rooster head around every odd corner when least expected. Tizzy was afraid to be caught snooping. As far as Tizzy knew, the tiny girl had not uttered a note since her cockydoodledoo on the grist-mill. But Tizzy took no chances. Button—and Button's odd behavior—did not inspire trust. Besides, there were other treasure troves to plunder. The kitchen cabinets were stuffed with pickled okra, home-canned tomatoes and relish, stocks of canned goods, and paraffin-sealed jars. Tizzy had seldom seen so much preserved, and never in a lone man's house. The apothecary chest held decaying secrets in its many nooks: pennyroyal, mustard seed, bloodroot, garlic, chicory, figwort, coriander, sassafras, alongside other dried bulbs and nightshades unknown to Tizzy. There was a long paisley curtain beneath the kitchen sink counter. Behind this curtain, down at one shadowy end—under a shelf—she discovered a pair of small padlocked cubbyholes. One could only imagine.

When she grew tired of this, Tizzy would leave Matthew snoring and roam the woods near the house. She encountered no country men nor country women there, bald or otherwise, and no Lychs either. Still, that threat always sat over her shoulder. She never ventured far beyond sight of the yard. She could hear a creek running somewhere nearby, but she never found it. Sometimes it was nice just to lie on a rocky crag and gaze up through the branches. Squirrels and bluejays would chide overhead, raising a racket through the pines. They reminded Tizzy of the mama raccoon and her coonlets back on the schoolyard. Tizzy wished she could have seen those other coonlets, just once. Other than the dead one. She prayed they were safe and growing fat for coming winter. Tizzy's coon-prayers were often broken by a steady echo, a ricochet sound, like someone chopping wood somewhere far off. Once, while Tizzy lay on her rocky crag listening to the chopper on the breeze, a brown cow ambled by without saying a word.

If the cow had spoken, she might have warned Tizzy of things any heifer or crow in these woods knew already. Tizzy might have learned that life thus far was prelude to things foretold, to a terrible blossom, and the most careless love of all.

One gold-burnished afternoon, Tizzy dozed on the sunny rock until she actually fell asleep. Hours passed. When she finally opened her eyes the sun was dipping toward darkness. Spooked by this, Tizzy brushed ants off her face and scooted from the rock. She made haste, returning to Nottingham's house. It was cool with dusk seeping in when she reached the homestead. The locust weathervane shifted idly as Tizzy arrived with the tart evening breeze at her back. The house looked asleep again, like it had laid down for a nap with Tizzy. All the windows were unlit. She saw Matthew asleep up on the porch, his shoes off, his dirty toes tangled in the swing's chain. Slipping around to the kitchen, Tizzy climbed the kitchen step and startled Mr. Nottingham.

Bob's eyes shot sidelong at the sound of her. He stood tall at the sink, his head back as he drank, gulping, draining the dregs of a fruit jar. The kitchen was in gloom and awfully still, the way rooms can be when draining the last dregs of light. Nottingham lowered the jar. He seemed a bit disturbed at Tizzy's sudden appearance. Disturbed in a way she had not yet seen.

"Oh—hidy," Tizzy said.

He wiped his pinkish lips, smearing them clean with the back of his hand.

"There you be," he almost whispered, laying the fruit jar in the sink. "I just knowed you was lost."

"I was just out walking."

"It's late fer that. That panther—he be bright-eyed and hungry come sundown."

"I didn't go far."

"Ever hear a panther scream?"

"No sir."

"He screams like a gal gitting kilt. If you ain't hereabouts, we don't know if' it's just a panther—or you at the wrong end of a panther."

"Goodness," Tizzy gasped.

"Best roust that boy, Tizzy June. Lazy, ain't he?"

"Yes sir."

Nottingham turned and went down the hall. Before

she woke Matthew, Tizzy went to the sink to wash her hands. Her hands were filthy from the woods. In fact, she was foul all over, inside and out. She had not seen a bathtub since the Saturday before her last night in a church. She caught whiffs of herself as she pumped water over her hands. The water gushing from the pump was clear and fresh smelling, but not Tizzy. She was a very dirty Tizzy. The water trickled through her fingers, swirling and mingling in the sink with the rusty red juice pooled around Bob Nottingham's fruit jar. Tizzy recalled many a dirt farmer telling her Preacher-Daddy that fall tomatoes tasted different, better. Fall tomatoes tasted best. Before leaving the sink, Tizzy washed the fruit jar, towel dried it, and put the jar away. Then she went outside to wake up Matthew.

After supper, Tizzy asked if she could have a bath and Nottingham said yes. Matthew took the big washtub down from the back porch rafters and brought it into the kitchen. They boiled four granite-ware stockpots of water on the stove. Matthew allowed how he would wait another week or two for his suds, then he left Tizzy to her business.

Nottingham had already retired to the parlor fire with his bonded whisky. The fire was a little hot, but it was too chilly out for no fire so they opened the front door. Matthew sat outside against the porch rail while Bob rocked his chair inside, stroking his Button by the hearth. Rebel Yell wished he had a good chaw of Day's Work. He asked Bob but Bob did not have a chaw. Bob kept to his liquor, not that he ever showed it. Matthew watched the stars and spat on occasion, chaw or no chaw, just for the fiddle fuck of it. He felt like spitting. That dark beyond the steps? That was the devil's dark he spat into. Matthew knew it and was not afraid. So he spat at it. It demanded as much of him.

After a while Matthew took off his County specs. He started rewinding the tired black tape on his spectacles' cracked earpiece. Matthew wanted to crush them instead. Maybe, after a Brinks job or two, he would buy some prescription sunglasses. They would be studly numbers alright, more his style. He replaced the eyeglasses on his nose, waiting for his eyes to adjust through one good lens and one chipped.

"Surprised ye don't keep no still somewheres, Bob," he said, scratching his ankle. Chiggers were thick as the third of June. "Never knowed nobody could drank store whisky on a regular deal."

"Don't know nothing about stills. Never learnt."

"Bet ye could buy ye some tempered lightning, from one of these hicks. Like that Lych feller Tizzy and me seen back down the road. Reckon he'd run a drop or two?"

"Ain't interested," Bob said.

Button spotted a snout beetle on the rug and started crawling after it, tracking it. She tracked it across the floor, out the door, down the porch and off into the night. Matthew waited till she was out of earshot, before his eyes rolled around, ogling back through the open door at

Nottingham.

"That little tadpole—she's missing a few rivets, ain't she Bob?"

"Really? What makes you think so?"

"Aw, I can tell. Got an eye fer it."

"Hnnn, smart too. You're quite a gangster ain't you, boy?"

"Better than that," Matthew bragged. "I'm bound fer red hot shells and glory. You must be perty dang sluggish, Odd Bob, if ye cain't see that. Hell's bells, if I ain't done ye another favor. Why, you'll be atelling your friends and neighbors how I once let ye live and holed up at your sty fer awhile."

"Where's that gun of yours?"

"In my bedroll, where I left her. Why is that?"

"Just checking your memory. That's all." Bob was grinning, sort of.

Matthew was not so sure what that last little crack of Bob's was getting after. Matthew was thinking maybe he had just been insulted or something. But he was not certain of it.

"You a real lugnut, Bob. Anybody ever tell ye that?"

Yes, this was Odd Bob's lucky night. A sure fire insult would have forced Rebel Yell's hand. He might have to take steps.

A cricket chirped in the dark yard so Matthew turned and spat at it. He grew lonely in his gut, watching the moonrise, listening to the stars twinkle and tweet. Distantly, he could hear soapy water sloshing, far off, behind the kitchen door. Damn, he hated taking baths. No, a night like this was perfect for a coon hunt and this made Matthew restless. The criminal life deprived you of the simple joys. He doubted Bob's hound was much of a tracker. No, that damn Judah was not fitted out like any coondog Matthew Birdnell had ever seen.

Matthew looked back over his shoulder again—looking back to ask Bob about his dog. What he saw struck Matthew kind of queer. It was something new and old and sideways about Bob Nottingham. And this time it was not his datburn bearcat teeth or reptile smile. Nottingham himself looked queer, even for Nottingham. Bob's little smile just hung there, suspended. His heavy lids could not hide how his eyes fell on something down that hallway. Something Matthew could not see from where he was sitting outside. Matthew was amused to see that—whatever it was—it made Bob happy.

Tizzy had climbed from the tub, leaving behind a truck patch of dirt in the murky water. She dried herself with a flour sack towel. She wanted to wash her hair but was afraid of coming down with the croup in this night mountain air. Her towel was stiff and did not dry very well. Earlier, in one of her bureau drawers, Tizzy found a linen nightgown. It was not really small enough but would have to do. Finally, Tizzy gave up on the stiff towel and pulled the gown over her damp body. The gown clung to her naked skin, her sprout of nipples budding through the thin, wet garment. Tizzy Polk did not realize that a draft had blown the door open a smidge, giving a narrow

view down the hallway. So she combed out her hair, unaware.

Unaware of Robert Lloyd Nottingham watching with
his whisky glass and cavernous gaze.

He had taken his mind off the boy and glanced down
the hall a few minutes before. The kitchen door had parted. The girl was bent in the narrow frame, her gown wet
and clinging.

Tizzy was innocent of any change. But out there in
the firelight, she had blossomed in the eyes of Bob Nottingham.

Later, in bed, Tizzy wandered by that deep honeyed
river, her eyes closed and dreaming. A heavy step entered her room. She might have heard it. She might have
kept her eyes shut, feigning sleep, afraid of the presence
which loomed for long minutes over her bed.

When she finally dared to look, by the honey morning
light, her pillow told the tale. It was the tale of a trinket
left beside her on the pillow. A gift. It was the tale of a
tarnished gold chain she hid in the toe of her buckletop
shoe. It was a tale she never told to Matthew.

STEP 14

"I'm gonna track him."

"Track him fer what?"

"I'm gonna tailgate that shitrag," Matthew said. "See where he goes."

"I doubt Mr. Nottinham would appreciate that."

"So what? He don't own this mountain. Leastways I don't thank he does."

Matthew sat astride the broken tongue of the upended buckboard wagon in Nottingham's front yard. Beneath the shady hawthorn tree, Matthew kept spurring the wild rocking bronc in his head. Tizzy could see he was building steam.

"But what fer, Matthew?" she asked.

"I'm gonna see what ole Bob is up to. You don't believe that line about swapping favors with these country cousins do ye? Ain't enough jaspers up here to raise a duckstand. Fergit all that mess about saltpeter Bob ain't got no use fer. Besides—"

"Yeah?" she pressed.

"I'm done stir crazy setting around this sty. Ain't you?"

"Well, sure, come to think of it."

Matthew nodded, slowly, squaring all the angles.

Tizzy saw some wisdom in Matthew's words, sort of. It was the morning after her first bath in ages but Tizzy was already ready for another bath. She could do without this awful mountain breeze, the hot rising damp, the insects. And today was just another dull rite in Mr. Nottingham's ritual. As usual, he was scarce when they woke up. As usual, shortly after grits and redeye gravy, he returned.

"He's regular, alright," Tizzy allowed.

"Hell, my Uncle Jack was regular. Bob's abnormal." Matthew looked at the plume of black smoke from behind the house. "Good ole Odd Bob."

"Hopefully he's applying himself and making good use of his time.

"Bullshit."

They could hear the high grinding whir of his sharpening wheel.

The man was around back at present, burning trash in the barrels while he put a new edge on more of his tools. Unbeknownst to Bob, while he burned things and whetted, Tizzy and Matthew were loitering out front under the hawthorn tree, red-hot for a plan.

Finally, Tizzy straddled the upended wagon's tongue, facing Matthew. She leveled with him.

"Boy, I know I pester you something fierce. But if something was to happen to you, I don't know what I'd do, stuck up here like this."

Matthew leant forward. He whispered in Tizzy's ear.

"Would ye miss me?"

"Yes. Yes, I believe I would."

"Few more days, ladybug, another week. Watch and see. We'll jump off this shitrag robber roost here, fer fancier digs."

"I still say, he ain't gonna appreciate nobody follering him."

"Well, I don't appreciate his shitrag personality. Come to think of it, I never have."

"Matthew—"

"Yeah, mama?"

"Please stop saying shitrag."

"Okay."

Matthew was still picking through Nottingham's backhanded digs from the night before. Matthew did not need Bob's little pop quiz. Matthew was one with his gun. He knew right where that weapon be and he knew how to use it. Yeah, Matthew figured he had been Dobber The Goat last night. He was pretty sure. That's why, right now, that loaded weapon was safe under this boy's shirt.

"But I'm scary," Tizzy begged, biting her lip. "Them woods is weird and unknown to us. He might—"

"Then you best stay here, Little."

"Little?"

"Little Miss Split-tail. Keep to your doll-babies and buckletop shoes."

For a split-second, Tizzy hated him again. She knew Matthew was utterly ignorant of her doll. But it still felt like he had just spoken ill of Lou-Lou, her beautiful broken friend. And these were the only shoes Tizzy owned, so what choice did she have? No matter. It was just hogboy prattle, the kind Matthew Birdnell was full of. Despite being more grown up than he was, Tizzy could not help but wish she had brought Lou-Lou along for the ride. At the rate he was going, Tizzy would not put it past this hogboy to up and get himself killed. If Tizzy had brought her doll-baby, at least she would not be left alone with Mr. Nottingham, like Button was.

"What if he hears you on his tailgate?"

"He won't. I'm wise to them woods, see. And I'm fleet of foot. You forgetting I'm part Injun."

"Just be careful, you gristlebone."

Matthew and Tizzy went back into the house. They watched Bob from Tizzy's window and they waited. Matthew was restless and ready now. The wait was much longer than he would have liked.

Bob Nottingham sharpened edges until his fiery barrels were down to a smolder. Nottingham doused them, then spaded the white ash over his dormant tomato plot. Matthew whispered that Bob was wasting time and good potash. Those vines weren't just wilted, Matthew whispered, they were dead already. Even deader than those beans and collards. Still, Nottingham carefully scattered his ashes until his spade scraped the bottom of the second barrel. With this deed done, Nottingham went inside, changed his work shirt, and left.

Matthew counted to fifty-nine before he followed.

"To hell with sixty," he said, "Leave the light on, partner."

Tizzy stood on the porch, shading her eyes.   She watched her wiry partner in crime slink into the pines downwind of the chicken pen. Her heart felt almost light for a moment. She had never had a partner in anything before. She certainly would not claim Matthew as a boyfriend. And she would never condemn herself to life as some pig slop slinger's girlfriend. The word "partner" had a nicer ring to it—even if it did sound like it meant more responsibility.   (More responsibility than being a girlfriend could ever be.) Of course, the two dollar question was: How responsible did this hogboy feel when it came to his partner Tizzy Polk?

Tizzy decided that was a question only a little fool would ask herself this far along and this late in the day. It was a question better left unanswered for the time being.

By the time Tizzy withdrew to the kitchen, she was already peeved at Matthew and kicking herself for not going with him. She was weary of this old home place, especially when she was left alone with it. Button might be around. But Button didn't count. The kitchen was dull and smelled of sausage grease from breakfast. Nottingham's soot-covered shirt hung on a chair. Tizzy washed it in the sink, then pinned the shirt on the clothesline. It would dry quickly in this sun. Tizzy had already forgotten they were into late fall down below. In the valleys, the hollers—and in Cayuga Ridge—the air was already crisp as green apples. But, up here, Tizzy absent-mindedly mistook the season for late July. Or August, when the cicadas and junebugs pitched a fit and the sky was pale yellow.

Perhaps the heat got to Tizzy's head. Or perhaps it was just curiosity that got the best of her again. She went searching for Button. Button might not count. But now that Tizzy had been laughed at by the crazy little tot, she thought she might be able to coax a thought or two from those dirty cupid lips. But Button was not in her favorite closet, or under the porch or crawlspace. The chicken coop held nobody currently but a pair of persnickety hens, the rest were out in the yard or strutting through the trees. A peppered ham and two slabs of bacon hung in the smokehouse, but no Button child was curing in its rafters. And all the while, Tizzy kept hearing a chopper. A chopper chopping far and away on the mountainside.

Returning to the parlor, Tizzy examined the child's big Victrola. She had never looked closely at the gramophone. It was an ornate, claw-footed, upright record player standing almost tall as Tizzy. In the shelves underneath, Tizzy found a stack of 78 r.p.m. shellac discs. Several were Doc Roberts and Vernon Dalhart, a few by the Pine State Playboys. One disc was cracked—*Down At The Cuckoo House* by someone called Spade Cooley (and His Orchestra). And, of course, there was the disc that already lay on the Victrola platter. Tizzy cranked the machine and set the needle. Scratchy notes began, in simple clusters. It was Button's tune, zithery notes, a lullaby twinkling from the speaker horn.

Tizzy smiled. She tried to read the dull yellow label going around and around, but she could not. The yellow label might have been cheery once. She did not want to stop the yellow label from going around. She just wanted to listen. It never crossed her mind to read the yellow label on the black record before she cranked it.

Why was her head so full of holes these days?

The longer the black record played on the green felt turntable, the more empty Tizzy felt. Soon, she was not smiling anymore. She was remembering things, shameful things she thought were tucked away long ago, buried for good. Buried in her baby days. Long ago. What was wrong with her?

Something zithery was pulling at Tizzy, tugging at her ... a sadness in the tune maybe...

The tune pulled at Tizzy and Tizzy fell. She fell through a hole in her head and found herself back in Bob Nottingham's bedroom.

His door was open. She had not looked for a Button in here. A pair of worn jock shorts hung on a bedpost at the foot of Bob's bed. Tizzy did not want to look at his jock shorts, so she did not. She trod softly upon his floor. She stood very still for a long moment, facing his oak chest of drawers. She slid open the empty top drawer and heard the rolling tiger's eye marble. But this time, it was not a marble rolling. It was a silver thimble. The silver thimble rolled toward Tizzy then stopped in the corner of the drawer. This silver thimble, it was familiar to her.

Button's tune kept playing, wafting through the parlor, zithering into this room, into Tizzy Polk. Without knowing the why for, Tizzy pocketed the silver thimble in her dress. She slid the drawer closed. The zithering notes slid past her as she turned.

Tizzy turned an uneasy eye toward the closet door, the yellow door that was closed and locked before. But now the yellow door stood open: wedged open with a rusty hatchet head. Why, it was not a closet at all, really. It was was a windowless storeroom, not big enough to be a bedroom. But it was Button's bedroom. Tizzy knew this. It was Button's room. The child's room was tiny and empty except for an iron bed-frame with bare springs. There was no pillow, just a twisted, dirty blanket atop the springs.

Tizzy stood there, empty. The music was sucking at her, sucking everything out of her.

Tizzy's eyes cut back and forth—betwixt the connecting rooms. Button's foul blanket—and Bob's olive blanket. His hanging jock shorts—the hatchet head—Button's bed springs—his jock shorts. Back and forth, sucking at her, in and out.

"*Stop it,*" she blurted.

Tizzy turned off her ears. Tizzy took steps. Fast steps. Faster.

She left the room.

She went straight to the Victrola and turned it off.

She ran out into the crackling sun.

This was child's play. The man's spoor was heavy in the forest. He was not hard to track, not for this Osage pathfinder. Matthew's specs required constant nudging. But he had no problem at all for the first twenty minutes or so. Until he crossed water, that is. Water always threw him. Matthew had never hunted much. Pap stopped letting him tag along after young Matt's first coon season. His Pap could tell fortunes and could tell one thing about this kid: Matthew Birdnell was too damn lazy to chase a varmint for long. Mainly, what Matthew liked was getting loaded with the hunters, drinking rookus juice and peeing in the fire. After a while he got left at home, unless they needed somebody to tote extra gear. The way Matthew saw it, maybe he would come back someday, after he was world famous, and kill one or two of them. That would impress his Pap. But this was no varmint Matthew was tracking now. This was just Odd Bob. Matthew smiled as he threaded through the pine, he was born to it. Being a young Osage buck, yep, that was his natural calling. He could track Bob on mostly-pure Osage instinct. Like a mostly-pure panther.

And he would have too, if crossing a creek didn't throw him every time.

When he left Tizzy waiting on the porch, it was a different story.

Not far from the house, on a wooded downslope, a footworn trail developed. Matthew actually sprinted ahead, catching glimpses of Bob on two occasions. Bob did not hear him, Matthew saw to that. Bob just slogged on, a hameheaded gait carrying him forward. He was unmindful of spry Injun trackers. Bob's bootfalls sank deep in the soft ground. It was easy to scout him along that burnt ridgeline. They dipped into a shadowy cool holler, then climbed rocky footings to a higher crag. Twin elms had fallen crossways there. Matthew slipped under a rotting elm trunk. They started down into another holler. Matthew's descent was quick and stealthy. He kept the man close.

Then, something terrible happened. He heard trickling water.

His heart sank. It was not a very deep or wide creek. But it was enough. If they were here to see it, Pap and his coondog buddies would be busting a gut about now. They should count themselves lucky, Matthew told himself. Otherwise, they would be laughing dead men with a slug in each eye. On the other side of the creek, Matthew tried to find Bob's bootprints again. He ran up and down the muddy branch for the better part of an hour. At one point, he turned around and the sun was not in the right spot anymore. That rock and that cluster of white speckled mushrooms seemed unfamiliar. Strange fern and spruce surrounded him now, quiet and whispery as a noonday prayer meeting. The woods were warming up. Bob Nottingham was long gone. And the Rebel Yell Birdnell was lost.

Matthew wandered in the trees for a few hours, his mouth drawn and thirsty. Why didn't he think to drink from that creek back there? He was asking this over and over and wiping sweat from his stinging eyes, when he ran hard into an unforgiving brush pile. It made a gonging sound and hurt like a bastard. Matthew looked down and saw his pant leg was torn. He had gouged his thigh. His blood dripped from a copper thump rod.

"Gotdammit," said he.

Hidden and corroding beneath the brush was a whisky still. The still was derelict and green and it looked like a lot of liquor had passed through it. Matthew was sure about this. He was not just one with the woods, he knew a moonshine still when he slammed into one. Bob might not be wise to it. But someone had run popskull up here then moved on, many moons ago. Matthew tapped on the big copper boiler. He enjoyed the hollow gong of it, longing for some sour mash to see him through this sorry day.

That's when someone moaned.

Matthew stiffened at the sound.

It was faint. A feeblish moan, like wind in a pipe organ.

Behind the derelict still, Matthew found a cow. The heifer was brown. She lay in a gummy lake of blood. She was ebbing away, bleary eyes almost shut, blood gurgling from the pierced vein in her neck. Matthew took care to avoid the puddle. He did not want stains on his white-top spectators. She moaned again, just barely, softly wheezing through the open mouth. Her lye-white tongue was coated with soil and rust. One hoof squirmed in the red slop. Was she resisting the end, in her death throes, or simply afraid of the figment of Matthew? Or was she still trying to ward off whatever had gored her? Her killer must be nearby, possibly due to return. She had not lain and bled for very long. Matthew's nostrils flared. It was an incurable situation. This heifer would be gone soon and so must he be. With rising dread, he moved on. But his head did not. He could not stop thinking about her. And, yes, a swig of corn would have been nice. A swig would have soothed his nerves.

Before the woods gave him up, Matthew saw a few more things. With each dark discovery, he kept leaving parts of his head behind. The sun went steadily and, after a hair- and shirt-snagging push, Matthew stumbled into a wild chestnut grove. In the broken light, white chickens scratched at the mossy mountain skin, milling about. They were just a smattering of dumb cluckers, not like Bob's flock. Nobody would know if he drop-kicked a few for fun. But right now, Matthew's stilts were wobbly, his shoes full of sweat and mud, his feet were raw with blisters. Seeing the chickens, he felt closer to the homestead, though: a whoop or two away. So he limped faster. His moves stringhalted now, thanks to the hole in his thigh. It ain't the gore-horn that kills you, he chanted softly. It's the hole. The hole. The hole. It ain't the gore-horn that kills you. It's the hole.

Another half hour of misery was still ahead of him. But Matthew finally took a wild left turn through laurel briar and around a wasp's nest and he came to a dead stop. What he saw down slope made him squeak like a rubber toy.

It was Bob Nottingham's smokehouse.

Matthew left the leafy steambath. He tripped down to the house. Tizzy was waiting on the wagon tongue. She sat there boiling in her own little popskull, in the late glare of day.

"I doubt you could catch a bug in a bucket," she said, once his tale of woe was told.

"He was sneaky. He threw me."

"Yeah, and I'm wily Delilah."

"I'm telling ye, Tizzy now—don't rile me up. He's a sneaky, backtracking shitrag and that's all they is to it."

"Take a rest, hogboy. You look thirsty."

"I told ye don't never call me no hog—"

"I'm sorry. I'm just hot, dern it."

"Let's git on in the house then. I need better shade and cool water."

"Nope," she said, chin on her knees. She would not even look at the house.

"And why not?"

"They's something *unfit* about this place. It's unfit, Matthew."

"Well, I ain't gone argue about that."

"I'm as much to blame as you."

"To blame? Fer what?"

"Well, I been thinking," Tizzy said, picking up speed. "Why do we always gotta be running from something or running after something else?"

"Huh? What's got into you while I was gone?"

"If we live backwards and upside down from the way of things, we ends up in unfit places."

"Doll baby, I'd give you a pill but I ain't got one," he said. She was going frantic on him.

"Matthew, I wonder sometimes if we ain't just whirly-gigs, for no good reason at all. You know? Whirlygigs. Seeds. We just is. And we fall. And we don't need no reason at all. And that's okey-dokey. Besides, they ain't none."

"They ain't no what?"

"No good reason at all."

Matthew tried to decipher her. But not for long. He gave up quickly and dragged himself inside where he drank six dippers. He almost stopped there, then decided to have a seventh. The seventh dipper finally slaked his thirst, so Matthew took off his shoes. He took out his pocketknife and found a bottle of red iodine in a kitchen cupboard. Then he tip-toed back outside, cussing the hurt of it all the way. His blisters got doctored while he sat with Tizzy and watched the sun go down. They bided slow time until the man's return.

Hours later, well into the evening, a weight still hung in the air. There was something changed about the place, something thick and stifling that Tizzy could not put her finger on.

Then, another stranger arrived. He arrived after dark.

He emerged from the woods and his eyes had nothing to say.

It was Mr. Nottingham. But it was not Mr. Nottingham. It was not the man who had left them earlier in the day. This Mr. Nottingham was screwed even tighter than the other one. The smell of onions frying in bacon grease finally lured Tizzy back into the house. But this other Bob did not seem to recognize them. He barely spake a word at Tizzy or Matthew while supper was fixed. This was not unusual, really. Only, this other Bob was almost vicious about it. He moved a little quick around the kitchen, like a man afraid he might hurt one of them badly if he was forced to speak. Soon he had Tizzy and Matthew screwed tighter too.

At the table Tizzy watched a moth flit at the hurricane lamp until it stuck, scorching on the glass chimney.

"Why's a moth do that?"

"Looking fer a moon," Bob said, looking at nobody.

Matthew worried that Bob might know now that he had been followed. But Bob showed no signs of such. The only thing this other Bob seemed interested in was his ham hock. In a prickly triangle, the three ate ham and butter beans (with fried onions) and canned nectarines. This Bob gnawed, gnashed, and sucked his teeth while Tizzy and Matthew sat there jumpy, afraid to even go for the salt.

In the middle of supper, Button crawled in from the back porch. On hands and knees she scooted under the table's oil cloth. Tizzy blinked, watching as one tiny hand appeared. Like a glove puppet sitting at the empty chair, Button's hand reached up and slid her supper plate off the table. Ham and beans disappeared below, beneath the tablecloth. Soon Tizzy and Matthew heard slurping and a smacking at their feet. Their eyes met, but neither spake a word. This was an exotic turn.

But not to the other Bob.

The other Bob Nottingham just sat alone in his kitchen and fed himself.

STEP 15

"*Buuuuu*-tton"

His bottomless gullet broke their kiss. Both faces turned in the moonlight. Matthew was confounded. He had just worked his sore thumb past Tizzy's obstinance and up to her tiny tit.

"*Button—*" the man was calling.

"There he goes again," she said.

"Yeah."

It was well past midnight. Matthew had pestered and nagged until he coaxed Tizzy out of her grump and out to his bed swing. Out here, they were less likely to be heard if Matthew got lucky. The things he had seen today agitated Matthew and kept him awake. Kissing seemed the answer, at first. But kissing only made it worse. He breathed heavy and lied into her mouth, seeking even more adventure. And he almost had some in his hand. He was on the brink of some serious titty. Preacher's-girl titty. Then Bob snatched it away.

"*Buuuutton*," Bob called, as he snatched it.

Matthew and Tizzy slipped off the swing. Quickly, they skulked down the porch to the rear corner of the house. Hidden behind the wringer clothes washer, they peered into the backyard.

Bob was near naked again. He was pacing out there at the edge of the woods, boney-footed, and fishbelly-white from the neck down. He was naked except for his jock shorts.

"Hyere now, *Buuu-tton,*" he drawled, looking up at the trees. "C'mon in here, girl."

Bob hovered, quiet for a moment, his eyes combing the moonlit thicket.

"Looks like Bob couldn't sleep neither."

"Yeah," Tizzy said.

"Looks like he shook off his grump too."

Yeah. But, Matthew, look—"

Tizzy was pointing.

Matthew followed her finger to a mesh of pine boughs high above Bob Nottingham's head.

There she was. Button's cupid face looked down at Bob from the nook of a tall tree. Perched in the cradle of limbs, against the night sky, all Button was missing was a pair of dirty wings.

Far below, Bob shook his head finally. He muttered something none of them could hear, then went back inside. So Button was safe. Or was she?

Tizzy was still wondering about this when Matthew grabbed her arm. He pulled her back down the side-porch.

"Listen Tiz," he shushed her, crouched in conspiracy. "I got me an idear."

"I don't care. I don't wanna hear it."

"C'mon, jist trust me," Matthew urged softly, thumbing a black fetlock from her wide chinaman eyes. "Do as I say."

"I ain't gonna let you mess with me—"

"Shhh. I ain't talking about no loving, gal. I got the brainstorm, see? I want you to do this fer me. I want ye to go in there, git yourself dressed, then wait under the bedcovers till I come fetch ye."

"Now, why in tarnation would I wanna do that?"

"It might be a hour or two," he whispered, ignoring her protest. "But afore long I'll be in to fetch ye. Now git after it—"

"But, why—"

He did not give her time to think out loud. Matthew took off, creaking down the porch to his swing. Tizzy was left dangling. She did not know what else to do. So she went inside and got dressed.

When Matthew shook her back to life, Tizzy was drifting on the sea and the sea was in the cup of her mother's hand. As she drifted, Tizzy's dress had bunched up around her, under the blanket.

"C'mon, hop to," Matthew said, tugging on her toe.

Honeygirl, you are so rare, so fine and refined...

Tizzy tried Matthew, and then some. She was not moving fast enough. Matthew was antsy while she wiped her eyes and fumbled with her shoe buckles. She was even humming dumb sea shanties while she took too much care with her buckles. Matthew reckoned it was just Tizzy being a girl. How could he know she was taking care of secrets? Tizzy was not about to tell him. And she was not about to spill her golden gift—the golden chain inside her shoe—by moving fast and reckless while only half-awake.

"I swear, Matthew," she yawned. "I'm tuckered out."

"I ain't. Never did git to sleep."

"Well, I *am*. Fess up and tell me what this is about now."

"Keep your voice lowly. I heard ole Bob knocking around in the kitchen."

"Dang it, what're you up to?" she demanded, her voice a bit lower.

Matthew slipped off the bed. He knelt before Tizzy, his hand caught her face. His eyes gleamed with righteous intent.

"You don't know it. But he carries a lantern when he goes."

"Who?" she asked. But she knew who. She was stalling.

"*Bob*. Who else?" Matthew said. "I seen the fire in his hand the last few nights. He takes that outhouse lantern. I can see it without even boosting my head off the piller. You can tell that kerosene wick burning fer quite awhile. Till he's deep in the wood."

"Yeah? So, yeah?" Tizzy was scared of what came next.

"So I reckon a lit lantern is a sight more simple to foller than some tracks in the wood. And we might as well be ghosts on his tail, since we'll be coming up behind with no light in the dark."

"Where—where you reckon Mr. Nottinham gets his kerosene from up here?

"Gotdamn, who knows where Odd Bob gits anything from? Stop asking fool questions."

Tizzy wanted to quarrel. But she only wanted to quarrel if it could change the shape of things.

"I want more time to think about it," she told him.

"People in hell want popsicles. We ain't got no more time. Bob's fixing to go."

The thought of venturing out on wild Riddle Top in the pitch of night scared Tizzy witless. But Tizzy did not need a divining rod to divine that Matthew was going, with or without her. His herky-jerky desires were tweaked, and Tizzy knew what that meant, where that led. Every grave-digger ends up in a grave. But Tizzy was not about to lie here in this house by herself, listening to every whistling timber or night hooter.

"I got to know where he goes," Matthew said. And that was that.

He waited for more of her fuss. But it did not come. A glum Tizzy finished buckling her shoes then stood up. Matthew was already watching out the window.

Shortly, the kitchen door-spring groaned. And there was Bob Nottingham, etched in moonlight. He moved across the yard, beyond the clothesline, headed toward the outhouse. From the windowsill, Tizzy and Matthew saw the match strike and the lighting of a hurricane lantern. Bob strode with the lantern, around the outhouse, then into the woods. Soon his flare of light began to fracture within the trees.

"Here we go," Matthew hissed.

They left out the side door.

Matthew set the pace, Tizzy scurried to keep up. They entered the pines but the moon did not. Despite this, Matthew's spectacles managed to focus—and keep focus—on the winking dot of light he saw up the trail. Tizzy felt like sometimes she saw more than she wanted to see, even in these dark woods. Every time Bob's lantern disappeared Tizzy would feel a pang of panic until it shone again. This was the only way to do it, Matthew told her again, the only way to go. Steadily, they watched that lantern swing and flicker and move farther up the mountain. And they moved with it. After a while Tizzy tried not focus on the lantern far ahead. She would leave that to Matthew. She was too busy fending off pine needles and unseen nettles.

Bob Nottingham was a relentless point man. This rocky path was obviously familiar to him and he never let up. But Matthew was cocksure again. He had this dicked. They would be fine as long as they kept moving fast and did not let Bob get too far ahead. As long as they did not lose sight of his light. They would be fine as long as Bob did not hear them crashing through the woods back here, trying to keep up. After all, this was the same old trail Matthew has scouted earlier, right? Hell, this afternoon was just a test drive. Tonight was the same, but with headlights. Same damn trail. Same damn Bob. These were sonic-speed decisions, maybe. But somebody had to make them. It ain't the gore-horn that kills you. It's the hole. It's the hole.

After a while, Matthew's attitude began to change. Soon he was breathless, with sweat dripping off his glasses. He had grown tired of Tizzy's grip on his shirttail. Silently, Matthew cursed the day Nursy Jane told him his eyes were weak. But he could not let on to Tizzy. Not now. Not here in this maze of shadowy timber and strange bug-life. He kept looking up, looking for the moon. The moon-spirit would have guided him, like it would guide any Osage pathfinder. But the moon did not want to go with Matthew.

Matthew's spirit revived briefly when they crossed the creek. It was the same creek that derailed him before and sent him on a dead cow hunt. This time, after splashing through the shallows, Matthew almost sang out a hallelujah. They reached the other side and Bob's light was still in sight. Hell, this was easy as tracking Baby Jesus by a star. Well, maybe not quite that easy. Matthew kept barking his shins on deadwood and boulders as the trail bent upward, climbing a grizzly crevasse. He knew Tizzy's bare legs were suffering even more. But she did not whimper or moan or gripe in any way. Yes, Tizzy showed some stern makings as she dogged his heels. Matthew had to give her that. Who would have believed it of a little flat-chested preacher's girl? Tizzy could really tough it after all.

It felt like they chased that lantern fire for hours.

Then things leveled out and got brighter. But not in a good way. Bob Nottingham advanced into a wide open glade of moonlight. Yes, the moon was out there again. Bob was briefly revealed and easy to see. Matthew and Tizzy hung back in the trees, afraid to enter the open field until the man's dark figure had forded the clover and foxtails. Bob disappeared into the woods on the far side of the field. But Matthew still waited, counting the seconds and rolling the dice. He did not want Bob to glance back and see them out in the open. Matthew waited as long as he dared. Then he lunged forward, dragging Tizzy by hand in a mad dash through the moonlit clover.

They hit the treeline and stopped just inside, breathing hard. Back in dark forest, Matthew's pop-bottle eyes darted and searched, desperate to find Bob's guiding light again. Quickly, he spotted it. Yes, there it was. Bob's lantern was winking up ahead, climbing the pike. Matthew and Tizzy charged hard, upward through the clutching tree, chasing the glow of that lantern. Tizzy could feel Matthew's fervor through his shirttail. He was desperate now, she could tell. Surely, the end of his race must be near. And so it was.

Matthew tripped as he ran. He tripped on an ant hill, but never knew what he stumbled on. He looked down as he tripped. And when he looked back up—he saw black.

The lantern's light was gone again.

And still, Matthew and Tizzy ran.

They kept going full tilt, their eyes searching the dark up ahead—their hearts pounding and begging Bob's light to reappear. But Bob's light did not reappear. After a full minute or more of pushing hard through the tangled blackness with no relief, Matthew started stumbling more and running into branches. And their hearts began to sink. Bob was gone. Their torchbearer was gone. Then, in a sad union, Tizzy and Matthew stopped running. They stopped, they bent, and they gulped for air.

"Matthew—"

"*Hell's bells—*"

"Where'd he go? Where we go now?" she asked.

"Don't know."

"Maybe you could—"

"I jist *don't know.*"

"You said he'd be easier to tailgate in the dark."

"Guhhhh—"

"Mathew, you're so dang smart," she snapped. "I ain't spending the night out here waiting fer no snake or bear-cat to git us."

Matthew said nothing.

Tizzy's hand could feel his shirttail trembling. She let go of it.

"What's the matter, Matthew?" she whispered finally. "We can jist retrace our tracks, back to the house."

"Unnnh—I—"

"Yeah? What's got aholt of you, boy?"

"I cain't see."

"Nary can I."

"Naw, I mean I cain't see *nothing*. It's like I'm in a coal mine."

"Nothing at all?"

Tizzy began to tune in a picture. She had never suspected his eyes were so datburn weak. Matthew's lies and deceptions never ended. He was blind as a mole and too ignorant to beg. Tizzy would also bet ten bright pennies that Mole Boy here needed thicker lenses than a mole's pride would admit. And now his chickens had come home to roost. Or, they would if they weren't so afraid of catching a bullet. Tizzy knew this was not the time to cry over spilt chickens. Besides, she did not feel as scary as she expected she would. After all, Tizzy did not share his affliction. Her eyes were pretty good. For the first time she realized she could make out trees and leafy shapes in this dark forest. There was not much light, but there was enough for Tizzy's chinaman eyes. But she had not noticed. It snuck up on her. She did not need six yards of daylight to find her way around. In fact—at her feet—Tizzy could detect a damp, worn trail. Just barely. But the trail was there.

"Lord amighty, son. Why didn't you say so?" She grabbed his hand and pulled him from his trance. Nudging up the path, Tizzy spied most of the low branches. She pushed them aside, warning Matthew of what he couldn't see. They made progress. Matthew did not resist.

Tizzy was wrung out. But she had not traipsed this

far to turn tail. Tizzy was no fool. If they went back to the
house now, Matthew would get over his shame face in the
time it took to take a nap. Then he would be back at it in
the morning, picking at this scab. Truth be known, Tizzy
had gotten nosy parker herself about Mr. Nottingham's
comings and goings. Especially after his rude and ungra-
cious behavior at supper. It was like breaking bread with
two different stagmen. Both of them were cranky stagmen. Only one was a little more cranky. Neither of them
knew please or thank you. And you never knew which
one was the one snurling at you to pass him the dern
biscuits. Tizzy figured it was time to find out what got
Mr. Nottingham's nose out joint. There were three—maybe four—more hours before dawn. If they did not catch
up to Mr. Nottingham soon, Tizzy could turn around and
find her way back down the trail. But there was no time
to fritter and Matthew was lagging. He was dragging
her back. Tizzy gave Matthew an extra rough *jerk*. This
gristlebone was too dern slow for Tizzy's temper.

"Stop your pouting," she said.

Matthew gave her no lip. He kept looking for the moon.
But the moon-spirit was not there. His eyes had betrayed
him. So he did as he was told. He had no choice really. He
wished he still had that field of bright clover back there.
He would have yanked a tooth for it. What he did have
was Tizzy's hand. He felt Tizzy's hand but he followed the
darkness. She led him up an invisible, blindman's path.
Stumbling forward, he followed her into denser thicket,
cracking his melon again on a lowslung limb. The limb

was invisible and dead—and it broke off, splintering bits into Matthew's shirt and down his sweaty spine. They dipped into a cutback. This was probably the same cutback that swallowed Bob's lantern light and robbed Matthew of all eyesight and dignity. Tizzy gleaned her way up a mossy rock grade. The trail grew slippery. Then the path began to confuse and become muddled over boggy ground. The path fizzled out until Tizzy paused in her pursuit. Matthew waited while Tizzy looked deep into the underbrush, casting about for some sign or a way forward in the dark. She listened deep. Matthew asked what she was up to and she shushed him.

The crickets got louder.

Tizzy scratched her elbow and admitted that they might have left the trail. No, Tizzy was not so sure of their bearings. Apparently the rocky upgang had thrown her off the scent. Too bad. It would be better for them to retrace their steps, she told him. Better than wandering even farther astray. They would go back down to the house where they might still get a few hours' sleep before Mr. Nottingham came back. Tizzy gave Birdnell the spur again. She reversed course and began to prod her dunderbilly partner back along the thick pine ridge. They couldn't be too far off the trail. The trail would lead them back.

Time was a funny thing up here. They both knew by now that time was like taffy on this mountain. Especially time spent in the early hours of eventide, the witching hours. It stretched, it shifted, it was hard to measure.

But they could not have been circling back more than ten minutes before this tide shifted again. The pines were singing above them, the wind on the rise. Then Matthew began to detect a soft glow. The soft glow grew, his eyes tuning to it. This was not supposed to be happening yet. Matthew was puzzled, but glad to be seeing anything again. Tizzy was just puzzled. They still had far to go, downhill through dark trees, before reaching the homestead. And that house would be dark when they got there. Yet, here was a light in the forest. And this light had worry in it. This meant Bob or some stranger or strangers unknown might be waiting just ahead. On the other hand—up here, with the shape of things—any light felt like mother comfort.

All these things spun in their heads as they approached like a pair of night-flying moths looking for the moon. Instead, they found a toy cottage and a candle.

They both stopped and saw it at the same time.

Tizzy let go of his hand.

"Matthew? Can you see that there?"

"Uh-huh. Sure do."

Matthew stepped up, shoulder to shoulder with Tizzy. His County specs glistened down into a tiny dell.

"Oh me. I do too," Tizzy said. She dropped to her knee. So did he. She pointed, "And they's a candle in that winder there."

The cabin glowed pretty and inviting beneath waning moon. It nestled at the bottom of a bowl of blue grass inside a crown of trees. Hewn of granite and notched rafters, the cabin seemed to sit down there waiting for them, lodged like a gemstone. And, yes, there was a candle in a window. Pickets of a grey paling fence doglegged up the slope to a rock-ringed well on the far rim. It reminded Tizzy of some grandpa cobbler's cottage out of her nursery tales.

"Git closer?" she asked in his ear.

"Don't you know it. What you waiting fer?"

Matthew was born again ready and tickled to boot. Hell, yes. Miss Uppity Tizzy Polk was slowing him down again. She was always slowing him down. And Matthew would have told her so right then and there if sunup wasn't still a few hours away.

They crept down into the hollow. No smoke curled from the chimney, but the acre looked well tended. The cabin was one room, maybe two. Approaching the blind side of the front door, Matthew and Tizzy stopped and crouched there for a moment. They could see the candle-lit window. It was a double window alongside the door, only a few feet away. Matthew went first. He and Tizzy scooted like Button, on hands and knees, until they were crouched beneath the windowsill. Already, they could hear his brogue. And they could see his face up there. His stagface. He sat in a chair. He was rocking, slightly. Through a parted gauze of curtain they could see the edge of his jaw. As he spake, his jaw moved, catching eerie candlelight.

Bob Nottingham would utter a few words then stop, as he listened to somebody—somebody they could not hear.

It was hard enough to hear Bob through this window. Tizzy made out a word or two—just snatches—about "secession" (or was it salvation?) and about "taking every wrong turn." It was hard to tell. Secession and salvation sounded a lot alike. She heard him distinctly say "I'll be bloody damned," then his voice dropped again, dull and steady. The conversation continued, but they still could not hear the other voice. They both wanted to peek up over the windowsill and see who Bob was talking to—but their nerve failed them. Another inch into the light and their reflected glimmer was sure to draw Bob's eye. If not for the rock wall, Tizzy could have reached up and touched Mr. Nottingham's scarred arm. They were that close. And Tizzy's blood was pounding so loud inside her it was getting even harder to hear him.

Captivated but ungratified, Tizzy and Matthew retreated from the window. They were wincing with the jitters as they soft-footed fast away from the cabin, and did not exhale till they reached the trees.

"Who was he ayapping at?" Matthew wondered.

"His big dog fer all I know."

Tizzy's eyebrows met. She stared back down at the cabin with nothing but more questions to show for all their trouble.

"You catch any of it? What was he saying?"

"I don't know," she said. "I heard a snip about secession and how he'd be damned."

"Yeah, I heard that. I heard that last part."

"Ain't much to go on." Adding, subtracting, Tizzy felt

like a catfish who just got hooked a little deeper. She did not like this feeling. But there was no stopping it now.

"Naw, it ain't much to go on," he agreed.

"Maybe we can take another peekaboo by daylight."

"Whoa now, Mizz Whistlebritches. What ye mean by that?"

But before he could reload, Matthew Birdnell was being led back down the mountain. He was blind again and being helped along by this big-headed Tizzy Polk. It would do no good to lock horns with her now. He would lock horns with her later though. That was for damn sure. Tizzy would be singing a different tune and he'd be there to teach it to her. Just as soon as the sun came up.

Button was crawling. She was crawling with ants. The ants crawled up through her legs and under her dress. They crawled in her hair. When they were angry, the ants crawled fast. Tonight they crawled fast.

Some folks had fool notions. They were fool enough to believe that ant soldiers marching onward as to war got angry only on the hot days. That's because most folks knew only their own worlds. They did not know the worlds of the kiltered. Button knew the kiltered. Button was kiltered. Most would never believe an ant army would swarm three houses high up a tree—a Blind Tree—long after midnight. But up here, high in this tree, on this mountain, everything was kiltered. Everything big and everything little up here was kiltered.

Button knew little. She knew little most of all. And, mostly, Button did not care.

She did not even care if these ants bit her or made her blister. They did not want her blood. She knew that much. And, up here, that was kiltered. Button could not remember the last time she cared about more than the next dawn. She could not remember the last time she felt a hurt. These things below, these souls, these ants, these hurts, they were small things to Button. She could not be bothered with them. Night after night, Button climbed, limb-to-limb she climbed, sleepy-eyed and streaked with pine tar. For Button, it was all in the eking until dawn.

Until then, Button was. And Button watched.

Tonight she had seen the Leg Dancer again. On the blue moon the Leg Dancer often came to dance. Button would sit up high and watch those ghostly legs—(and they were only two legs, nothing else)—dancing in the foxtails. Button did not know whose legs they were. The Leg Dancer danced in lady's shoes. So they might have once been parts of a lady. This is all Button knew but never told about the Leg Dancer.

Button knew little. She only knew what her eyes and ears told her. And that was a lot. But she never talked or told about what they told. And she never slept before dawn.

Most nights on Riddle Top were bad nights, some worse than others. The worst were nights that began in anger but ended without glimmer of hope. But Button had never known hope. So she did not care. How could she? She was born to dead folks.

Button just moved from tree to tree, watching leg dancers and lost children and the Man far below. His Man smoke was very strong. Sometimes he was close by her. Sometimes in a room she smelled his smoke. Button did not smell his smoke now.

Soon Button would climb these trees to Hulep Choat's Peak. First thing, every purple morn, Button would wait in that lonely tree on Hulep Choat's Peak. A Willerswitch Witch once danced circles around that tree, and sang her song to each new dawning. But no more. The witch came no more, and neither did her song. This is all Button knew and never told about the Willerswitch Witch.

The Man would soon pass below that Hulep Choat tree, just before dawn. Button was his Button. So Button would be there, waiting to see him pass. Then she would go crawling after his smoke.

Button had also waited in this Blind Tree tonight. She had seen the boy and the girl pass below. After the dancing legs were gone, they passed, not so long ago.

They passed down there, through the sharp needles and claws. The boy was gone blind now, passing beneath the Blind Tree. The girl was a Wrong Girl. She was one of them. That girl would tell you so. Tonight that girl led that Blind Boy by the hand. She led him from up the mountain. In this dark, the two never saw the ant hill when they kicked it and hurt it and made these souls so angry. And they did not care. Why would they?

Button knew where the two were going. They were going back to the kiltered home. But this even they did not know. They were going back to that place where the smoke of the Man was strong.

This is all Button knew and never told about that Blind Boy and that Wrong Girl.

STEP 16

"Two heads?" Matthew spouted, oaf-legging it through the meadow grass and clover. "Why did ye have to make it with two heads?"

This field was brighter than it had been last night by blue moonlight. He liked leaving the land of the blind.

"I figured it to get his attention," Tizzy said, trailing behind.

"Yeah, I reckon you done that awright. You don't think ole Brer Rabbit kyping his undies would of been sufficient?"

The truth was, Tizzy was beginning to think maybe that two-headed part had gone a head too far. The truth was, everything had gone so far since they went tearing out of Cayuga Ridge until Tizzy Polk could not tell a likely thing from an outer space thing anymore. Earlier this morning, an extra head seemed like divine inspiration—a good idea at the time.

It was Matthew who cooked up the cockeyed notion of a wild hare stealing Bob Nottingham's underpants. After

they got back down to the homestead, in the dark early before dawn, Matthew flopped on his swing and went
straightaway to sleep. But not Tizzy. Oh, she tried and
tried, and Lord knows she was bone weary underneath
it all. But the long night of skittish chaos still had her
screwed too tight and her mind still racing. Dawn began
to bloom with unnatural autumn heat. But Mr. Nottingham still had not returned. Tizzy quit tossing in her unfit
bed and decided to get back up without one wink of sleep.
She even built a breakfast fire in the kitchen stove so Mr.
Nottingham would not suspect they left during the night.
Everything would look normal.

Full morning arrived, but still no Bob Nottingham.
Tizzy did not feel like fixing breakfast just for herself. She
noticed it in the hall mirror, on the way back to her room.
She was looking more and more hungry these days, but
feeling it less.

It was only then that Tizzy began thinking that Mr.
Nottingham might have never come back on any nights.
That possibility was a revelation to her. Maybe he left
each night after midnight then did not return until almost
noon the next day, every day. Just in time for dinner. So
Mr. Nottingham had not been getting up and leaving early before Tizzy and Matthew were awake. He had actually
been leaving late of an evening and returning late of a
morning. That would be highly peculiar behavior in most
folks. But this was Bob Nottingham, wasn't it?

That was when Tizzy began stewing up a plan to drive
Mr. Nottingham to distraction. She needed something to

distract him long enough for Tizzy and Matthew to revisit that pretty cabin and find out who lived there.

"We can write a letter and leave it for Mr. Nottinham to find," Tizzy told Matthew after he finally awoke mid-morning. "We'll tell him we got called away. If we can think of a good excuse."

Matthew yawned, drank strong coffee, and began to percolate on that a bit. Odd Bob had still not returned, but that was just Bob being Odd Bob. This was his ritual. If Bob was still not wise to their shenanigans last night then he would probably return at his usual time. That would be in an hour or so. Bob always came back to feed at mid-day. This meant that Matthew and Tizzy did not have long to drum up some cock and bull that Bob might swallow.

"We need to get out of here," she said. "I know I keep telling you that. But, before we go, I got to know who Mr. Nottinham spends nights in that cabin with. If I don't, it will haunt me all my days. I just know it will. Listen, Matthew—you just had to go traipsing up there after him. I put my shoes on like you told me and I went with you. I didn't even fuss about it much. Well, it was you who got me up there to that place. And it was you who put this hook in me. All I'm asking is fer you to help me get unhooked."

Then, to prove her point, Tizzy finally took Matthew and showed him Button's little unfit room, inside Bob Nottingham's room. She knew both would be empty, and they were. Even Matthew seemed a bit bothered by those bare bed springs and the connecting door, though he said nothing about it out loud or in so many words.

"Bob needs to stop smoking in bed," was all he said. "This room reeks."

Matthew also got his first gander at a pair of Bob's jock shorts, still hanging there on the bedpost.

"Ye know, Tiz," Matthew told her, when they were both back slurping coffee on the swing, "I got me a girl cousin, up Coffin Holler. Ever time we get together fer Yule she swears she once had a wild hare come thumping in the house when her door blew open on Yule morning. Blew wide open, the way she told it. Looked like a long-haired bunny. She said that frosty hare thumped in jist long enough to take off hopping with her daddy's red union drawers in its teeth. She swore it was a big damn hare and, afore he died of consumption, her baby brother Jack used to back her up on the tale when we scoffed at it. Baby Jack said he come running when she hollered and caught sight of that wild bunny jist afore it hit the trees. Her daddy—my Uncle Cob—he says he don't know what to believe. But Uncle Cob says he do know his best and only long johns went missing and never come back. What do ye think of that mess?"

Tizzy thought it was worth a shot. Yes, it just might work.

Matthew had never spent much time in the Cayuga Ridge schoolhouse or learned his letters. So Tizzy soon found herself at the kitchen table with a chunk of charcoal, crafting a note on brown paper. Despite the poor instrument, Tizzy tried to use her best handwriting.

Dear Mister Nottenham,

A hare with two heads run out the door with your jock shorts. It run into the woods. It run down for the road. Matthew and I are gone to hunt it. We will bring your jock shorts back soon.

Your friend sincerely,
Tizzy June Polk

Tizzy read it over and over more times than she could count. Then she showed it to Matthew who said it looked booging good to him even though he could not read it at all. It would have to do. They were too curious about that cabin and Tizzy was all out of ideas. Besides, Tizzy took a certain pride in the construction of the note and had always been proud of her curly letters and pretty cursive hand. She had been told that it was a skill which ran in the Polk family. It was the only good thing her Preacher-Daddy had ever said to her. Or the closest to a good thing.

Tizzy did not know why she decided to write it up as a two-headed hare snatching jock shorts. It seemed like a good and provocative idea in the heat of the morning. Two heads seemed better than one. And she had seen a two-headed calf once. Matthew was highly skeptical to the point of snurling at it. But he did admit to having heard of such things advertised by carnivals passing through. That was enough for Tizzy, at the time. Perhaps Mr. Nottingham had heard of such things as well. Perhaps Mr. Nottingham would go down to the road below, to see what was up with his stolen underpants. Or to see a two-headed varmint. Or, at the very least, he might stay at this house a good long while, waiting for Tizzy and Matthew to return from their hare hunt. Either way, it could win Tizzy and Matthew enough time for another round trip up the mountain.

"But what about his jock shorts in there?" Tizzy asked. "They gotta go somewheres and I ain't touching em."

Matthew got some loud chortle out of that.

"You think Bob's got the pod cooties or something?"

"This here is unfit, Matthew," is all she had to say.

Matthew got off the swing and went into Mr. Nottingham's room. He met Tizzy in the kitchen with the jock shorts hanging on his pocketknife. They both watched the shorts burn in the stove.

A half hour later, with the sun beating down, Tizzy and Matthew were no longer in the house. They were hiding behind the chicken coop. From there, they both watched as Bob Nottingham came striding out of the woods at last. He hung the lantern back in the outhouse, then climbed the steps to the kitchen, going inside. A few minutes later he appeared on the front porch with Tizzy's note in his hand. He walked each side of the house, checking the entire porch. Then he stopped and stared down the slope toward the lower woods—the woods which led to the road and the blue Packard. Then he scanned the note in his hand again.

When Tizzy saw this she breathed a sigh of relief. Mr. Nottingham could read. The notion that he might be as unschooled as her partner in crime came late to Tizzy. But too late to do anything about it. They were already hiding behind the coop by then. Now, it seemed a frivolous concern. After all, he was a worldly man. Wasn't he? Anybody could see that.

Tizzy was even more relieved when she saw Mr. Nottingham carry the note down the front steps and head into the lower stand of trees. The wild hare chase had worked.

But that was not good enough for Matthew Birdnell.

No, here they were, headed back up the mountain and Matthew was still mocking Tizzy's words. She could have written down a rum cake recipe for all he knew. At least Mr. Nottingham could read those words. Mr. Nottingham knew it was no rum cake recipe. Mr. Nottingham was no half-baked fool in a field of clover.

"Naw sir," Matthew railed on, flushing quail as he went, "she cain't jist bear false witness in a believable or timely manner or do as she's damn well told. Nope. She has to go telling the man that they's *freaks of nature* loose in the vicinity." Matthew waved his arms in the air and spake at the sky. "Well, I don't know about you, biggun. But I about had *enough* of her feisty-bitch lip. What you think, Santy Claus?"

Tizzy thought about splitting his head open with a

rock. They left the field and entered the woods again and this was Tizzy's opening of opportunity. She could see it. She could pick up one of these big speckly rocks. She could frame her aim betwixt those two jug ears poking out the sides of his bobbing head. She would put a new bloody mouth in the back of his head and then, maybe, the one in front would shut down. If he did not die, that is. That would be the Birdnell style, wouldn't it? Matthew would up and die on her and leave her alone up here to fend for herself. It was no use. Tizzy could not rely upon hogboy for anything.

Fortunately for Matthew, they dropped into the trough of the cutback. The abrupt change of scenery changed the conversation. It was easy to see now how these high dewberry brambles had snuffed out all light from Bob Nottingham's lantern last night. Matthew slowed. He was being dainty about the thorns on either side.

"Remember, we cain't tarry long," she said.

He flipped flies away from his mouth. This day was rotten hot.

"Yeah. I'm remembering how fast Bob can move up this mountain."

"Matthew—when's the last time you eat any ice cream?"

"Mama, I ain't had no iced cream in a good long while. Our ole cow don't pump enough milk. Never enough sugar or eggs. Been over two year I reckon."

"Wisht I had some now."

"Hell, yeah. Wisht I had me some too. Sweet Elberta peach cream. Cain't beat that."

"I'm partial to chocolate, myself. Your cousin Willy Jay's got it down at his store.

"Yeah, we don't talk to him no more."

"Don't like strawberry."

"Naw, I ain't big on no strawberry cream neither. Spent too many summers on my knees picking them stinging red bastards."

"Orange sherbert is good."

"Ain't never licked me no orange sherber."

"You oughta try it."

"Anybody been alicking on you lately, little gal?"

"Hush, Matthew. You are utterly depraved."

"Wonder what kind of iced cream ole Odd Bob likes."

"Chocolate, I expect."

"Yeah? Why ye say that?"

"I dunno."

"Damn that strawberry though."

"Yep."

"Strawberry. Hmmph. I'd rather eat me some hairy monkrat iced cream."

"Yep. There you go. Utterly depraved."

They spilled down into the grassy dell again. A spray of yellow butterflies danced ahead to the cabin. Sheltered in the pines, the place looked drowsy and quiet. By daylight they could see much of the ivy lacing the chimney had gone brown and the fence was missing slats. A winch hung clearly over the rock-ringed well up there.

"They's no animals on the place, Matthew."

"Yep. I can see that."

"Never took notice of it last night."

"No milk, no eggs. No iced cream around here nei-ther."

"And they's no road."

Matthew made his way to the cabin door. As the last moment he sidled over to the double window to take a peek, drawing his pistol as he went. But now, the cur-tains were drawn also. He could not see in.

"*Put your thing away,*" Tizzy hissed when she saw the gun.

His County specs blinked back at her. The pistol went back under his shirttail.

"It don't look habitated, do it?"

"Knock on the door," she said.

"What if somebody answers?"

Tizzy threw him a look. Matthew caught it. He didn't like it, but he caught it. He knocked on the door.

When nobody answered Tizzy began drifting back out from the doorway. She looked around for signs of life.

"Want I should knock again, Elberta?"

"Nope."

"Well, what now, Elberta?"

"Matthew—could you jist blow your nose and *think*? Could you possibly help find an open winder or some oth-er avenue to *gitting inside this house?*"

"I swear Tiz, one of these days your lip is gonna meet the broad of my hand."

"Try it, hogboy."

He lurched sideways, back to the front window. He tried to force it open, pushing and rattling it.

"Don't break the glass," Tizzy said, joining him. The room in there was murky. Through the thin embroidered curtain, Tizzy could only make out the candlestick and a bedpost. She shrugged and went back to try the front doorknob. It was plumb typical of this gristlebone here to not even test the door. Okay, it was locked. But this gristlebone didn't know that. And wasn't this a darling doorknob? It was tarnished brass. Old-timey with scrolls and curlycues. Even the keyhole looked fancy. Too bad it was locked.

"Wonder if they's a skeleton key hid somewheres," Matthew said, sidling up to her.

"Might be. Let's go around back."

"Don't ye wanna look for the key?"

Tizzy was already wading through the ivy, disappearing around the corner of the cabin. She would not be denied.

In back, a short split-log kitchen or storeroom was attached to the stone of the main cabin. Cut into the logs, a second door hid behind a wild white rose bush. Only the top of the door could be seen above the rose blooms. It was sealed shut and there was no outside knob or latch.

Flanking the door on the right was a high shuttered window, smaller than the window out front. Somebody had closed this window for keeps by crudely hammering the shutters together in the middle. The rusty nails were crooked and bent. It was a sloppy job but good enough to keep most folks out. Tizzy was surprised to learn that Matthew Birdnell was not one of them.

"Lookee here," he said, slipping his knife blade under one of the right shingle's hinges.

Rainwater had leaked down that edge of the window and was rotting the wood. With his knife, Matthew jimmed off both hinges on that side and swing open the joined shutters. Tizzy was reluctantly impressed. Matthew might not be redeemed, exactly. But it was easy to forget he robbed schoolhouses at night when nobody was around to stop him.

Matthew was already poking his head inside rain-stained burlap curtains.

"Just the kitchen in here," he echoed, goose-necking through the glassless window.

"Well, git on in," Tizzy said, worried about the clock ticking inside Mr. Nottingham's head. "Then help me through so I can take a gander."

"Awright, you little witch," Matthew said. He hiked up and shinnied in over the windowsill.

Tizzy heard the clank of a bucket. She heard him fall head first and curse. She tried not to smile too loud lest he hear it. It had already been another long day with the Rebel Yell. Too bad they still needed each other. Tizzy reached up and grabbed the windowsill. Before she could start to strain, she heard the backdoor. It scraped. The hinges whined. It cracked open and shed white rose petals. Matthew pushed from the other side until he broke the briar seal. Soon he had the door open enough for

Tizzy to squeeze through.

As soon as she was inside, Tizzy saw the empty milk bucket he had spilt. Matthew was squeezing on his left shoulder, making a big show of it.

"I might of popped my socket," he said, wincing.

Matthew had climbed in over an oilcloth-covered counter. There was a tin water pan, but no pump. Tizzy hated to think about fetching water day after day from that well out there. Rust-pitted pots and blue pottery plates gathered dust on a shelf. Across from the back-door was another door. The door was padlocked. Most kitchens had a pantry, but most pantry doors were not padlocked. Why bother to lock up a pantry way up here?

Matthew looked at the door like it was just another window shutter on a schoolhouse. He jiggled the pad-lock, then tried his knife in it. Then he tried some of the extra keys on the car-key ring. The fourth key he tried broke off in the keyhole. He was pondering whether he should shoot off the lock when he heard Tizzy's voice.

"Matthew..."

"Whuh?" he said, squatting with the padlock. He tried to suck out the broken key blade.

"Come in here..."

Matthew stopped sucking the lock and cocked an eye at Tizzy.

She was murky in there—standing beyond, in the front room. Something was wrong. She was talking too quiet.

Matthew got up and went in after her. He stepped into the flat shadow of the room. There was a small stone cavity in the wall ahead. That was the fireplace. And Tizzy. She was facing him, looking past him at the wall beside the kitchen door. She stood fast, staring. She was staring at the bed. Matthew came to the foot of the four-poster bed, where Tizzy stood. Then Matthew turned around to look at the bed. He nudged his glasses, trying to see in the brackish light. Then he did.

Somebody was lying in the bed, somebody small and very still. Nobody was breathing in the room. Nobody spake in the room for a very long time.

"She's passed," Tizzy whispered finally. "Ain't she?"

Tizzy walked over to the window. She parted the dusty curtains. Sunlight crept in across the bed and across the sallow face that lay in it.

It was the face of a woman, no, a girl. It was pretty Vistalynn Ray.

"Oh, my word."

Tizzy felt herself gliding to the girl's bedside.

There she lay, eyes open, resting in unpeaceful slumber.

She was so beautiful, so womanly pretty. But she would never be a woman now. She was Vistalynn Ray.

How could Tizzy ever forget her? She was the new girl from Ewe Springs, from Tizzy's last day at Cayuga Ridge School. The tentacles of Vistalynn's raven hair spread out across the pillow. Her widow's peak crested over her open blue eyes. Blessedly, the rest of Vistalynn Ray was covered. The quilt was tucked under her chin. Tizzy remembered her well. She remembered this slender throat, and the parted lips of this lush mouth. She remembered the cream in these cheeks and the curl of these black eyelashes. Yet nothing in Tizzy's memory of this pale girl equaled the beauty she saw here. Vistalynn Ray was more comely in death.

And Matthew Birdnell was leaning over her deathbed. He had crept forward while Tizzy was entranced.

"Matthew, don't—" Tizzy said, searching for better words.

Matthew set the keys on the bedstand and reached for the quilt. Vistalynn's heavenward stare did not care. But Tizzy did.

"Matthew. Don't," she said again, more feeble this time.

She watched his split thumbnail brush that slender neck as he slipped the covers from Vistalynn Ray's body.

She was naked. She was naked and nobody was surprised.

The quilt slid smoothly down her smooth skin. Two dusky nippled mounds appeared, then her ivory-sloped belly and, finally, the sparse nest betwixt her legs—legs flanked by bloodless stumps and white bone.

Vistalynn's hands were missing. Her hands were cut off clean at the wrists.

"Matthew, *stop*. Don't look no more."

Matthew tossed back the rest of the cover as Tizzy caught her breath. Then, with relief, she let go. Vistalynn's pretty little toes were still there. Only her hands were taken. There was not much mercy in that. But Tizzy would take it.

"Ain't she something..." Matthew uttered, without question. He was scarcely there himself, until the back of his hand grazed a dead toe. He flinched and let go of the quilt. But his eyes never stopped feasting on the girl..

Tizzy could smell the venal sickness in his mind.

"Ssssss—" she warned him.

But Matthew wanted more. Matthew's specs kept shining over those marble bosoms, the bee-stung mouth and bit of white teeth. The dry blood drop on the full upper lip. Tizzy could see how far gone he was.

"Who is she, by God?" he asked, wiping his mouth. "I wonder."

"A girl I know. From school. A Ewe Springs girl."

"Well I be damned."

"That's what he said."

"Who?"

"Mr. Nottinham."

"You thank he done this?"

"Yes," Tizzy said.

She leaned over, only inches from Vistalynn's face. Their noses almost touched. Tizzy studied the girl with great earnest. Vistalynn's upswept eyelashes were perfect in death. They were probably still growing.

"But—" Matthew squeaked. "But what's he gone and done with her hands?"

"Go ask him."

Tizzy didn't even hear herself say those words and Matthew did not laugh.

Tizzy was peering down into a tiny blue glass world. A dead schoolgirl's eye. Folks said the eyes of the dead still held reflections. They said if you looked hard enough—and knew the way—you could glimpse the horrors the dead had seen, the sufferings of their last moments, this side of the veil. Tizzy thought she might find a glimmer of these things, frozen in the depths of Vistalyn's right eye. Was that a blue dragontail Tizzy saw in there? Was sweet Vistalynn a maiden thing? Was Tizzy? Tizzy did not know. She could not be sure. To her own naked eye, Vistalynn's naked flesh looked virgin and unsullied. Except for her missing hands, of course. But who could tell for true?

"Tizzy? I thank we best light on out. Git on outa here."

"So do I."

"Off'n this here mountain."

"Boy howdy."

"You agreeing with me on that?"

"Yep." Tizzy was serious as a preacher's girl, her memories roiling.

"Maybe he didn't do it. But I ain't one to hang around here waiting fer whoever did."

"He done it."

Tizzy raised up from the cold face. She glanced down the bed.

"You awright, Tiz?"

"I do declare..."

"What?"

"She sure was a perty thing."

231

"Yeah. She is that. You know her name?"

"Yes. I do."

"Well?"

"Her name was Vistalynn Ray."

Matthew covered the poor girl back up. Tizzy drew the sash. Her elbow hit the empty rocker and Tizzy left it rocking. They rigged the shutters back in place and fled the weird cabin. This damned dell had no charms left to speak of.

They raced down the mountain, panting, planning out loud as they ran. It was too late. Much too late. Even if they sprouted wings and flew, Tizzy and Matthew could not land back at Bob's house in time to leave today. By then there would be only an hour or two of sun left on Riddle Top. They agreed to depart first thing the next morning—no matter what. They would leave somehow, some way, before Bob Nottingham returned for dinner at noon. Matthew swore he would sit up with Tizzy all night if need be, to protect her from nightwalkers and sleep-walkers and any other walking things. Tizzy made him promise that much.

Tizzy's head was racing too, with fervent glimpses of bubble-blowing babies, dancing childerns, her Preacher-Daddy Polk in his bed, Shonda Jo's sloppy hips, that lippy Ludlow Prather, and mean Mr. Wainwright with his drawers full of nastiness. The good folks of Cayuga Ridge. More than anything, Tizzy kept hearing the bubbles of laughter from sweet Vistalynn Ray—that ravishing new girl. The unspoiled spoiled tart who stood up at show and tell with her grandma's opal ring and heartbreaker's vixen eyes and made Tizzy hate her so quickly. Tizzy did not know much about Vistalyn Ray, but she knew one sure thing about her. Nobody, no matter who they were, ever deserved that fate of that girl back there in that cabin.

Was it a week or two weeks or a month since Tizzy Polk stood on that playground? Seasons had come and gone inside her in the wake of their little crime spree. Her world, the seasons in her heart, they all changed when Tizzy heard the report of Matthew's pistol down at Hayden's Crossroad. And what did they have to show for it? Seventy-one dollars, no cents. Tizzy had not once thought of that money in Matthew's pocket since the moment they started up this mountain. But Tizzy had no trouble conjuring up a glimpse of the fear in that old woman's eyes: Miss Doobelle, who did nothing but mind her own business. Tizzy knew, if she could have looked deep into dead Doobelle's glassy eye, it would have held one clear reflection. Matthew with a gun. Tizzy's partner in crime.

"Probably he kilt her in that place," Matthew called out, well behind her on the trail. "So's nobody could hear."

"It's doubtful."

"Why the hell not. Nobody to catch her screams, way up here—"

"Nope. They's no blood on the bedcovers."

233

"Awright, awright. I git ye. Still if we'd poked around much longer last night, we would of heard it happen. Sure enough. After he was done talking at her. We would of heard it happen. Damn, what'd we of done then? Hearing her screams before dawn?"

"Blow your nose, Matthew. I'm perty sure she was already dead."

"Then who was he atalking at? Who was he talking at when we spied on him?"

"You figure it out—"

"And what you think Odd Bob's gonna say now? When we roll back in so late from this wild bunny hunt?"

She did not answer, avoiding more thorns and gruesome questions. Tizzy led the way, scurrying down the rocky path, the path leading over a deep chasm. Matthew fell further and further behind until she could not even hear his feet behind her. She could hardly even hear his mouth flapping. Nothing back there mattered anymore, Tizzy told herself. Everything mattered up ahead. Saints alive, what if the car had been stolen? What if—before they found the car—what if the rapture came down?

"What's the man gonna say, huh?" Matthew called, way back there.

Hurrying alongside a wall of rock, Tizzy's head overflowed with these mad what-ifs. She rounded a ledge and gravel started falling like rain in front of her. A landslide of rock and dirt followed. Then a creature dropped onto the trail with a loud thumpity-thump.

It was a huge hare.

Tizzy *screeched.* She revolted in mid-stride—sucking the screech back inside as she recoiled.

It had two heads. It was a two-headed hare. It had a horrible four-eyed stare.

The two-headed hare had long dirty brown fur and it had two flipping heads. Yes. Each head had black marble eyes, two long yellow shards of teeth, and two long hanging ears. And claws, yes, it had claws.

The two-headed hare took two thumping steps toward her, with four long ears flopping.

Tizzy took two steps back.

"Watch your step, honeygirl," one harehead rasped, in her mother's scratchy voice. *"You ain't so rare."*

"You ain't so refined," the other harehead said, in her mother's scratchy voice.

The two-headed hare thumped forward. Then it began to spit up dirty jock shorts.

Tizzy screamed. Tizzy stepped backward.

Tizzy fell off the mountain.

STEP 17

"*Matthhhhew,*" Tizzy shrieked, tumbling over the mountain scarp.

Falling and flailing, her right hand snagged on a hairy root. The washed-out root held—almost yanking her arm off—but her hold on it stopped her fall. Pain seared through Tizzy's shoulder socket. She hung high over the chasm, suspended and hurting. Loose dirt showered down over her face. Tizzy spat gravel and yowled. "*H— help.*"

Half-blind, her eyes full of grit, Tizzy swung herself until she could fling her other arm up and grab the root with both hands.

"*Heeelp.*"

She dangled, her buckletop shoes kicking at the air. Suddenly, she heard Matthew above her.

"*Take her easy, Tiz. Take aholt of me—*"

Leaning over the ledge, Matthew got his hand on one of Tizzy's wrists. He tried to hoist her upward.

"Let your *other* hand go. *I got ye.*"

Tizzy's other hand was now clawing blind and wild at Matthew. Tizzy hit Matthew's glasses. Quickly—just before they could slip and spin away—Matthew yanked his glasses from his face, tossing them back over his shoulder to safety. For a moment, his fuzzy eyes thought they saw a tiny, blurry lake down there, far below. With no time to ponder this, Matthew finally got a grip on both of Tizzy's hands and gave her a final heave.

They both collapsed back onto the mountain path, hearts exploding, guts afire. Tizzy was spitting out grit. Matthew started feeling about for his glasses.

Suddenly, Tizzy sat bolt upright. She gaped up and down the path.

"Where'd it go?" Tizzy demanded, her mouth as dirty as Button's.

"What ye mean?"

Matthew winced, rising onto an elbow. He slipped his glasses back on and looked. He saw nothing worth looking at. The critter was gone.

"That thing. That thing with *the heads*."

Tizzy did not dare tell him.

She did not dare tell him it was a hare. He would say she was as touched as Button. Tizzy kept checking the path, up and down. Was that thing still hereabouts or sneaking around behind them? How could that thing even be? How could a hare Tizzy and Matthew conjured up in their two heads be here talking at Tizzy with its two heads? How could a hare with even one head be talking at her?

"What ye mean—that *thang*?" Matthew asked, working his sore shoulder. Yep, he had popped the socket. "What heads are you yapping about? He jist got one head. And that's one too many."

Tizzy's head swung around and gawked at Matthew. Her eyes were so big and round they didn't look chinaman anymore.

"*You seen it?*"

"Sure, I seen it."

"But, Matthew, it had—it had two—"

"I don't blame ye fer being scary. But it was jist that ole dog."

"Doggy?" Tizzy's heart pump fumbled. Her torn fingers caught a blood drop from her lip. Tizzy looked up again. The path was still empty.

"Jist that ole brindled dane. That Judah. Bigger'n a bull ox and thrice as ugly. He run off when ye screamed."

Matthew laid back, pillowing his head in a clump of foxtails that sprouted from the ledge. The sun felt good. Lying there, Matthew pondered this girl Tizzy. With her stringy jap hair, cut like a mushroom cap, and her woeful eyes so scared and scoping hither and yon—Matthew felt bad for her. She had never had nothing and didn't even know what nothing looked like. Nothing worth having, that is. She was lucky to have him along to show her.

"It din't look like no doggy" Tizzy said, sounding like a crib baby. She could still hear her mother's sickly voice. "Not to me it din't."

Tizzy's mind went adrift. She was looking for a ship

she could sail away on. Oh, any ship would be fine.

Matthew let her drift on her secret sea, but not for long. That big damn Judah might have been spooked off by Tizzy's screeching. But that big damn Bob would still be wondering where they were. And Bob would come looking for them up here—if they didn't get back to that house and beat him to the punch. Tizzy would be okay in a minute. She would have to walk it off.

Tizzy picked herself up and Matthew helped her. Together, they brushed the soil and twigs from her dress. They began to move down the path again. Tizzy started working the sore shoulder of her right arm—the one that stopped her fall. Yep, she had popped the socket.

They did not dawdle and they did not meet Bob Nottingham coming up the trail. The trip back down seemed an eternity, yet they returned more quickly than ever before. They had to. They had little choice. Tizzy was the first to notice how funny time was getting this afternoon as, once again, they rustled through the clover field.

"Looky, Matthew," she said, pointing at the sky.

"Looky where?"

"I swear. I swear I can see the sun fall. It falls so fast."

She was right, of course. Not that Matthew wanted to admit it. But he did pick up the pace, leading the way. He had little choice. Because the sun began going down fast. Too fast. It seemed like the sun was falling from the sky. They began to move faster, so the sun fell faster, like it was racing them down the mountain. The sun finally disappeared down the path, ahead of Tizzy and Matthew.

When they finally got where they didn't want to go, another long night was there, waiting for them.

And so was Button.

And so was Bob.

STEP 18

Button sat with her knees up, watching from the back stoop. She looked a mite worse for wear, but she always did. Some ragdolls are born worn out. The next dawning was a long ways off. Until then, sleep was out of the question.

Behind her, lantern light shone from the kitchen window and screen door. The rest of the house sat dark and smelling of hickory. Smoke paid out of the parlor chimney and the kitchen stovepipe. Button did not care as the two came out of the night and passed her, climbing up the step. She did not care even a little.

Inside, Bob Nottingham bent over the sink. He cut a quick glance at the backporch door. Tizzy shrank outside the screen.

"Evening, Mr. Nottinham," she said, then dry gulped.

Bob pumped more water. For a moment Tizzy was scary that he might be washing Vistalynn Ray's pale hands in there.

"You must of been dranking," he said, staring into the

sink.

"What?" she asked.

"I figured you must of been into my good hooch. You tell me you're seeing double. You tell me they's wild hares in my house. Hell. Ain't many hare left in these parts."

"Aw, you know how it is, Bob." Matthew came geehawing from over Tizzy's shoulder. "We was mistook. Turns out, that was a monkrat we was hunting. He must of come in under the house."

"Kinda like you, huh?"

Nottingham smiled a bit, without looking up. He pumped more water into the sink.

"What's that you say, Bob?"

Matthew pushed past Tizzy. He opened the screen door and came inside. Tizzy came after. Tizzy kept her distance from the man. She took a chair on the far end of the table.

Nottingham shook water off his hands.

"A .38 rod like yours ain't so good fer drilling monkrat, boy. Or didn't you know?"

"Naw, ye see Bob—here's how it is," Matthew bragged. "When I was a young'un I'd drop a monkrat, squirrel, or a jaybird jist about ever day. With a flat-ass rock. I'm lethal when it comes to flat rocks. I never miss."

"So where's your monkrat?"

"Didn't see none."

Bob turned around, toweling off his hands.

"Hell of a sight better with chickens, are ye? Chick-abiddies don't never thin out. Not around here they don't."

"Naw, they ain't too scarce," Matthew allowed.

Bob Nottingham eyeballed Tizzy. She tried not to cringe.

"You being might quiet. Ain't you?" he asked. When she shrugged, Bob made his little smile again. Then he made a little joke. "Well, you're looking underage to me, daughter."

"Oh? Uh—" Tizzy stammered, wringing her hands under the table. "Whatcha mean?"

"Girl your age. Better lay off them hard spirits," he said, enjoying himself. "Else you'll turn to harlotry."

"I—we—we might of been confused. A little," she began, trying to speak slowly and clearly. "But we din't wanna let that ole hare—I mean—we din't wanna let that monkrat light out with your jock shorts."

"Jock shorts," Nottingham reflected. "Yeah, I read that part."

Matthew was shaking his head, acting like he gave a damn.

"Sorry we couldn't save your drawers, Bob. Looks like mister monkrat got em after all.'

"Yeah," Nottingham muttered to himself. "That never happened."

"But it did, Mr. Nottinham," Tizzy urged. She needed him to believe. "It was them jock shorts out of your bedroom. He took off arunning with em."

"Cain't be, girl. I only got the one pair."

"Oh, yeah, Bob? Well, where is they?" Matthew was

stupid enough to ask.

Nottingham looked at him evenly. Too evenly.

"Why, you know the answer to that, boy. I'm awearing em. Now."

Matthew stopped smiling.

"You wearing em now?" Matthew asked again, even more stupidly.

"That's right," Nottingham said.

Tizzy did not know what to make of this or how to test the theory.

"Really?" was the best she could do.

"Uh-huh," Nottingham answered. "Really. You must of been mistook."

Tizzy dropped her fretful eyes. She saw her hand wringing in her lap. Never before had she liked those hands so much. She was glad to have them.

Matthew braced himself against the water tub to keep from staggering. No more tall tales leapt to mind or offered him a way out of this.

"Sure," he mustered. "Sure. We must of been mistook."

"It happens," Nottingham granted.

Matthew began slurping a dipper of water. He spake in dribbles.

"Say, we sure appreciate the comfort and kindness, Bob. But looks like we best be moving on tomorry morning. It's time we git outa your Brylcreem."

"Aw, you two jackanapes cain't leave now," Bob said, with a hint of playful. "I jist got word from the lady of the house. Or, her what used to be. She's acoming home tomorrow afternoon. To visit with her Button."

"Button?" Matthew sputtered. "That one out there, Bob? That little stone troll's mama?"

"That's the one," Nottingham said.

"I don't think Button's gonna notice, Bob. I surely don't."

Bob Nottingham ignored this.

"How did you hear she was coming, Mr. Nottingham?" asked Tizzy, sitting on her hysteria.

Matthew hung his head and met her eyes.

"Neighbor brung me the news. He been down to the parcel post. Brung me a letter. Ain't that somethin'? Two letters in one day. One from you and one from the perty lady. Didn't I tell you she grew up over in Johabeth Holler? Not far from here. Her daddy is gonna fetch her in his truck."

"You sure about that, Bob?" Matthew asked, looking for a way out.

"Sure, I'm sure. Her daddy is gonna fetch her from the station. Then I'll fetch her up here to see the baby." He looked at Tizzy. "You're gonna like her. She reminds me of you."

Nottingham's lips pursed, like that was something to think about. Then he went to the cabinet over the water tub. He elbowed Matthew out of the way, took down a skillet and shuffled it onto the stove.

"Naw—naw. We done wore out our welcome," Matthew told him.

Had there really been some neighbor by here, Tizzy wondered? Did Mr. Nottingham even have any like a neighbor? Could that have been the forlorn specter who came to knock on the door then return to the woods? Tizzy knew the answer to all that, but hated to face it. There were no neighbors. There were no neighbors left, if there ever were any. There was only this man and that girl and that horrid hound. Suddenly Tizzy remembered her bad spook back up the mountain trail.

"Ain't seen your dog about Mr. Nottinham," she bleated.

Nottingham was sprinkling cornmeal into the greased skillet. "Judah be with me. All afternoon. I do believe he's in by the fire."

Matthew was a distrusting soul. He slipped backward into the hall. Nottingham paid him no mind. Matthew turned, took some quick steps and a queasy peek into the parlor. The fire was burning. *Rrrrrrrr*. Judah growled low and Matthew could respect that. He went nowhere near it.

In the kitchen, Tizzy kept protesting.

"I doubt we can even stay fer breakfast come morning," she insisted from her chair. "That way, you can git back to doing whatever it is you got to do, that really needs doing, I mean. Once you're shed of us, that is. Oh, my word, yes. We'll just say our goodbyes come crack of dawn. Why, they weren't no way you could've done a dern thing worth doing today after you spent all that time hunting us. I mean, hunting us and that sneak-thieving wild hare." Tizzy faltered. "That monkrat, I mean."

"Aw, that wild hare," Nottingham said, nodding at his skillet. "He might not of had no extry head. But he weren't so sneaky."

"What you mean?" Tizzy heard herself riddle. There was no wild hare. There never had been.

"He was an easy catch. Kilt him right quick."

Nottingham reached into the sink. He grabbed a pair of long ears. A fat brown hare landed hard and dead on the table in front of Tizzy. Tizzy and the chair both jumped. The blood-flecked snout and pronged front teeth were wrung around backward from the hare's body. The neck was broken, almost twisted off.

"Clouted him. Wrung his neck. Just inside them trees. Took me no time at all."

Tizzy felt sick. Matthew returned from the hall.

"It's no sweat, Bob," he spouted loud without seeing the longhaired carcass. "We're history, see. We jist don't want our welcome wore out."

Nottingham glimmered, his jaw crawling. He shook his head, slow.

"Me and mama, we won't have it no other way," he said. "You'll see. I wager you come around come morning. You got all night to sleep on it."

STEP 19

Betwixt supper and dawn, the screen door never squeaked open or slapped shut.

Shortly after midnight, Tizzy took the tarnished gold chain out of her shoe. She wrapped it in tissue paper. She tucked it into the jewelry box amidst the lace tablecloth and old photographs. Then she closed the bureau drawer.

Matthew had joined Mr. Nottingham at the kitchen table. He ate a fried hare plate with plenty of grease gravy. But he was utterly depraved. Tizzy felt much too sick in her belly for that. When Mr. Nottingham flopped that wild thing on the table in front her, gooseflesh had swept over her holy being. It ran honking through her brain and heart and soul and made her never want to sit at that table again. She wanted nothing to do with that lopeared abomination, even after she watched them skin it out over the sink. Tizzy begged off, using mewling words she forgot as soon as she said them. Then she went to bed early so she could lay awake all night. She did not ask Matthew to sit in her room with his pistol to protect her. With his night blindness, he was more likely to shoot him a Tizzy Polk if she made any sudden moves before dawn. No, Tizzy would go it alone. She would tough it out. She blew out the lamp then pulled the covers over herself, fully-dressed.

She lay there knowing there would be no nighttide dreams down rivers of honey, for to sail away to sea. She would not be cupped in the hand of her loving mother, perhaps never again. Tizzy felt as if her dreams had been skinned out over a sink. She was no longer so rare nor fine, nor was she refined. She was most definitely not refined. And she was almost as unfit for chains of gold as this house was unfit for slumber. Just like that wild bunny who was given birth by Tizzy, and just like Matthew Birdnell—Tizzy was a thief. She was unfit, born in sin, and could not be trusted.

That man in there knew. He seemed to know everything without being told. Perhaps he saw the same stain on Vistalynn Ray. Perhaps she was a thief too.

For the first time since they came knocking on his door, Bob Nottingham did not leave his house all night. It was like he knew his tenants were about to bug out on him without paying what they owed. When his usual time of departure had come and gone, Tizzy finally turned the knob and peeked out of her bedroom. She could barely see Mr. Nottingham's room across the dark parlor. She could see his door hung open. Tizzy could also see a red ember flaring and fading, then flaring again. With some faraway glimpse of hellfire in hand, the man sat unseen in his bed, blowing smoke into the darkness. Tizzy was afraid. She was afraid that if she could see him better she would see him rolling those smokes, while he sat there in his only pair of jock shorts. She hoped he was, anyway.

Why he was—or what he was up to—she could not cipher and did not want to cipher. He was a riddle she no longer wanted to solve, for fear that she might have to face some riddle within herself. She might have to ask and answer her reason for being. That was the greatest riddle of all, for Tizzy. She had always wondered how she came to be. But she was even more afraid of the answer. Something about the way Mr. Nottingham looked at her sometimes made Tizzy feel like he knew the answer.

So, now, she did not want to know Mr. Nottingham too well. She did not want to visit the places he might take her.

STEP 20

They were tired, Mr. Nottingham. They were cross. Both Tizzy and Matthew forewent all breakfast.

"No, I still ain't so hungry, Mr. Nottingham."

"Hell's bells, Bob. I was up with the trots, running back and forth to that privy all night."

They were afraid to say they were still leaving. Afraid of what he might say or do next. So, without a word betwixt them, Tizzy and Matthew both knew they would bide their time. He would go again. His comings and goings were the blood that coursed his veins.

They quickly devoted themselves to a game of jack-straws. The two nested in the hen-scratches beyond the gristmill. They dropped the straws. They picked them up again. They dropped them. They picked them up.

They thought he would never leave.

There was the odd clink, thump, or rattle-rattle from the house, usually from back toward the kitchen. Nottingham made a couple of trips to the chicken coop and corncrib, saying nothing to either of them, leaving the boy and girl to their dirt play. It began warming up early, with flies abuzz, Button who knew where, Tizzy cranky, and sweat slithering down Matthew's nose. They whispered and waited. Tizzy doubted jackstraws had ever been played so long or so poorly. Neither she nor Matthew were working with a steady hand.

Close to noon, Nottingham appeared on the front porch. He called out to them.

"Off to git mama," he trumpeted. "Anybody shows while I'm gone, you tell em sit tight."

Then the man left. Nottingham strode carefully up into the pines, disappearing above the smokehouse. Tizzy dropped her jackstraws. Head down, Matthew started picking them up. Tizzy was ready to quit playing games. There was something in the tone of Mr. Nottingham's voice—some joke beneath the surface—that told her nobody would be showing up while he was gone, or when he got back.

But they pretended to play for a whit longer, until they were sure the man was out of earshot. Finally, Matthew dropped his straws again. Tizzy did not move. Their eyes met. They leapt up and ran inside.

Tizzy only wanted her buckletop shoes. Or so she said. Matthew took the German army trench knife he had fancied from the pantry, along with a whetstone from the kitchen drawer. While Matthew was getting the whetstone, Tizzy filched two candles, slipping them into her dress pocket. She had already taken a matchbox, so that way they would not be caught in the dark again—no matter where they were.

Matthew slid the knife into his belt as they slunk off down the hill. Their feet made too much noise skidding down the steep wooded slope. It could not be helped. All this rustling might alert every monkrat and fox squirrel in creation. As long as they did not alert the stag-faced man, they could still beep the car horn. Suddenly Tizzy remembered a day on the playground, years ago, with Shonda Jo Biggs. Tizzy stopped and knelt. She swept away dry leaves and drew a criss-cross in the hillside with her finger. She spat in its crux for good fortune, then leapt up and ran to catch Matthew. Who knows where Shonda Jo got such a silly consecration. But Tizzy was casting pride to the winds. Every little bit helped. The day looked hopeful so far, didn't it? Nothing jumped out of it or grabbed at them.

When they slid down onto the road—Tizzy began to see things differently.

The blue Packard was in a worse jam than Matthew had let on. The back end of the car sat disturbingly low, sunk to the passenger taillight in dry mud. The bumper was now baked into the mud gully by all this heat. To Tizzy, it did not look much better than that half-sunk tractor they passed coming up the mountain.

"I suppose you got a fast fix fer all this? You got a Big-mouth Birdnell fix fer this?" She was fed up to the gills.

Matthew was circling the car. Even he was shocked.

"Dang. It weren't this bad when I come down here before," he grumbled. "It was still wet. The mud weren't set up hard like this."

"You know he's most likely watching us, don't you? He probably right over there, or over there, or over there. In them trees. Watching us and laughing it up. And if he ain't, that dadburn Button is."

"Naw, he ain't. He's off somewheres, fetching whoever or doing the Odd Bob. He ain't gonna spend no second day down here looking fer us on this road."

"You don't know that," she said, sitting down on the running board.

"I don't have to know it. I feel it."

"You feel it? Where? In your dirt digger feet?" She made a face at him.

"Yeah, maybe I do" he snurled back, jumpy as a Mexican bean. "It jist might start there and work its way up."

"Okeedoke. Well, you let me know when it finally gits to the top."

"Aw, c'mon, Tiz. Jist shuddup. I got this figureed, see? Done it a hunert times before. Have a little faith in the Rebel Yell here."

Tizzy could think of no words worth wasting. She could tell he was as antsy about Mr. Nottingham as she was.

Matthew opened the trunk and took out the jack handle. He spent a lot of antsy minutes trying to gouge and route a moat around the trapped tire. The sun got higher in the sky while he did it. They both kept looking around and over their shoulders. Eventually, Matthew got so sun-drunk and delirious in his zeal that he would jump and yipe out loud every time a pinecone fell. Tizzy took over and made him sit in the shade for a spell. With the tire dug out pretty well, Tizzy moved on. She began to scrape some clearance beneath the car's chassis. A half-hour became an hour, but she worked smart, with more mother wit than Matthew. He came out of the shade and stood in the ditch beside her, standing sentry. Or, that's what he called it. Mainly, he got underfoot. Tizzy had to stop once and make him put the gun away, back under his shirt. He was waving it around a little too much, jabbering constantly while she worked. It drove her ding-batty and Tizzy was still afraid he would trip or slip and shoot her in the back while she did his dirty work.

Tizzy and the jack handle toiled until the Packard stood a real chance of escape. Finally, she stood up and stood back.

"Battery's probably low," she advised, scraping hair and sweat off her flushed cheek. "Don't wanna have to crank it too many times."

"She'll run like a top. You jist watch me." Matthew bopped out of the ditch, acting the fool. "Hill-a-billy, hill-a-billy, hillbilly *bop*—"

Matthew flung open the car door, his hand in his pant pocket. The keys never crossed his mind until that moment.

"Whatcha mean you *ain't got em?*" she exploded.

"Whoa. I, uh—I jist ain't got em on me, doll baby."

"You best start *thinking*, boy. You think *hard*. What was it you done with that ring o'keys?" Tizzy wanted to cut his head off with a harp string.

"Don't *holler* at me. Let's see. I, uh—"

You know how to cross-wire a car?"

"Uh, naw. I ain't never—"

"Me neither. So damn your hide, Matthew Birdnell, *think*."

"Godawmighty—*wait*—I set em down on that doily up there."

"And what doily would that be?" Tizzy demanded, un-clenching her fist.

"In that rock cabin up yonder. Where that dead gal is. Or was."

"*Cryyyminitleee—*"

Matthew ducked behind the side mirror—before she could come at him.

"Back off, Tiz. I'll go fetch em. I'll fetch them keys. Be back in a jif. You jist wait right 'chere."

"This is a broke record. You'll git lost again."

"Naw, I won't. I know the way now. I can take a jag, around through that stand of black oak yonder, and hook up with the trail. You take a little nap in the car and dream about that cold drink I'm gone git ye soon as we're off this mountain."

"A cold drink? Who you gonna kill to git it this time?"

"I'll fetch them keys from that cabin and be back down here to kiss your foot in under a hour."

Tizzy eyed him. This was iffy. His track record was broken too.

"I'm going with you," she said. She started past him,

headed for the trees.

Before she could get past—Matthew shoved Tizzy *hard*, knocking her off her feet to the ground.

"No, goddam ye," he barked. *"I got the Osage in me. I move like the panther and I'm more fleet o' foot on my own."*

Tizzy came off the ground as fast as she hit it. She came spitting hot rivets.

"I ain't gonna set here like no titmouse getting *owled at*."

"Wait fer me back up at Bob's place then," Matthew spat back.

"I ain't agoing back to that house *neither*," she yelled in his face while wiping her own.

Matthew got real quiet. He wasn't sure how they got here or how it came to this. Neither was Tizzy.

"Okay, then ye gotta trust me," he spake from the heart. "Jist take a load off here. I got to do this right. Fer once. I'll be back. I promise. By the time you count nine hunert and ninety-nine, this Birdnell will be back with them damn keys. Then it's Memphis and all points in betwixt. And that's the gospel truth."

"Matthew," Tizzy sagged. "You swear?"

"Course I swear."

"You won't be long from here?"

"Watch me. Hell, we got plenty of time still. We got all afternoon to pick our way back down this road. Sure, we do. I can hear it. Cain't you?"

"What?" She blinked up at him.

"It's the sound of the git rich. And the chrome-plate boogie."

Before she could tell him to be careful, Matthew loped off, climbing up into the trees. For a few minutes, she heard him rustling in there, headed for that blackjack rim. Then she did not hear Matthew anymore. Tizzy crouched under a pine tree until its shade covered the blue Packard. Ants began to bother her so she went and sat in the car.

STEP 21

Cluck, she said.

The cluck you say, Matthew clucked back.

Cluck, she did say.

Go cluck your red rooster, he clucked.

Cluckity-cluck-a-cluck-cluck.

Damn these chickens clucking and pecking underfoot. They had all best cluck a way out of here before he went berserkers and popped a few more.

This neck of timber did not hook the way Matthew had thought it hooked. Shouldn't there be a ridge rising on his left, a climb where Matthew could hook up with the footpath to the rock cabin? Unless his radar was off—which it was not—that creek cut right down through these woods and Matthew should have already crossed it. He was not going to worry it too much. Not yet. He had a satisfied mind. If this detour did not pan out, he only had to go upslope along that tumbling creek, until he reached the point where Bob's trail jumped across. Right. And, hopefully, Matthew would reach that creek soon. Before he went berserkers. Because these white tail feathers were everywhere, clucking underfoot. And that creek ought to be behind him by now. Not ahead.

After Matthew took his leave of Tizzy and the Packard he felt strong again. It was always that way, wasn't it? How could he let himself forget? Once again, Matthew felt the sinews of ancient hunters in his stride. His pap had warned him. A woman can sap a man and distract him. Why, forgetting those dadburn car keys was a freak, a joke. He would never have let that happen if Tizzy had not been around, pecking at him. That's why, as soon as Matthew left her back on the road, he felt much better. The panther in him was reborn, the Osage buck. He knew in his loins he would return within the hour, keyring in hand. From now on, things were going to be different. No gal, naked or not, pretty or not, dead or not, was going to trip up this pathfinder twice. Yes, he knew this as soon as he got shed of Tizzy back there.

Fifteen minutes later, Matthew Birdnell was lost again. In no time at all, he was lost and thirsty and cursing Tizzy for letting him go.

It was Riddle Top. Riddle Top was to blame. Only Riddle Top could betray his radar like this. These woods kept twisting, darkening, most sunlight cut out by the high spreading branches. The earth was bred dank under here. More than anything, this place made you feel alone and abandoned. Left alone with yourself. That's why Riddle Top could put the panic in you, if you let it. But Matthew was not going to let it.

He must not lose his temper with these woods, or with himself. No good could come of it. His temper was his Pap's temper. His loud, half-breed, teat-sucking daddy. His daddy who was too scared squirtless of the big world to be a worthy sonofabitch. But he was just the man for your daily, pint-size dose of sanctimony. Pap never needed any church for that. He had an outhouse. And that outhouse had *The Queen's Saxonican Juris Dictionary.* Pap worshiped at the altar of that book. He wielded its words—a lot of words he did not understand—like a bully with a club. Words like "pertinaciousness" and "fortitude" and "moxie" and other things Matthew was missing, according to Pap. Matthew was not sure if "little four-eyed bastard" could be found in the pages of that book. He even had his doubts about "moxie." But Pap wielded those words too. And Matthew knew better than to doubt him out loud. Zeph Birdnell was known to stomp toys to death and drink heifer's milk straight from the heifer. Sometimes he drank hog's milk from the hog. He also drank everything else. As a result, Mommy's face was a bombed-out war zone, worn out by too many brats and too many collisions with those pig-farmer fists. Mommy's face stayed so swollen you could hardly see her eyes anymore. Matthew had never seen her cry, and what little sense she had when she married Zeph Birdnell had been knocked out of her long ago. She was stupid. No wonder Pap hated her for holding him back.

But Matthew was not going to let that happen. He was fast, he was lean. He had a .38. He moved like the panther.

Even in weird woods like these, he would never panic. A panther spirit could smell water—he could sniff it out from miles away. His eyes and ears were sharp.

Yes, Matthew would soon catch the creek scent. He would sniff it out, or stumble over it by chance. And this time, the creek spirit would help him. He would follow the creek spirit farther up the mountain to the trail, to the rock cabin.

Soon, he hoped. Because the air under these trees was thick and disturbing to him. It seemed like these blackjack oaks had never breathed, nor drawn life from anything fresh on this mountain, or in it. This air smelled rotten. If he had not been an Osage buck, possessed of the panther spirit, this rot might go to work on his nerves.

Matthew could not carry a tune. But that wasn't going to hold him back. Nothing could hold him back. He was whistling soft through his teeth as he walked on, looking for the smell of water.

As his teeth whistled, old strange words kept noodling through his brain.

O watch your step, step, step...

Krrr-rickkk. Something dry snapped back there.
Matthew reeled around.

He nudged his glasses and looked. No one went there. Only these crazy chickens underfoot. Zeph Birdnell hated chickens so Matthew kicked a hen. She went squawk-

ing. Matthew turned back, and she was still squawking.
As he went back to walking, he was about to start whistling—-when he heard whistling, soft whistling. Far behind him. What the hell was that? Matthew cocked his
head sideways, looking back, still moving, still moving.
He did hear whistling, didn't he? Who's that whistling?
That you, brother Weldon? Let me in on it.

Matthew reset the trench knife under his belt—she
was still with him, razor sharp and deadly. He had the
pistol of course, but she could backfire and alert Bob.
Bob was sure to hear any gunshots. Matthew could see
it play out in his mind, clear as well water:

Rebel Yell hears a no-good whistler. Rebel Yell shoots
a whistler. Bob comes running. Bob grins. It all ends
before it gets started. And there might not be any more
escapes in Bob's master plan.

No, if some triple-jointed Lych or any other hill crazy
was to jump Matthew, Matthew would have to jug the
rascal with this trench knife.

Matthew struck a trot, picking up his pace through
the black oaks. He kept searching, searching, for any
sign to help him. A creek, something, anything. His radar was no help.

This cowl of leaf was too thick. No, he could not see
clearly and he knew it. Sometimes that was a good thing,
but not so much right now. Some things were best left
unseen, some were best left untold. Matthew had never
told Tizzy everything about his last lost afternoon. He
had spared her. It was the manly thing to do. With her

kind of pap, she didn't need any more invites to madness. Matthew never told her about the gory cow. He had seen the gory cow. He remembered her well. Just another lost afternoon. He had never told Tizzy about the little spine-bones wired together around an ash-littered altar. Matthew had seen that too. He never told her about the monkrat skull in the red patent leather purse. The purse hung on the tree limb. To protect Tizzy, he had kept things sketchy about that lost afternoon. This was the strength and power and fortitude he found in the panther spirit.

Right now, the panther spirit was trotting along, faster and faster, until his lungs were burning. Matthew was almost running now, running from a whistle he was not sure he had really heard.

Then—abruptly—he landed atop a high crest.

Matthew stopped, chest heaving. He scoped out the lay of land below. Here, the woods dove at a steep angle then leveled off again, far below. It was so steep, though, that Matthew would have to descend slowly. This meant that whistler back there might gain ground on him. If there was a whistler. Time was wasting. Matthew had no time to dawdle or hesitate. He had to reckon the most forgiving course—down the slope— if he was to make it without a tumble. He had to reckon it quickly. Time was wasting. Struggling to see better, Matthew took another step, up to the very edge of the crest, onto a lip of sunken logs.

And the earth broke loose.

Splinters and mulch went sliding fast down the incline. Matthew Birdnell went sliding and racing down with it. Upright on his feet—he was forced to run faster, faster, eyes frantic—getting ahead of himself, faster—down through the slide of soggy leaves. He fought to keep up with his white-top shoes. He was still fighting when he finally reached the bottom and smashed into the tree.

He might have lost an hour or a day or a few days. If Matthew had been gone only that long, he could have gotten over it. A handful of hours or days missing in the life of a Jesse James was part of the blur and heat of the adventure, the price you pay for being notorious. That kind of blackout was no worse than a bad drunk on bad corn liquor. As long as it did not do you brain damage or make you blind for life, you would get over it.

But, waking up with a nasty ache in your melon, under a six-hundred-year-old blackjack tree, surrounded by stone trolls was harder to take. And they were baby stone trolls. And they weren't smiling. It got worse after that. Matthew looked down and saw the rusted outline of his pistol in the grass. The pistol's handle was rotted off, leaving only the iron frame of the handle. What had he just been robbed of, he wondered? What kind of queer deal was this? It got worse. When Matthew woke up and looked down and found he had a long white beard to his knees, it was a different tale altogether. His fingernails were gnurled yellow, a half foot long or more. This would take some getting used to. Then his face began to feel wet. Really wet and slimy. Dripping with slobber. And the baby trolls weren't smiling. He reached to wipe away the wet from his face—but poked himself in the eye with a long twisted fingernail. Down there at his knees, the tip of his beard was dripping with slobber. Why, this was no long-whiskered tale at all. It was just a sorry, sour mash dream.

Matthew woke up feeling like a salt lick. Wet. His face felt wet. His tongue tasted another tongue. His noggin hurt bad. He first saw specks of sunlight through the high leafy dome. Then he saw the blurry, mottled snout of Judah. The big dog bent over Matthew, his sandpaper tongue licking and slobbering over Matthew's cheeks, nose, and lips. Matthew didn't mind for some reason. He tried to get a fix on where he was. Yes, there was that sneaky tree that attacked him, that blackjack oak. It was old alright. But it sure weren't no six hundred years old. Then that sour dream poked its fingernail in his eye long enough to remind him. Matthew reached up to check his face, catching a handful of Judah tongue when he did it. Judah kept licking. Matthew was relieved to find no beard to speak of. The knee beard was a dream too. He had never been able to grow a good beard, to his consternation. Matthew had always wanted some wild-ass sideburns. Wouldn't that look studly in the newspapers?

Matthew's hand reached up and fondled the great dog's ears. Then he remembered the car keys. Time was wasting. Matthew made an effort and raised himself. Judah stopped licking Matthew's face. Judah lowered his tail and sat, watching Matthew prop his back against the tree. Matthew's County specs lay there in the grass. He picked them up and put them on.

There was little new to see. Nothing earth-shaking. No last minute changes. The woods twittered and sun sprites danced across the dark forest bed. Those white biddy hens were still out there clucking about.

So much for dreams with long whiskers. But how long had he been dreaming? How long had he been out? Not long, he hoped. Matthew knew he needed to skeedaddle. Tizzy was waiting on him.

In fact, Judah seemed to be sitting here waiting on him too. A whimper came from those drippy, goofy jowls. A needful whimper.

Matthew was having second thoughts about this old hound. Judah did not seem so bad after all. Kind of friendly. The giant dog sat there panting like any other dog. His eyes were keen and bright, and curious. Ready for whatever. Maybe Judah would scare off any strange whistler's on Matthew's tail. Maybe he already had. Maybe it was time for them both to skeedaddle together.

"Aw," Matthew said, "We gittin' fast and nasty now. Ain't we?"

He reached out to scruff Judah's pointy ears again.

Judah snarled. His eyes went mean. A squelch burst from his belly. He lunged.

Matthew threw up his arm. Judah went for soft throat and face. Matthew felt the rush of hot breath from the dog.   A ripping growl and the dog attacked Matthew's exposed gut as Matthew jerked away.   The fangs drew blood, shredding flesh and shirttail.

Matthew slid and ran, four eyes blitzing terror.   Chickens scattered.   Matthew ran for his life, Judah close at bay.

The boy peeled through the brace of trees, aiming for a high blackberry thicket at the corner of his eyeglass, slightly upslope.   Judah chomped into Matthew's left calf. A horrible rutting howl ensued as the dog's anvil head thrashed, tearing at the muscle.   Matthew wrenched free, slinging dirt and fever.

Matthew flew into the thicket.   Briars and twigs popping, ripping at his body, Matthew forced himself through the brush.   It was thorny chaos.   His heart tried to punch through his chest.   His whorefucking specs kept slipping down his nose.   He plucked them into his pocket.   He slashed his way through, using his hands and arms like dull-edged cleavers. Blood roared in his ears, bloody voices roaring at him, you can't stop, you can't think, it ain't the gore-horn that kills you.   Then—Matthew exploded out the other end of the thicket—cut to pieces and stumbling.

Matthew flipped around.   Judah did not break from the thicket—where was he?   Matthew turned and bolted away from the thicket.

Guhhhrowwww.

Matthew's head jerked aside. Judah tackled him.   The dog went for the spastic boy's throat. Again. Again. Judah kept on coming.

The dog had skirted the bramble. Matthew got that in a flash. Locked in the fray, Matthew kicked and scrapped for every inch of life betwixt him and those jaws, that foul breath. Dust churned. Judah sicced like a dervish.

Matthew suffered as Judah's jaws tore into him, roaring, slobbering. Ahead was a root-ledged ravine. Matthew kicked and squealed, dragging them both toward the ravine. Judah went for Matthew's face again. Matthew's hand flew up into the dog's fangs to stop them. Dragging. Blood spewed from Matthew's hand.

Matthew dug in his heel and kicked hard—

They pitched over the edge—into the ravine—joined in hellish embrace. They tumbled down. A hind paw shredded Matthew's cheek. A sharp tooth seared into his groin. Boy and dog fell and exploded apart at the bottom of the ravine.

KRRRR-ACKKKSSSH. A dead-falling pine bough crashed down, barely missing Matthew. The limb broke at the bottom of the ravine, beside him. Supersonic pain shot through his thigh, high-voltage agony blew out his eardrums. Matthew scuffled backwards, yelping, his fuzzy-eyed panic blinking in every direction. Looking for the dog.

But the dog was *gone.*

Dog was gone.

For a moment.

But dog would be back, oh yes, dog would be back, oh no, this dog don't scare.

Matthew's leg was broken, he was sure of it. His leg felt broker than this dead pine. Don't stop. Don't think. It ain't the gore-horn that kills you, it's the—

He leapt up screaming. With each step came a jolt of fire through his leg and groin as he gimped away fast down the ravine. A root tripped him. He hit hard. Hand over fist, he began to crawl—then scramble—like a sprayed cockroach.

Dog will be back. Yes. No. Dog don't scare.

Ahead, the mossy hull of a big tree trunk lay against the ravine wall. Matthew saw a long hollow beneath it. Quickly, quickly, he burrowed under. He hustled through the molder and spider webs to the center of the woodbark tunnel. Still, he heard no dog. No dog out there. Nobody growling at him. Nobody. Safe, he was, by grace of nothing. He was safe. But where was that Judah bastard? Tracking at the lip of the ravine, maybe, just overhead?

Matthew coughed up dark sputum and looked down. He smeared the thick cake of blood off his groin. Christ, so his leg was not broken after all. No, it was not a tooth-hole that burned and bled alongside his privates. It was the trench knife blade. The silvery tip was snapped off in his right thigh. The rest of the knife—the handle, hilt, and most of the shank—was still under his belt.

Cringing, Matthew twisted in the tight hollow space. He pulled the knife handle from his belt and dropped it beside him where it would do no more damage. His finger pressed around the oozing wound. He could see the knife tip glinting deep in the bloody center. He was hurting bad. He tried not to whimper or make any sound. He wanted to stay off the hound's radar.

But, *wait*. Hold on, dog-dang it. (*Dog-dang it? Who used to say that? Who?*) Wait, dog-dang it, Matthew had *his gun*, his .38.

He reached around back for the pistol—and found nobody home but his tailbone. Frantic, he searched the surrounding mulch. No, the gun wasn't here. His mind flew backwards. Where could it be? Where? Why, he could have lost the .38 anywhere in the tussle or the underbrush. Oh, sweet Judah, he wouldn't be surprised if he lost the pistol way back—when he first tumbled down that slope into the tree. Before this dang-dog found him. It was only in the whiskery dream Matthew saw the pistol, rusting and rotting. Fuck. He never saw the gun again after he really, really woke up.

Rrrrrrggg.

He once was lost but now was found.

Rrrrrggg.

Matthew froze. He sure heard the Judah now. Yes, the dog was down beyond his feet. He heard sweet Judah snarling and sniffing down at that end of this log Matthew hid under. He heard him—and then he didn't. The big brute bastard shut up again.

There was silence.

Except for the buzz of flies and the buzz in his brain. Except for the blood pounding from his pain. There was silence.

Matthew listened, not daring to suffer or breathe.

Then he heard the dog again. Heavy paws clumped around outside the log. Then clumped out there in the grass, down the length of the tree hull then back again. Matthew heard skidlick of leaf then—thump, thump, thump—Judah was on top of the tree trunk. The dog paced back and forth atop the trunk's shell, scratching and clumping directly over Matthew's head. Matthew felt like he was inside an ancient tom-tom. Seconds passed. Matthew sweated and clinched his stinging eyes. Why hadn't he stayed back there—stayed and tried to hotwire the car? Why hadn't he told Tizzy about that red purse on the limb with its tiny skull? Why hadn't he told her she was pretty too?

RRRRRGGG. His worries flew out the bottom of the log. *RRRRRRRRRGGG.* An ear-splitting *growl* come down the shaft from the top of the log.

Judah was *inside* the log. Judah was crawling in, snarling in through the spider's den—angry, hungry— hungry for Matthew's face.

Matthew backpaddled like a demon out of the wood cocoon. He came out the bottom and leapt atop the old log. The dog was out too.

Judah's teeth were crushing Matthew's ankle by the time Matthew got his arm around a sapling up on the ravine's edge. Hoisting himself—in grinding misery and hurt—Matthew pulled upward out of the rut, bringing his legs and the dog with him. Judah dangled by his jaws from Matthew's leg, dangled in mid-air. The veins in Matthew's neck were about to burst when the sick clench of boy and beast finally rolled and spilled onto the grass above.

There was little fight left in Matthew. He was out of the ravine now, but he doubted it mattered or would make a difference. He was almost spent, his wad was shot. Judah was coming at him again. Matthew kicked weakly at Judah's dripping jaws.

Judah reared up, lunged, then fell back. Judah took a frothy *snap* at Matthew's cods. Matthew yanked his cods clear just in time. The hellhound's wicked eyes flared.

"Please—" Matthew heard himself beg.

Then Judah stopped. Judah stopped and turned and galloped away.

In a fetal curl, hands over his head, Matthew heard the hound fading off, rattling off through the leaves. Soon the beast was nothing but echo.

Judah was no more. He might have never been there.

The sun-speckled oaks went quiet. Shadows swam together. Matthew lay shattered in the grass, cut and bloodied. He waited for more abuse, more terror. He waited for the dog to return. But dog did not return.

He began to uncurl. A low breeze moaned through the pine. There was some damn bird making a noise up there. And he heard the idle cluck of chickens, fucking chickens.

And he could smell something. It was not water or a creek, he smelled. It was not a clean smell. It was the fevered hush. It was death, probably. It smelled familiar. It was a bad smell.

The boy rolled over on hands and knees and threw up. Retching until his frothy cods wanted to heave out his gullet, Matthew finally got empty. His spasms ceased. Ague chills swept through his flesh, his sweat dripping in the dry grass. The boy slowly got up off his knees. Matthew stood bent with a stringhalted splay to his gimp leg, his brain sloshing. What was this stink? This boogery odor—the one that soured his guts—what was this stink all about?

Matthew took a game step. The pain shot through him. But the pain almost bored him now. He was getting used to it.

Besides, this was abnormal. This place here. Odd and abnormal. Look how these oaks formed an open-ended circle, a shadowy alcove near the ravine. Beyond the oak tree circle was a rock-rimmed well and winch. Where had he seen that well before? From his pocket, Matthew took his bent spectacles and looped them onto each ear. He hobbled closer. It was good he could not see himself. He knew he was a crazy-quilt of bloody scratches, gouges, and mud. But he did not care. Pains and scars were easy to forget in a place like this.

Betwixt elder oaks in the circle were rough wooden tables. They were worktables—jointed betwixt their support trees so long ago that the bark had grown and burled out around the crude planks. Hung on horse-nail pegs in the bark and stacked upon open-air shelves were all manner of cleavers and saws. There was a host of old forge-hammered implements for cutting. There were crusted knives, barbed-wire coils, and iron pokers. And jars. Empty glass jars.

Yes, this place was enough to drive all troubles, dogs, car keys, and Tizzys from Matthew's brain. This place had a pure fascination. Like a cancer. It was an open wound and right there was the hole.

The oaken cluster bowered around a great pit, a deep pit. A pit so deep you could not see its black-mawed bottom from where Matthew stood. It was big enough to swallow a dump truck or milk wagon or pickup truck or even a Packard convertible. Damned if it was not bigger than any godawful hole Matthew had ever dug. The stench oozed out of it.

It ain't the gore-horn that gets you, he chuckled inside himself. It ain't the gore-horn that gets you. It's the hole.

And this hole seemed to be asking things of him.

Matthew came forward, moving into the ring of trees, closer to its lip. His fingers smeared the blood and sweat on his lenses, trying to make his glasses to see better. He winced and took another step, to the edge of this rent of earth. His hand went out, steadying himself against an old oak. He took no notice as ants swarmed over his fingers.

"Watch your step now," he told the hole, "I'm the Rebel Yell. I was borned bad, daddy."

Yes, and he was borned to see this pit. This pit, she was deep. This was the big dig. She was the mother hole. And, damn if she didn't look almost—*empty.*

He never heard the 20-pound sledge raise up behind

him. A pair of hard, gritty hands swung the sledge. The first blow smashed into the back of Matthew's skull and blood burst out his ears. His lank frame teetered upright and twisted a bit. His eyes were dull ahead, his motors were cut. The sledge swung again. The second blow demolished the rest of his brains and sent his glasses flying. The County specs ricocheted off the oak tree. Matthew gave up the ghost.

STEP 22

By the time Tizzy reached the biggest tree on Riddle Top, her day was almost done.

She had pricked her finger. It was getting harder to see the thistles and nettles that troubled her path. Her hair twined in the nettles. Her fingers kept raking them away. And she pricked her finger whilst raking them. Didn't she? Her memory was not good. Tizzy was glad to finally leave the worst of the thicket and pass onto more barren ground beneath the trees. She was glad to no longer have woodbine stroking her bare ankles. She did not like being touched down there.

"Matthew—" she called.

There was so little light left. Was she past the point of no return? She suspected she was. It was hard to say. Time was so funny up here. Whether she found him or not, she barely had time enough to reach the cabin—if she had to go that far. She did not want to go that far. She doubted she had time enough to return to the car. Yes, Tizzy had come too far to turn back. And she was beginning not to care anymore.

Tizzy felt like something inside her had begun to drift and crumble, like the earth was crumbling beneath her. She felt as if she were neither here nor there, yet part of the everywhere. Arrivals no longer mattered. There were strange and familiar mists moving through these woods now, and she moved with them. She knew these mists, knew them by name. These mists were Loneliness and Neglect. The mists came drifting out, from inside her. They knew her too well. And they knew her name. They must have whispered her name to the magpie. Her sad old misty friends must have told on her.

"Matthew? You there?"

The magpie kept leaving. The bird spun up through the trees, flapping, swooping to great heights. With black wings flapping, with their flapping streaks of white, the magpie seemed so carefree, yet so careless. Yes, these were careless days indeed, more fragile than Tizzy first realized. Now this day was almost done, crumbling into dusk. Then the dusk would crumble away too. And what would be the remains? Tizzy's memory was not good. But she knew the answer to that. If she did not find him soon, nothing would remain of her. Tizzy Polk would crumble away alone, lost in guilt, lost in loneliness and neglect. And nobody would know how she went.

The magpie awakened her.

Tizzy. The magpie knew her name.

She had dozed off, waiting back in the blue Packard. Hours went by without Matthew. Long shadows crept over the car as Tizzy began to drift. A pity, it was. She had spent a sleepless night in the house of Nottingham. But the night and his house had left her weary, in a weakened state. Now, the late sun lulled her. Tizzy nodded off.

A mountain chill was creeping in when magpie feet came hopping, hopping across the Packard hood. She rubbed her eyes open. The road and woods around her were nearly blue as her chariot. She felt she must do something. Something. But what? Tizzy never really considered returning to Mr. Nottingham's house. Not now. Not alone. For all she knew, Matthew had broke his leg or his filthy pencil neck. He was always fouling somewhere. He might be lying near death in some stump hole, moaning for Tizzy to save him. Well, no angel of mercy was she. But, maybe she should run fetch Matthew anyway, before it got too dark to do it. Partners weren't that easy to come by. At least not for Tizzy Polk, they weren't.

The sprightly bird perched on the windshield, rattling at her. Suppose, just suppose, this bird-rattle was a spirit. Hadn't Matthew told her of such things? What if this bird was a spirit come to fetch her to Matthew's ailing side?

"You ain't telling me nothing," she told the magpie.

Tizzy put her shoes back on and abandoned the car.

Now, here, deep in the mists of this spectral forest, the

mists and magpie were all that moved. Where had all the chickens gone, she wondered? Had all the stray chickens gone home to roost, along with all other birds and beasts and the chattering bugs? Naturally. Wasn't that what chickens did come nightfall?

Tizzy wanted to go home now. Back home to Cayuga Ridge, where she was not rare and she was not refined. She even wanted to go home to her Preacher-Daddy. She wanted to suffer sharp words and hell-stinging thunder-bolts and the Preacher's wrath of ages. She ached for the scorn of silly children and stern elders. Yes, she must go home now, to the fires of Cayuga Ridge. As soon as she found her lost boy.

Up ahead, the magpie was hopping about the ground, beneath a colossal oak tree. The magpie started pecking at something there betwixt the roots. Tizzy approached. The bird flew away.

Tizzy stopped and stood beneath the oak. A bloody acorn lay betwixt her toes. It was the only acorn beneath this great tree. Tizzy raised her head and looked straight up into the spreading limbs. This might be the biggest tree Tizzy had ever seen. She could see strange fruit up there, high in the heavenly skein of branches and leaf. The tree was filled with strange shapes. Were there other birds roosting up there? It was too dark to see. The light was fading.

But she could see her magpie, swooping back down. Her magpie was returning from that endless tree. Again, her magpie landed a few feet ahead.

Tizzy dropped her eyes back to the ground. Who was she beguiling? This was not her magpie. Tizzy had no place for cur dogs or magpies. She was guilty enough to know that. It was time to learn her lessons.

The magpie hopped along, silent and twitching. The magpie's rattle had stopped. The bird no longer spake her name. Tizzy told the bird to scat and skeedaddle. And it did, flapping away.

"Matthew—" she called. "Matthew?"

Tizzy walked on in her unwashed dress and buckletop shoes. Her astral voice echoed and faded.

"Matthew Birdnell?"

Soon, she was swallowed by familiar mistings. Soon she was only a tiny voice. And soon after that, her tiny voice was almost gone too.

From high above, Button watched Tizzy go. Button also watched the vesper magpie.

The magpie winged up into the giant spreading oak. Higher and higher, upward into a tangled tree of hands. Scores, nay, hundreds of hands, putrefied and withering, were hung here like the strangest fruit. Each hand had a spike through the palm, dangling by wire from scores of spindly limbs. The birds knew. So did Button. Button sat perched on a nearby sycamore limb watching that Tizzy girl, watching this silly bird, and watching this monstrous tree.

This was the undying Tree Of Hands.

Button could not remember this life without the Tree Of Hands. She could tell by all bushels of dead fruit it bore, that the Tree Of Hands had probably been around forever.

Button watched as the magpie lit on a slender hand with a spike through its palm. The spiked hand hung on a wire. The bird pecked at the opal ring on the pale finger. Then the magpie sprang, flapping, to the dirty hands dangling nearby. The snippet's beak began to tug and tug on a bloody split thumbnail.

"Matthew?" a voice was calling.

By the time Tizzy reached the toy cottage, her day was almost undone.

An old wind had risen in the pines and Tizzy was afraid. Where had her mind gone? Her memory was not good. She could never hope to sleep the night in such a pretty rock cabin. She could see the front door stood open, whistling for her, whistling, singing with the old wind, singing just for her.

Tizzy, Tizzy, sang the darkling door.

Entering strange upon the threshold, Tizzy began to repent. Repent.

"Matthew? I'm sorry, Matthew."

She went a few steps into the pale grey room, looking for the pale dead girl. No one sat in the gnurled rocker. No ember warmed the hearth. Lo and behold, Vistalynn Ray's corpse had taken leave of this place. The bed lay empty now. The naked schoolgirl was gone. Perhaps the girl had come to her senses.

For Tizzy, with repentance came hope. There was always hope. Perhaps the girl had come to her senses.

Perhaps Vistalyn Ray had gotten up and gone home too. Or had the last shred of her been spirited beyond the veil? Tizzy might never know the answers. She only knew the bed was empty, with pretty patchwork covers folded in place, ready for the next sleeper. She only knew the clawfooted bedstand stood empty, with no keyring left upon it.

She only knew her ears had never whistled so sweetly—this old wind whistling from behind her, through the open door. This is all Tizzy knew but never told about the old wind.

She stumbled back outside, where the wind was.

The wind, it sang the praises of that well up yonder. That rock-ringed well and winch just up the rise. Yes, that well might save her, if she would let it. Perhaps Tizzy Polk could draw from the well a cool drink or throw herself down its wellhole. She began to ascend toward it, upward she went, toward the well.

As the well drew near, a ghostly white peak loomed behind it. Beyond the well's winch grew a towering ring of oak trees. And within that oaken ring, the ghostly white peak rose, half-hidden within the ring.

Tizzy moved beyond the well and stepped into the ring of oak trees. Now she saw more clearly. The ghostly peak was the up-jutting corner of a big white box. It was a box as big as a Gospeltime Milk wagon with its nose in a hole.

Tizzy Polk got slower, and slower.

287

The great hole opened wide for her. The white panel truck was tipped over the edge, nosing down into the fathomless pit: **GOSPELTIME MILK - "Sweetest O'er The Land"**

The old wind sang a horned hosannah. Tizzy heard it so clearly, she heard it so datgum well.

The truck had no tires. The truck's cab was buried down in the pit, in a squalid nest of bedsprings, scrap iron, and char-blacked bottles. The truck's rear doors angled skyward and off-kiltered. At the edge they leaned, like double doors into the hole.

Tizzy had wandered so far. Now that she arrived at these doors, there was little she could do.

She had to open them. So she did.

Tizzy lifted open both of the milk truck's screeching doors. Inside was reeking.

A zither-buzzing chord struck. A thick clot of flies whooshed out past her.

She turned her head away, shooing with her hands inside the fly-blown exodus.

Then Tizzy June Polk turned back to look. To see. To see clearly.

She looked inside the truck's innards and saw the oxen heads and corpses of strange critters, Matthew's rude face and torso, the remnants of folks, folks gone by, arms, legs, breasts with black nipples and pieces of Matthew. Lou-Lou's cracked doll face nestled nearby (or was it her mother?). Yes, inside was the reeking. But no hands were left here to rot, all hands were hanging high and accounted for. Deep and resounding was the slaughter within, and the slaughter without. Sweetest O'er The Land.

Tizzy's mouth opened like a wanton harlot.

She was howling but nothing could she hear.

Shrieking silence tore from her lips.

Like her throat was slit.

Like her tongue was split in two.

She was slit like those horrors she saw inside.

Tizzy turned and Tizzy ran. She ran blithering and making baby chatter, back downhill to the cabin. Flying inside, she bolted the front door behind her. She jumped over the bed. She heard a dark voice calling, calling. The night had just got rich on Riddle Top. Yes, the night was here. Tizzy knew what this quick rich night was wanting. The night would be wanting its whore.

Crunch, crunch. Tizzy heard boots on gravel out there, heavy boots on gravel.

BOOOM-BOOOM-BOOM. Someone was pounding on the front door, pounding as she shrieked. Outside, in a shrill wind, the shape of man kept shifting past the windowpanes. Blind with panic, Tizzy fled into the kitchen.

In here—in here she saw sanctuary. A dangling open padlock. An inner door ajar.

Tizzy raced inside and pulled the pantry shut. She pulled back into the black of her hidey hole. She plundered her dress for a stolen matchbox. She struck a match. There was a deadbolt on the inside of the door. She slid the bolt, locking the door. Flame scorched her fingers. She shook out the match. She lit another. Here was a lantern on a shelf amidst jars of preserves. Frantic, Tizzy lifted the lantern's glass chimney and put flame to wick.

She stood up with the lantern and began turning in the tight pantry. A fine mist of coal dust filled the air. She could smell it.

And she could tell that these were not fruit preserves or jars of stewed tomatoes after all. These shelves were rife, packed wall to wall with jars of the deepest red. Red like the red in a jar one early evening. Like the red draining into a Nottingham gullet when Tizzy Polk arrives and surprises him.. This pantry was jam-packed, with these red quart jars, up, down, surrounding Tizzy. Tizzy wanted to shrink from them, but everywhere she shrank from the jars, there were more red jars behind her.

BOOM-BOOM-BOOM.

Now the night was banging on this pantry door.

BOOM.

And the night would be wanting its whore.

BOOM.

Tizzy went squealing, twirling inward, inward, crashing into shelves. *BOOMBOOM.* Walls of shelves collapsed— *BOOM*—jars breaking, spilling forth. The lantern shattered and snuffed out. Tizzy slipped on the bloody slime, collapsing in fever. She cried. *BOOM* the horned god spake. Do you love the blood of the lamb? *BOOM* the horned god spake. Tizzy wailed. Tizzy writhed on the floor on a sea of blood and broken glass. The hosannah rose from within her and all booming doors fell away, fell away, into this deep red sea. All night she tossed in this tempest, in her boat of baby angels, who sang an old refrain:

> *O watch your step, step, step,*
> *Watch where you wander little lamb,*
> *O, to a promised land*
> *where you began,*
> *Unto the hands of Nottinham...*

STEP 1

Dawn was replete upon Old Riddle Top. It was hot, crackling hot. Sweetest o'er the land. The cabin sat still. The cabin door hung open, as she had left it.

Tizzy emerged, trudging into the light. It was morning, with chores to be done, time to scatter her acorns. Tizzy's face was cut. Her arms and legs were pitted with glass and blood. Her dress was slashed in tatters. Her buckletop shoes had gone missing. Tizzy Polk moved as a broken thing moves, a puppet with one severed string.

She traversed wood and briar until, a day or a moment farther along, she found herself in an open field. Flies and locust chittered around her bare ankles. Coming toward her through sunburnt grass was the stagman, the brooding man, the man with tattoo scars. He bore a broadaxe. His smile was thin with reassurance. Dry blood flecked the corners of his smile.

She did not flinch, for she was not afraid. He stopped and took her in, a cacophony of locust swirling around them.

"Ain't you a human man?" she asked, her voice a husk.

"Mostly."

"Was I a bad girl, Mr. Nottinham?"

He squinted in the morning sun, his face grizzled with strange kindliness.

"No. No you were not."

"No?"

"Maybe to your god. Maybe. But they's lots of gods up here. He's yourn, I reckon."

"I'm guilty. I know I am."

"We all got the guilt for what good we ain't done. You ain't no different."

"Ain't I a born sinner then?"

He shook his head slowly. The heat, the insects, they did not faze or interfere with his being.

"You never had no choice. We born. That's all."

"Born in sin..."

"Born. Ordained to die. Ordains ye to suffer, he does, to suffer for how he done made ye from the git go. All so's he can git his loving. Ole boy's a selfish bastard, ye know. Needs his loving. He don't give a good dawg damnation who he hurts to git it. He wants it both ways."

"He? M-my Lord?"

"Uh-huh. Yup. He got that real wicked temper." Nottingham smiled a bit more. "I don't tolerate him."

"You ain't near as bad as he."

"Judge fer yourself."

She gazed wistfully into Nottingham's eyes. She understood him now. The breadth and beat of his soul had been there all along, so near to her since baby days, through the storm and suffering.

"Mr. Nottinham?"

"Yes?"

"Can I stay here? With you?"

"Surely. Do as you will."

"Thank you Mr. Nottinham."

She shed a tear.

"None of that," he said. "Tears don't shift nothin. Is a hallowing here. Always been a hallowing here. Always will be."

"Forgive me."

His hand reached out. His eye held a grievous glimmer.

"Don't worry it, daughter. Home never was. They's only this mountain. And the haint o' the gods hangs on this mountain."

The man took her tiny hand and she was led away, through the gentle grass. They went quietly to a cool place, together. Later, he would ask if she was thirsty and she would say yes.

STEPCHILD

Button hunkered on the back stoop. I been seeing it done for years. Those woods were sooty black beyond the clothesline and a silver moon had risen.

Her toes gripped the edge of the plank step, you know the kind, chin resting on her knees. The trees held hands and the hands were alive out there, for now and for to-night. This was all she knew and all she knows. Behind her, in the kitchen, the man was clattering tin plates, fixing to feed himself. Button sniffed and bristled. A smoky old wind worked its way up the hollers, binding like a coven of breezes around this house. She heard the faint squeal of the weather vane, shifting. Who knew where dog was as night crept in. Dog could be anywhere. Everywhere was his where. Who has seen any blind boys lately? Not she. Or that guilt-eyed girl. No sign of her either. You had to watch for the signs. You had to wait. They all came back when the wind howled mournful enough and bitter memory flooded the air. You had to be ready. You had to watch careful. Or they would eat you, drink you.

The man's boots are behind her now, shuffling heavy on the dark porch. His tattoo-scarred arm drops a rattling plate beside her on the top step. It smells of tin cans and cities and far-off folks she has never known.

"Don't worry it. Eat," I say. Then I go back inside.

But the rag-doll baby does not eat, not tonight. She does not move or slide or expect revelation. She shall not sleep. She waits, she watches. She will watch out forever if need be, her moonface breathing in these woods, as they seethe, she draws breath, button eyes darting at every feathery fit and titter, at every midnight moan and tizzy.

Other Riddle Top books by Randy Thornhorn:

THE KESTREL WATERS
A Tale Of Love And Devil
(sequel to *Wicked Temper*)

HOWLS OF A HELLHOUND ELECTRIC
Riddle Top Magpies & Bobnot Boogies

THE AXMAN'S SHIFT
A Love Story

Visit Randy Thornhorn online at

www.thornhorn.com

Printed in Great Britain
by Amazon.co.uk, Ltd.,
Marston Gate.